
THAT NIGHT I GOT DRAGGED HOME BY A WEREWOLF

A Transbian Monsterfucker Novel

AUTUMN WOLFF

This book is dedicated to my amazing wife, Meghan, who passionately supports all the wild words I slap down on the page. It's also dedicated to Em, my bestie who bakes me wicked sick cookies and encourages me to write whatever my depraved brain conjures up.

Chapter 1

Autumn arrived early this year, smacking down any ornery temperatures in her wake and reminding the people of Pine Springs that Maine is ruled by winter. And she'd be on her way to greet everyone soon enough.

The smell of smoked meat and cooking oil filled the air as I walked down First Street toward Benny's Grill. Benny himself was standing outside next to a commercial grill flipping burgers and rotating red snappers over a propane fire.

My mouth watered as I imagined the hot dog that awaited me, striped with ketchup and mustard and wrapped in a split-top roll.

I stepped off the sidewalk and into the road to avoid a gaggle of teens dressed like dogs and cats laughing and walking by. When I hopped back onto the curb, I caught sight of my reflection in the Remys storefront window.

The thin black lines I'd drawn for my whiskers were still exactly where I'd placed them when I left the library staff restroom. My nose was still painted a light shade of pink. And the cheap set of bunny ears I'd panicked and rush ordered from Spamazon sat fastened to the top of my head, long black hair spilling around them and drifting down past my shoulders.

Making sure no one was watching, I spun in my white bouffant dress and checked to make sure my little poofy tail was still sewn onto the back. Check. Check. Check. Lilith the Bunny was perfectly intact, just the same as I was when I left work.

My powder-blue heels, the same color I'd painted my nails, clicked on the sidewalk as I rejoined the crowd of folks taking part in one of our town's most bizarre celebrations dating back centuries.

Storefronts were decorated with paintings of pine trees and moose. A fresh lumberjack mural in the style of Paul Bunyan had been finished just yesterday on the exposed brick wall of Bangor National Bank. The lumberjack overlooked Longfellow Park, which the town had spent a few thousand dollars cleaning up for the festival.

I dodged left to avoid a few screaming toddlers dressed as raccoons running around their mother as she held ice cream cones and looked for a place where they could all sit.

Getting her attention, I pointed over at Longfellow Park and said, "I see a bench free over by the swings."

Her eyes widened as she sighed in relief and mouthed, "Thank you," maneuvering her noisy little trash pandas across the street that'd been closed to traffic.

"Look! A bunny! She's a bunny! Can I be a bunny?" one of the kids asked, turning back and taking notice of me.

The mother glanced over with a smile and said, "Maybe next year, Kait. I bet she's been planning her costume for months. Now c'mon. Let's sit down and eat these before they melt."

A surge of joy and euphoria swept through me as I stifled a giggle and a joyful little dance.

She, I thought. *They called me 'she.'*

That was slowly growing more common here in Pine Springs, and it only made my evening all the more exciting.

My stomach grumbled, and I soon turned back toward my initial mission of getting a couple red snappers and a beer from Benny's.

The smell of grilled beef and pork flooded my nostrils, and I honest-to-god licked my lips. A pair of crows cawed and flew down into the street, picking at the remnants of an abandoned popcorn bag from Blue Star Cinema.

"Ugh, being hungry is for the birds," I mumbled, feeling a pang of emptiness in my stomach as it growled again.

I chuckled at my awful joke and got in line behind a husband and wife dressed as a buck and a doe. His antlers were a little crooked and appeared to be made from paper towel rolls.

He actually made his costume, I thought, looking it over. He'd sewn together some thin brown and white fabric to make an oversized onesie but had chosen to forgo a tail. Ironically, the tail was the only part of my costume I'd made, bunching up a wad of lace and sewing it to an old dress with WAY too many threads.

"And I only poked myself twice," I muttered.

The line moved quickly as I found myself facing Benny Nelson, a sweaty, heavy-set man in a pair of overalls with a Boston Blue Sox baseball cap covering his thinning hair. He ran the town's main greasy spoon and was directly responsible for the 20 pounds I'd gained since moving to Pine Springs.

A worn yellow awning with the words "Benny's Grill"

painted on it covered the glass front door of his restaurant. I came in to have lunch on Wednesdays and usually brought a book to read at the counter while I ate. Sometimes we'd chat about literature. Benny proved that appearances can often be deceiving and was a die-hard fan of writers like Agatha Christie and Jane Austen.

His brown eyes found me as I stepped up close to the grill.

"Evening, Lil! That's a wicked cute costume," he said.

I giggled.

"Thanks. But it's nothing compared to your beaver getup. You look like you're ready to dam up the Penobscot," I said.

In truth, the fry cook had only slapped on some oversized plastic teeth and hung a spray-painted cardboard beaver tail from a thin rope tied around his waist. But that was the beauty of Wylde Night. Everyone in town dressed up as animals however they could. On the walk over from the library, I even saw a grandma with tiger facepaint being pushed in a wheelchair by one of her grandkids.

"Ha! You're a sweet kid. Most of the brats who come through have given me shit about it," he chuckled.

Some fat dripped from a couple of the burgers, and crisp yellow flames shot up to singe the beef.

"Kid? C'mon, Benny," I laughed. "I'm 25. I pay taxes. I work full-time. And drive a shitty car. That all sounds pretty adult to me."

He sneered.

"Aw, don't think nothin' of it, bub. Once you pass 60, almost everyone turns into a kid," he said, adding some cheese slices to a couple of the burgers and waiting for them to melt.

Before I could retort, someone bumped into my shoulder on his way toward the restaurant door.

"Whoops. Sorry, sir," a cruel voice called.

Ah, there it goes. All the joy of being called "she" earlier flushed down the drain by a single asshole. Benny's older brother, Wilson, was the primary reason I only ate at the grill on Wednesdays, his day off.

Wilson was taller and thinner than Benny. He'd somehow retained almost all his hair and was usually seen wearing khaki shorts and tank tops. Unlike Benny, who lived every day with a heart of gold, his brother tended to walk around town looking like he spent every minute of every day being sprayed by a skunk. I never saw the man smile aside from the spiteful sneers he passed my way after intentionally calling me "sir."

He'd find any chance he could to slip that into a sentence. Wilson didn't care how unnatural it sounded, either. With him, the cruelty was the point. He wanted me to know that I'd never be a woman in his eyes. And while I wanted to mash his face down into the grill for all the hell he caused me, I instead ignored him.

They say ignoring bullies who are starved for attention is the best way to get revenge, but it's never as satisfying or relieving as they make it sound. I always wind up pissed, and the bully usually walks away laughing.

Benny snapped to and whipped his spatula around, smacking Wilson in the elbow with it. Hot grease went dripping down that fucker's arm, and he growled and grimaced.

"Hey! That ain't no way to talk to a lady, Wil. Now get those buns inside and grab me another propane tank. We've got a whole line of animals to feed," the fry cook yelled.

Before he slunk through the front door with the burger buns he'd been holding, Wilson spat at the ground in front of my feet.

We both heard the older brother whisper, "Fucking trannie," before he vanished from sight.

That was a fresh dagger to my chest, and part of me wanted to spin around and run back to my apartment. Alan wouldn't be home for hours, and I could just sit and watch *Howl's Moving Castle* and hold my Blåhaj while I waited for these shitty feelings of inadequacy to fade.

Dysphoria's a bitch who visits often and doesn't take the hint that he's overstayed his welcome. Wishing him away only seems to make things worse as he spreads his legs across the couch and reminds you of every single time the world says you ain't right.

"I'm sorry about him, Lilith. I can't control the words that come out of his mouth. Wish I could, but I can't," Benny said. "What can I get you this evening? You want burgers or snappers?"

The urge to flee back to the empty library or home to my shitty apartment grew wild, spreading through my noggin like a vicious black mold. And just before I sighed and left the food line, a small tug on my dress brought me back to reality.

"Excuse me, miss?" a child called from down below.

Turning, I spotted a familiar raccoon with chocolate ice cream stained across both her cheeks.

"Y — yeah?" I asked, trying to force my throat back open and sound normal. No, I wasn't about to cry. Why do you ask?

"Can you tell me where you got your bunny ears?" the kid asked. "I think I want to be one for Halloween."

I stood there flummoxed, noticing her tiny hand still hadn't let go of my dress yet like she was determined to hold my attention until I shared the sacred knowledge of this treasure's origin.

Looking up, I saw the mother holding her other child,

also covered in chocolate ice cream stains, waving at us with a smile.

A small spark of hope was relit somewhere in my heart, and I just huffed, shaking my head.

"They're, um, from Spamazon. I think I just searched for 'rabbit ears costume,' and these were the first option."

The kid's eyes widened.

"Did they come in other colors?" the kid, who couldn't have been more than four, asked. "Because I want some red ones."

She didn't seem to have any sense of stranger danger, so long as the individual she was talking to was dressed like a cute animal. The ears I'd ordered were white, but I thought I remembered seeing other colors.

"They had some different colors. I think red might have been on there, but I'm not sure. Sorry."

The little raccoon's face lit up with a huge smile.

"Okay, thanks, miss! Bye!" she yelled, running back to her mother. "Mommy, she said they had red ones on Spamazon! Can we get them?"

Putting aside the fact that those weren't my exact words, I turned back to Benny with a renewed smile on my face. My faith in humanity was restored by about 12%, just enough to stick it out and enjoy the rest of Wylde Night.

"Cute kid," Benny said, chuckling and flipping a few more burgers on the top row of the grill. More smoke drifted up into the air, and behind me, the line had doubled, filled with people dressed as moose, lions, and even a lobster.

"Yeah, see, that's what an ACTUAL kid looks like," I chided the cook. "I know it's been 3,000 years since you were one, but —"

He interrupted me.

"Har har. Do you want some snappahs or not, Lil? This is the food line, not the joke line, bub."

I rolled my eyes and held up two fingers.

"Enjoy!" Benny said, handing me two red hot dogs on a paper plate. "Good luck not staining your dress."

Laughing and grabbing a can of beer from a nearby ice chest, or "chilly bin," as I'd seen a Kiwi call it on Reddit, I went to look for a place to sit and eat.

Rounding a corner and coming to the town square, I found a dozen picnic tables had been set up. A red and blue bouncy house full of kids (and one unfortunate adult) blocked most of Eastern Avenue. On the opposite side of the square, a small stage had been constructed for whatever local band they'd hired to play the Wylde Night concert.

All around me stood picnic tables full of costumed families enjoying a beautiful sunset and chilly evening breeze. Bug zappers were hard at work hanging from the awning of a large blue tent that'd been erected to protect party games in case of rain. Thankfully, there wasn't a cloud in the sky.

I spotted skee ball, some sort of fishing game with mechanical plastic fish swimming around an inflatable pool, a ring toss booth, and even a dunk tank off to the side with a guy around my age dressed in a full cartoon leopard fursuit.

Jack Rossler, the Pine Springs High School football coach, was redfaced and frustrated, trying to sink the leopard. But every throw he set loose missed the dunk button by a few inches.

"Oh come on, Coach! Did they teach you to throw like that at Dartmouth? I thought you were a rookie of the year quarterback in '79?"

Another missed throw had the coach angrily grabbing

his wallet and slamming another $5 on the counter before being handed a basket of red rubber balls to throw.

His face was dripping with sweat.

"Hope you have an oxygen tank in that stupid costume, Pete because you're about to take a dive!" Jack bellowed before missing another throw.

"Oh, don't you worry about me, Coach. I can hold my breath. Of course, with the way you're throwing, I won't need to."

I found an empty seat at one picnic table as every eye was turned toward the dunk tank. I ate my food and noticed everyone was eager to see whether that leopard was gonna swim. I didn't have anything against Pete. He was a chill guy and worked the afternoon shift at Reggie's Pizza a few streets over. His personality boiled down to being a furry and being a stoner in that order.

Pete used his library card to get manga and comics delivered via interlibrary loans. I always liked when he came into the library, and he'd tell me about what he was reading. The latest trade paperback from *X-Men* or another volume of *Jujutsu Kaisen*. He never had an issue with me transitioning and got on board right away.

His exact words to my coming out were, "That's wicked cool, Lilith. Do you know if the *Uncanny X-Men* volume I ordered came in yet?"

After five baskets of balls and at least $50 raised for the Pine Springs Animal Shelter, Coach Rossler finally nailed the target and sent Pete into the tank below. He spun and pumped his fists into the air as everyone in the square cheered and applauded like he'd just won an Olympic medal.

I snorted, threw my trash away, and walked up to the dunk tank as a black and gold leopard climbed out of the water and sat back on his platform.

"Your suit gonna be okay, Pete?" I asked.

He waved a paw at me and said, "Yeah, Lil, it'll be fine. This is just a spare suit I designed to get wet. I've got a guy over in Bangor who will dry clean it for me."

I nodded.

"Need a beer or anything before I go?" I asked.

He shook his giant fuzzy animal head.

"Nah, I'm good. Ate before I climbed in here. You go enjoy the event. Cute bunny costume, by the way."

I smiled and nodded at him.

"Thanks. I hope you have fun tonight. I think there's a whole line of your former high school teachers ready to take their shot at you."

"Eh, I was a bit of a shithead back then. I'm sure they'll earn every dunk they get, especially Mrs. Whizzler."

I flinched at that name. Pete had only told me once what he did to piss her off in 10th grade, and I still shivered remembering it.

Being a rural librarian didn't exactly pay much, but I had good health insurance through the state that covered things like my hormones and bloodwork. Still, I pulled out $5 and played a round of ring toss, walking away with a little candy bracelet as a prize.

Passing a walking tour of historical buildings run by the head of the Piscataquis County Historical Society, I heard an older woman named Regina Bells talking to a group of mostly senior citizens.

"And this here is the Wylde Postal Office, constructed in 1812. Lord Jameson Wylde arrived in Portland in 1799. Traveling north, he eventually made his way into what we now call Piscataquis County and helped fund this town's beginnings. He invested heavily in the first bank and two separate mills. A decade later, Pine Springs was incorporated as an official town."

One of the men walking in the group slowly held up an iPad and took a photo of the aging brick building that now served as a community studio, courtesy of some federal grant the town had won to expand rural artist opportunities.

"Lord Wylde went on to build the town's first school in 1816 and the Pine Springs Community Library in 1823. In his older years, he became obsessed with all manner of strange things like the occult and animal spirits. He told odd stories about a hidden graveyard that brought creatures back from the dead, a place he was determined to find," the tour guide went on. "And then, in June of 1830, he went missing. Some folks said he wandered into the woods muttering to himself. Others said he skipped town and sailed back to England. But no one was ever quite sure where he ended up."

I decided to check out the art gallery. The old wooden floors beneath me squeaked as I walked around and glanced at paintings by local artists.

OUTSIDE, the walking history tour continued. I overheard some folks discussing Wylde's disappearance and trying to solve the lingering mystery from the 1800s.

And that's why we dress up as animals on the first night of autumn to honor his legacy, I thought, stopping myself from mouthing the words. I'd heard that tour more times than I cared to admit. Most of the people in town did.

The artwork I walked past consisted mostly of landscape portraits. Rocky sides of Mt Katahdin. The shores of Caribou Lake. The forests of Baxter State Park. I was impressed with the majority of them. Then again, I couldn't paint to save my life.

I turned around to find myself being sized up by a

stout man who appeared to be in his late 40s or early 50s. His blue eyes looked me up and down before he said, "Well shit. I was asking myself whether you looked as good from the front as you did from the rear, but then you went and settled that question for me."

"Excuse me?" I asked, involuntarily pulling my arms in tight. Unease crept through my chest as this man, who was dressed like a bull, took another step toward me, breath smelling heavily of wine.

"You know, if you like artwork, I have a private studio at my house I'd love to show you," he said, offering me a hand.

I slowly shook my head.

"That's okay. Maybe another time," I practically squeaked, turning to leave, only to have my path of escape cut off by the bull.

"Up, up, up, hold on. I know I appeared suddenly, probably startled ya, but I promise you I'm a decent guy. My name's Ezekiel. I just want to get to know you. And can you blame me? Pretty girl like yourself, obviously into art? What a score. C'mon, give me a chance to change your mind," he said, raising his hands.

I shook my head again and tried to turn him down. My heart raced as sweat started to form around my temples. Fear arched through my chest like lightning. What should I do?

If I tell him I'm trans, will he leave me alone? I thought. *What if that just makes him violent?*

Taking a step backward, I managed a shallow breath.

"Wow. I didn't think it was possible, but you look even cuter when you're a little scared," Ezekiel said, wearing a grin that said the man knew exactly how I felt, and he reveled in it.

Before I could say another word, a strong arm slipped

around my shoulder and pulled me backward into the embrace of a taller woman whose hazel eyes swept from me to Ezekiel.

"Huh?" I stammered, shoulder pressed against her tits.

"There you are, Little Cottontail. Sorry, I'm late. I've been looking everywhere for you."

Her husky voice speaking next to my ear sent shivers down my spine, and all I could do looking up at this towering, muscled goddess was blush and nod. Heat rushed to my cheeks and chased out the fear in my heart.

The woman who had one hand comfortably resting on my shoulder, pulling me in close, smelled like cinnamon and dry leaves. Her smile was warm. And a silver porcelain wolf mask perched on the right side of her head, secured with some kind of string or elastic. It hung over some of her long, wavy hair the color of tree bark.

She rocked tight jeans and a large gray tank top with the sides cut open. Those cuts revealed a black sports bra and enough muscles to short-circuit a Terminator. Er — at least enough muscles to short-circuit a librarian, a librarian who, at this moment, was realizing just how thirsty she was.

Ohhhhh fuck, I thought as Ezekiel seemed to snap out of his stupor.

"Hey, we're a little busy here, lady. Why don't you find another bunny to—" he started before the stranger tucked me tightly into her grasp and brushed right by him. She didn't pay him any mind whatsoever, escorting me outside and back to the picnic tables, most of which had been cleared away for dance space.

A band of four middle-aged men were warming up. From the looks of it, they had a drummer, a bass player, a dude on the keyboard, and a guitarist who would be doing most of the singing.

Looking behind us, I spotted Ezekiel stepping out of the studio with his arms crossed. His face was almost as red as the coach aiming for the dunk tank earlier.

My escort stopped in front of the stage and put herself between me and Ezekiel, effectively cutting off my view of him.

"Relax. You're safe with me. He can't do shit," she said. "I'm Mars, by the way."

"Lilith," I practically whispered, still feeling like I was in a daydream. This bodybuilder had snatched me away from a creepy dude, and I wanted nothing more than for her to sling me over her shoulder and carry me back to her cave for snu snu.

My cheeks re-heated at the thought, and I attempted to scold my mind. It was a weak attempt.

Mars placed a finger under my chin and raised my eyes to hers.

"You still with me, Little Cottontail?"

I stupidly attempted to nod, forgetting where her fingers were.

She chuckled something wicked.

"Would it be okay if I told you that your little starstruck act is wicked cute?" she asked as I felt my heart sputter and threaten to give out altogether.

"I think any girl you called 'cute' would be at risk of melting into a puddle," I said.

A much louder belly laugh.

"Well, then I guess we should move away from that sewer grate. I'd hate to see you disappear before I got a dance or two out of you."

Something in my brain clicked when I recognized her words.

"You? Me? You want to dance with me?" I asked, feeling every bit the idiot I'm sure I sounded like.

"Would that be okay?" she asked.

More people were beginning to gather in front of the stage, but my gaze was locked on Mars. Her eyes were wild and hungry, yet she demonstrated nothing but absolute control in the way she stood, despite towering over me.

"I'd love to, but I'm kind of lousy at it," I said, looking down at my two left feet.

Mars stepped closer, and I got another whiff of her cinnamon lotion.

"Well maybe you could just follow me," she said. "You look like the kind of girl who's good at doing what she's told."

Yup. That sent my heart into a tailspin as a feverish desire overwhelmed me. I wanted to be in Mars' arms, rubbing up against her, feeling her lips against mine. And from the look she gave me, Mars was picturing all those same things in her mind.

The band's guitarist finally spoke into a microphone. He was a tall Black man wearing a denim jacket and ballcap.

"How are you fine people doing tonight?" he asked.

Loud cheers from all around us erupted as people yelled things like, "Great!" and "Really good!"

"Fantastic!" the guitarist said. "Well, my name is Caleb. Me and my friends are called The Dad Bods, and we'll be playing a mix of classic rock covers I'm sure most of you grew up with. Any fans of Journey out there?"

The crowd erupted into cheers.

"Lovely. We're gonna kick things off with a little song called 'Any Way You Want It.'"

And, true to his word, they launched into their cover, which sounded about as good as anything I'd heard over the speakers at Benny's.

Mars winked and stepped closer.

"Are you okay being touched a little while we dance?" she asked.

"Given how long it's been since I've been touched by a pretty girl like you, it's safe to assume you have permission to touch me however you want," I responded with a surprising amount of honesty.

With all the grace and strength of the apex predator she appeared to embody, Mars put a hand on each of my hips and pulled me close. I yipped.

"If you want to play the part of the bunny running from the Big Bad Wolf, you're going to have to watch the things you say in front of me," Mars leaned down and whispered in my ear.

And, again, with a brutal amount of honesty, I whispered back, "Who's running? Maybe I've waited a long time to be caught by the Big Bad Wolf."

Mars made a biting motion with her teeth and started dancing against me. I was alive for the first time in weeks. Fire built inside of me as this beautiful woman who seemingly came from nowhere ran her hands against my hips and then over my breasts for a moment. It wasn't long enough to cause a scene, but we both knew what she'd done. And I was suddenly so hungry for her to do more.

The woman in the wolf mask led me, and I followed helplessly in her charming gaze. If she swung me left, I went left. If she swung me right, I went right. And by the time we'd each had a beer or two, The Dad Bods was deep into its playlist of things like Deep Purple and CCR.

My body wanted to be tired, as the sun set, and darkness took the dance floor with us, but instead, I found myself hungering for more of Mars. She never quite seemed to tire, at one point leaning close and asking, "Are you ready for a bigger dance move?"

What could she possibly mean? Again, though, eager

to give myself over to the Big Bad Wolf, I nodded. She flashed me a wicked grin, made sure we had plenty of space, and then lifted me straight up into the air, spinning me around.

I felt weightless in her arms. And she made this look so easy like I was nothing more than a spare pillow to her strength. I laughed, and people around us cheered and clapped.

Then, I was back on the ground and looking up into Mars' eyes. Her bright, golden eyes that were so inhuman I froze entirely. Was I seeing things? Her eyes were hazel earlier, right?

She lingered there with her gaze on me as if knowing exactly what I saw. And then she blinked, and her eyes were hazel once more. Static seemed to build over my arms as gooseflesh raced toward my elbows.

"What's the matter, Little Cottaintail? Are you done dancing with me?"

Sweat ran down my forehead and back. I was suddenly flooded with pheromones I couldn't even begin to place. I was far from a virgin, but this was the first time I'd felt so hungry for. . . for. . . whatever it was that Mars seemed to have going for her.

Was it the alcohol? My mind was a little buzzed, but I felt otherwise in control. As control as one could feel when they've been dancing with someone like Mars for an hour.

As if she could sense my desires, Mars moved her face closer to mine and said, "If you're bored of dancing, I can think of. . . something else we can do. Would you like to go do something else? Just the two of us?"

There's nothing I wanted more at this very moment when a red alert started blaring in my mind. And it's not because of anything Mars had done, but rather, the situations I've found myself in when other girls have asked me to leave with them.

Anxiety must have flashed across my face because Mars seemed to lower her charm and soften her voice a bit.

"Or not. I don't want to pressure you. We don't have to go anywhere you don't want to."

I caught my breath.

"No, it's not that I don't want to. It's that, I'm worried about how you'll react if we do."

Mars said nothing.

"I'm. . . probably a bit different than other girls you've taken off the dance floor to a more private place."

My dance partner waited patiently for what I struggled to get off my chest, and fear grabbed my heart in an icy grip that knew she was going to leave as soon as I told her.

Taking a deep breath, I said, "Mars, you're fucking beautiful. And I'd love to run off someplace quiet with you. But before we do, you need to know that I'm trans."

Her expression was patient but otherwise stoic like she was waiting for more words to come.

With a sigh, I said, "Look, you seem like the kind of woman who likes other women. And I'm a big fan. That's the kind of woman I'd like to be someday, too. But there are people here in this town who would tell you to your face that I'm not an actual girl."

And then Mars did something that simultaneously caught me off guard and rekindled the fires of my hearth. She buried her nose in the crook of my neck, sniffing deeply before running her tongue over my skin and lightly biting me.

I gasped as electricity raced between us, and I was once more melting under the full weight of her raw and animalistic attraction.

With a voice only I could hear, Mars whispered, "You smell and taste like a woman to me."

Where I probably should have been freaked out, I was suddenly hot and bothered like I'd never been before. Her magnetism and soft affirmation of my femininity aroused me in ways I couldn't even begin to describe.

And as I succumbed to her touch and taste, I whimpered, "Then why don't you take me somewhere and do to me what you do with all the other girls."

Her warm breath and slight nibble on my ear only left me more desperate to get away from this crowd and somewhere alone with Mars.

Fuck! I thought. *I need her.*

The last cicadas of the season sounded in the distance as Mars practically dragged me out of the square and away from the eyes of people who were otherwise decent. But at this very moment, I didn't want to be decent. I wanted to be under Mars as she did filthy things that would burn the ears off of a nun.

My only desire at this moment was for her to take me somewhere private and then take me herself.

"My truck is parked a few blocks away," she said, as we waltzed up the sidewalk. There wasn't a soul around. Everyone else was back near the stage. Without warning, Mars got in front of me and then picked me up, slinging me over her shoulder.

I laughed and gently kicked my feet.

"What are you doing?" I snorted.

Mars tickled the back of my legs and said, "You just seem like the kind of girl who likes being carried."

"How the fuck are you so strong?" I asked, admiring this view of her ass. "I know I'm not exactly a twig, yet you keep hoisting into the air. You don't even sound like you're out of breath."

"I wouldn't worry about ME being out of breath, Little Cottontail. I actually intend to leave you breathless tonight."

So, when we rounded a corner and came into view of an old beat-up pickup truck, Mars set me down and pushed me against the passenger door before locking her lips with mine.

I was beyond ready for Mars to take me as I let my instincts and desires drive.

She deepened her kiss and scooted my ass away from the door handle as I giggled. I buried my fingers into her hair as more heat built between us. I knocked her wolf mask off and leaned down to grab it.

"Forget it," she said, pushing me back up against the truck. "I don't need the mask to be the Big Bad Wolf for you."

Mars kissed me again, her tongue finding mine and claiming every inch of my mouth for herself. She could have it as far as I was concerned.

Bottoms gonna bottom, am I right? I thought.

She grabbed my hair and pulled my head back as I gasped and felt the back of my skull slowly touch her truck window. Then, she kissed the side of my neck in a storm of passion that nearly melted my legs.

When she stopped, I was breathing heavily with desire. I needed more. I wanted this fucking dress off and her tongue on me.

"Do you want to come home with me?" she asked. "It's a small farm not far from here."

"If you keep using your tongue like that, I suspect I'll come wherever you bring me," I hissed as she opened her truck door and let me climb inside.

This might have been the stupidest thing I ever did, but

right now, in this moment, I couldn't think of anything I wanted more.

Chapter 2

It wasn't a graceful fall, but I tumbled backward onto a soft king bed with a wooden headboard that looked big enough to have been torn from the side of a galleon. The way Mars leapt onto the bed had me wondering if she'd been an Olympian jumper in the past.

Wait, are her eyes —, I started to think before her weight was thrown atop me. Fuck! I loved the feeling of a sturdy woman on top of me, pressing me into the bed with every fiber of her desire.

Smother me with your heat. It's my favorite place to be in the world.

Mars settled her hips on mine and leaned down to kiss me again. Her lips almost seemed warmer than the rest of her. And the way her tongue swept over mine as though the muscled butch had complete dominion over my mouth left me breathless. After a few seconds, she pulled back, and I caught my breath.

"You keep panting like that, Little Cottontail, and I'll have to assume you're in heat," Mars laughed, running her fingers down the side of my cheek.

I managed to surprise her by pulling her thumb into my mouth and sucking on it. I wanted to taste her, all of her. She shivered and grinned as my tongue draped itself over her thumb before I lightly bit it.

"Biting, Lilith? Are you sure?"

"I'm sure that if you don't sink your teeth into my body at least once before we're done tonight, I'll be leaving you a three-star review on Her."

Mars pressed her hips a bit tighter against me and started to grind slowly before lowering her lips to mine again for a long, breathy kiss. While our lips were locked, she ran her hands over my breasts and gave them a gentle squeeze, eliciting a moan of pleasure from yours truly. I was under attack on multiple fronts, and I couldn't surrender to her fast enough.

"Fuck," I hissed, finally pulling away from her lips to breathe. Even though her hands had to work through my dress, Mars still managed to make my nipples hard and ready for more.

She suddenly stopped and asked, "How much do you like this dress?"

"My affection for this dress is far less than my desire for you to keep fucking me, Mars."

With a shocking display of speed and strength, I watched Mars grin and sink her fingers into the fabric, tearing it wide open like tissue paper.

"How did you —?" I started to ask before my horniness flared up again, and I pulled the beefcake of a woman back down on top of me. I needed her to use those muscles on me, to hold me firm and deflower me like I was an innocent virgin kidnapped on the night before an arranged wedding I didn't want.

Really, Lilith? I thought to myself. *You've known this woman for an hour or two, and you're already building fantasies in your head?*

I wasn't sure if Mars could read my mind, but she chased any coherent thoughts I had left when she unhooked my bra (because those are too fucking expensive to shred) and lowered her tongue to my tits. Goddamn! It was even better without a top on. Of course it was. How could it not be? She licked my right nipple while fondling my left breast with a free hand, and I could do nothing but melt under her.

I lifted Mars' tank top off and removed her bra so I could return the gesture, and she hissed in pleasure at my touch. I was surprised to find our tits were around the same size. And when I took a break from playing with her breasts, Mars buried her face in mine and took turns nibbling on each while continuing to gently squeeze and rub my nipples.

Pleasure ran through my entire chest, and my brain was flooded with oxytocin. Like — my skull was probably a fishbowl of oxytocin at this point, and I was the happiest woman alive.

It was when Mars started to peel away the lower half of my dress still clinging to my body that I grabbed her wrists. A surge of panic shot through me, and suddenly, I was horny and dismayed. It was a strange combination where I wanted Mars to do things to me, but I had a border wall that needed to be respected.

She stopped immediately, her expression of pure desire changing to soft concern. I was impressed by her sense of control. We were both still panting, but that oxytocin had started to drain from my brain as dysphoria took root. I remembered one or two particularly disastrous sexual encounters where girls I'd gone home with said they were cool with me being trans until they got my panties off.

"Are you okay?" Mars asked, still breathing heavily and

sweating a little. God. She was like a furnace! How did she run so hot?

I tried to catch my breath and remember how to form words.

"Y — yeah. Listen. You remember that I'm trans, right?"

She nodded.

"And while my insurance from the state is good, it's not THAT good."

Mars cocked her head to the side in confusion.

"Like — sure, HRT is covered. Bloodwork is easy. But. . . surgery? Not so much. And being a rural librarian doesn't exactly pay enough for me to drop $20 grand on a basement renovation if you get my drift."

As my new friend's eyes softened even more despite her maintained look of hunger (seriously, how did she look sympathetic while wanting to devour me at the same time?), she ran her fingers down my cheek again.

I was just now becoming aware of her saliva covering my tits, and fuck me if that wasn't giving ammunition to Team Horny to overwhelm Team Dysphoria in my brain.

"Lilith, if you think this is my first time handling girldick, you're gonna be surprised."

And, to be honest, I was.

"I've dated a few transfemmes from Montreal. Cute girls. Fucking brats, but they were great lovers. But they hadn't had surgery either. I assure you, we each had a great time. They taught me a few things. I made them scream my name in ecstasy. It made the six-hour drive worth it every time," Mars said.

And while a bit of relief started to peek out from my nervous noggin, the stubborn bit of dysphoria remained. I heard the frustrated sighs and the disgusted groans of a few memorable cis lesbians I'd gone home with in the past, women who swore up and down they were perfectly fine with girldick. And midway through what started as a great night of sex, they just. . . stopped.

"I'm sorry," a girl from Rockland said. "I can't do it. It's just too much."

And I drove home crying, my heart feeling like it wanted to jump out of the moving vehicle and smear itself on the interstate.

Mars was giving me all the right signs that she really would be fine. But every time I closed my eyes, I heard Robin and Natalie quietly apologizing and leaving the bedroom.

"Look, I trust you. I have no doubt you'd deliver me a fabulous orgasm or two if I let you venture down there. But I have some mental scars and dysphoria that just won't let me revisit that area. I'm sorry, Mars."

She nodded.

"I completely understand. And I'm not going to pressure you. I promise."

How on Earth did I manage to wind up in the home of such an amazing and patient partner? And why did my dysphoria have to ruin a fantastic time? Among all the questions I was asking myself, I found an unexpected inquiry making its way into my mind.

Are we fucking on fur? I thought, placing a hand on. . . yup, a large fur blanket covering the entire bed. *Am I getting fucked in a hunting lodge?*

Mars lightly grabbed my fingers running over the blanket.

"Yup. That's real. Hunted and sheared it myself," Mars said.

And. . . I could see it. This ripped queen of a lady stalking through the woods, hunting her prey, and tanning a hide in front of a large campfire. Er — I dunno what the blanket-making process involves. That was just the hunter fantasy my mind chose to imagine.

Team Horny was back in action. Mars, impossibly aware of my rekindling desire, flashed me her teeth before looking over at a nightstand drawer.

"Okay, Little Cottontail. Front door's blocked due to your desired renovations. I can respect that. How do you feel about being taken from behind?"

My eyes widened. And new images flooded my mind of Mars bending me over and — shit, yeah, I wanted that.

"What did you have in mind?" I whispered.

She chuckled. It was a husky laugh that did filthy things to my brain and only made me want her more.

"I'm thinking. . . some lube, a strapon, and you bent over like the naughty girl you're so keen to become under me," Mars said.

A surge of need ran through me, and I just nodded.

"Have you done that before?" she asked.

"A few times. It won't be my first rodeo being ridden from behind," I said.

Then, a new thought flooded my brain. I'd been freed from the top half of my dress, torn in two, arms pulled out of their sleeves. But the bottom half of the skirt remained mostly intact.

"A minor request?" I asked.

"Yes?" she asked.

I swallowed nervously.

"Can you. . . keep the skirt on and lift it when you fuck me?"

Mars licked her lips.

"You've got a filthy mind, Little Cottontail, and I'm happy to oblige. You're not the first girl I've come across wanting to get railed in a sundress."

I shivered in anticipation while she stripped entirely,

pulled out a harness with a moderate purple strapon, and got them on and ready for our activities. My eyes took in her chiseled form from her toned thighs to her damp pussy to her biceps that were probably thick enough to snap a tree trunk in half.

"If things get carried a little too far, just say something, and we'll stop," Mars said, turning me around and bending me over the side of the mattress.

This wasn't my first time doing anal, but I was far more excited for this time than I had been for the past few instances. Mars was a goddess, and I had faith she'd make this a memorable experience.

"I'm pretty sure I'm going to be limited to words that start with 'M' while we're doing this. So, expect a lot of 'Mars' and 'Mommy,'" I said as she moved in behind me.

With a slow, quiet laugh, she said, "I'll keep that in mind."

She lifted my skirt, pulled down my gaff and I waited while she slid a finger inside me to make sure I wasn't bluffing. Then, Mars took that purple dildo, made sure there was plenty of warm, clear gel on my rim, and pressed its head to my puckered entrance.

I stayed still as my anus resisted the toy at first. But Mars was determined, and I was patient while she worked the tip inside. A deep moan rumbled from inside my chest as Mars advanced the dildo inch by inch inside my hole.

Shivering with pleasure, I felt Mars siddle right up to my ass, and I knew the entire toy was inside me now.

"You good?" she asked.

A guttural noise of appreciation and affirmation rolled from my throat.

That's when Mars decided to pump, and I exploded in ecstasy.

She'd pull back a little and then thrust forward, riding

me like the little bitch I was thrilled to be. And if I didn't think Mars could get any hotter, I was wrong. Every time our flesh made contact, my new friend seemed to burn all the more. Was sex fever a thing?

"How do you feel?" Mars asked me after another thrust, and I keened.

She slowly grabbed a handful of my hair and pushed me down toward the bed. I was fighting to keep my eyes from rolling back into my head. I wasn't far from orgasm at the pace she was taking me.

The mattress didn't squeak, so outside of Mars' words, I only heard the gushy sounds of juices now dripping down my body.

I raised my ass higher, and Mars grabbed my hips, actually pulling me back, and goddammit, I was gay. I was so fucking gay for this woman riding me like there was no tomorrow.

"Tell me who owns you in this moment, Lilith."

She pulled my hips back toward her again, and I saw stars before my eyes.

"Mars! Fuck, Mars. Mars!" I screamed her name.

She didn't stop, but picked up the pace, riding me and bringing me so close to the edge that I could see over the cliffside and into the orgasm chasm below.

"That's it. Good girl. You just keep taking me for as long as you can," Mars said.

I sighed in bliss feeling more heat rising between us.

"Oh shit," I heard Mars say out of nowhere.

"I know!" I hissed. "I know. Mars, you're so fucking hot. I want you inside me again and again."

That was all I could take before I came against Mars' bed, and I felt her come not long after she uttered a series of curses that would have left Zeus blushing.

Carefully, I felt Mars pull out, and I collapsed onto the

bed, quaking in the throws of an orgasm that no amount of money could buy.

Mars didn't say anything. She slipped off the harness. I heard her panting somewhere behind me. Without warning, Mars pulled me closer than before, standing me up straight. I felt her tits pressed against my back and. . . were her arms always this hairy?

It was hard to think. So goddamn difficult as that flood of oxytocin from before was back in my skull and had reached high tide.

"How?" Mars asked, her voice taking on a bit of a growl.

"Good! It was so fucking good," I said, completely misunderstanding her tone and question.

My partner held one arm wrapped around me under my breasts and used the other to push aside my hair.

"I — I can't believe this," Mars started as she sniffed my neck and then licked from my shoulder up to my ear.

Shivering again, I moaned.

"Mars. . . how do you make that feel so fucking good?" I asked, closing my eyes and feeling renewed tingling race down my spine. I was never big on licking before, but when Mars did it, I didn't want her to stop.

My partner's voice dropped more as I felt the tall drink of water bury her face in my hair and sniff it deeply.

As I sighed in contentment, I felt wrapped in something strange. There was a queer energy in the air between us. And not just in the "getting assfucked by a dyke" way.

Gooseflesh crawled down my arms, and I noticed a strange static building between us. Unbelievable feelings of peace and security washed over me while I was in Mars' arms. These weren't one-night stand feelings. These were feelings of mad love and passion. Goddamn. What was in that beer?

Feeling giddy, I kept my eyes closed and taunted, "Hey, Mars. That was fantastic, but I thought you promised to bite."

While I snickered, I felt a lumbering growl build from behind me. And Mars' voice, which somehow seemed to plummet further in tone, now spoke from about two feet above my head.

Did she fuck me in Dolby Surround sound? I thought.

Mars' arms pulled tighter, and my mind inexplicably knew what she was going to do before she did it. Her mouth hovered a few inches above my flesh.

"Do it," I said, unsure of what exactly would happen.

She snarled and sank her teeth into the space where my neck and shoulder met. Blood ran down my flesh as some new force of energy sparked inside of me. Pleasure anew raced down my spine, and I threw my head to the side and moaned.

"Mars. . . Mars Dubois. . . Mars the farmer. . . Mars my lover. . . Mars my. . . my, oh, fuck!" I shouted as she released me from her jaw's grip.

Human teeth don't feel like that, I thought. *Why the hell am I bleeding?*

Images of Mars ran through my head, playing like a film. I watched her running across the farm, tending her animals, and protecting the herd. Then, she was in the woods, and a creature that no longer resembled the girl who took me home filled my mind's eye. Darting between trees. A massive furred beast. A wolf. Bigger than any I'd ever seen in a canine sanctuary. Glowing golden eyes that left shadows so thin they held no secrets. This beast didn't look like the woman who'd slung me over her shoulder and made me giggle. But I knew it was her all the same.

What's happening to me? I thought, my mind reeling from all these images and raw information.

Turning, I faced my lover and discovered Mars to have been replaced with a large bipedal beast covered in mahogany-colored fur.

Those golden eyes were out in full, piercing things that seemed to follow you down into your soul. Blood dripped from her mouth, a jaw filled with razor-sharp teeth. My blood. Her teeth.

Mars was probably around six-and-a-half feet tall. But this creature stood closer to eight-and-a-half feet, head just a stone's throw from the ceiling fan. Long claws hung from each finger. They looked like they could rip through timber.

And where I should have been screaming my head off and running for the door, which I noticed the creature had yet to block, I instead found myself half-sitting and half-collapsing onto the bed, just a foot away from our combined juices staining the blanket.

My heart rate was a little elevated given the mind-breaking thing I was looking at, but I couldn't bring myself to be afraid. It was the strangest sensation, knowing you *should* be terrified, but simply not being scared. Instead, I felt. . . at ease.

"I suppose that's you, Mars?" I asked, feeling like an idiot. What exactly did one say to a large creature like this?

She didn't speak for a moment.

I took that time to look around the room at all the heavy wooden furniture. A chair next to a bookshelf filled with titles of all sizes, both paperbacks and hardbacks. A nightstand with a small blue lamp. Above me hung a ceiling fan that was currently turned off. Though as warm as I was, I wanted it on.

Long blue curtains covered a large bay window opposite the bed.

My eyes spotted a series of carved wooden animal

figurines over on Mars' dresser. They seemed to be mostly deer and moose.

When I turned back to the woman who thoroughly fucked me, she was shrinking. I watched her fur recede and inexplicably vanish beneath Mars' tanned peachy skin. Joints, muscles, and ligaments popped and squelched as they resumed her human form. This happened in, maybe, five seconds.

Then, a nude butch stood over me again. The girl who had thrown me into her pickup truck and dragged me out of town to her farm (with consent).

"I'm sorry, Lilith," Mars said and looked to the floor. "I didn't expect that to happen."

"Well, if it's any consolation, I didn't either," I said with a surprisingly snarky tone. What tone was one supposed to have in a situation like this?

She stood there with her arms crossed, eyes back to their normal shade of hazel.

"Okay. . . I've never been in a position like this before. So maybe. . . I should just ask some rapidfire questions and let you answer them to the best of your ability."

Mars cleared her throat. I couldn't imagine someone as powerful as her looking awkward. But there she stood, somehow managing it.

"That sounds fair. Shoot," she said, finally locking eyes with me.

I nodded.

"Question one. Did you poison my drink, causing me to hallucinate all this?"

She shook her head.

"Okay, horrifying. That means what I witnessed was real. Cool. Question two. What are you?"

Mars sighed and scratched her head.

"I'm a werewolf."

"And that's not like. . . just a giant wolf. You actually do the whole Lon Chaney Jr. thing."

With a rather weak shrug, Mars kicked at something I couldn't see on the thin gray carpet below her.

"I mean — I can take the form of a more traditional wolf, too. What you just saw is kind of a merging of the two. I don't change that way very often."

I crossed my legs, which seemed like a weird thing to do given that I was still mostly naked. But I felt awkward just sitting on the side of the bed like I was.

The next question I wanted to ask was a bit more awkward, in that, I didn't know if she'd have the answer. But I decided to fire it off anyway.

"Do you know why. . . I'm not scared of you right now? I mean, I should be, right? I should be screaming my lungs out. But I'm not. And I find that very strange," I said, verbally tripping over myself.

Mars just scratched her head again.

"That's. . . complicated. And I'm still struggling to understand it myself."

Switching my crossed legs, I paused and thought.

With a softer voice, I asked, "Can you just tell me what you're thinking, at least?"

Her eyes found mine, and a shiver flew down my spine. The fiftieth one tonight. An inexplicable desire for her to see me fully roared through my heart.

Seriously! What's wrong with me?! I thought, scowling.

Mars took a long time to answer my question. I patiently waited while she gathered her thoughts, and I appreciated her form, even in the mess we'd landed ourselves.

"Okay, Lilith. If you'd stumbled across any other werewolf, I reckon you'd be screaming and frozen in panic. But you aren't. I can only imagine what's going through your head. But I can tell you what's going through mine. I'm hungry for you in ways I didn't know I could be before tonight. I know your full name is Lilith Emily Chambers. I know you aren't from anywhere near my territory originally. I know that if you had a tail, it'd wag like mad when people call you things like 'ma'am' and 'miss.'"

I started to put together what she was saying. Mars knew things about me that I hadn't told her. And some kind of unknown force placed this knowledge in her head. I experienced the same thing after she. . . bit me. I almost came to orgasm all over again, and for some reason, I couldn't stop thinking about her sinking those teeth into me a second time. . . and a third time.

But this went way beyond the stereotype of the trans puppygirl. There was a goddamn metaphysical force at play here.

"I saw things about you, too. I know you don't have a middle name. Your mother named you Mars after her favorite celestial body. Your family name, which you also got from her, is Dubois. And you have a huge herd of deer on this farm. Two, actually. You guard them well."

Mars rubbed her jaw.

"All these things would seem to point to one undeniable fact. You and I know things about each other without speaking a word about them. That's part of The Binding."

My eyes widened.

"And The Binding is something that only happens between a werewolf and her. . .," Mars said, her voice trailing off.

I suddenly found myself standing, feeling like I was on the edge of a cliff.

"A werewolf and her what, Mars?"

With a pained look in her eyes and clenched fists, Mars let out a deep sigh before saying, "Her mate."

Chapter 3

Sitting on the edge of a bed where I'd been assfucked by a werewolf, I should have felt a lot of things. Elation, because of the aforementioned activities. Horror, because the butch, it turns out, was a werewolf. Confusion, because I'd just been called her mate. Any number of these things SHOULD have been running through my brain.

Instead, I wondered if Mars kept coffee in her kitchen and wrestled with an unknown emotion burgeoning inside my chest. It wasn't something so simple as joy, nor anything negative like revulsion or fear. No, this feeling shook itself clean of anything easy to understand.

My mind poured through the strange emotion, and it felt like I was examining a geode under a microscope.

Ah, yes. I thought. *This feeling is comprised of 87% gratitude and 13% fear. Quite an elementary compound, really.*

Mars seemed to take this as a good sign and stepped a little closer.

"Watcha thinking about, Little Cottontail? Besides the obvious, I mean," she said.

I shook my head, giggling.

"It's really stupid."

"Try me."

Shrugging, I sighed.

"You asked for it. What do you call a trans Sherlock Holmes?"

Mars' expression scrunched up, and she cocked her head to the side like German Shepherds did when they were trying to puzzle out your words.

Oh fuck, I thought. *I'm going to be comparing everything she does to dog behavior now, huh? Mars will absolutely kill me if she finds out. Can mates read minds?*

That last thought flew around in my head like a deflating party balloon someone tossed into the air.

"Okay," she puzzled. "That's not what I was expecting you to be thinking about. But I'll play along. What do you call a trans Sherlock Holmes?"

I couldn't help but snicker as I said, "Femmedict Cumberbatch."

And we both just sat there laughing our heads off like a couple of goobers. Was the joke that funny? Or were we both still too overloaded from the amazing sex and a post-orgasm monster reveal?

Shivering as another wave of afterglow ran through me, I felt my brain go a little fuzzy.

"I mean — I should be freaking out."

"You should," Mars agreed.

"But I'm not."

"No?" she said.

Suddenly, that emotion that'd been inflating my chest made total sense.

Goddamn. Post-nut clarity is real after all, I thought.

It was gratitude for being desired and fear that the being wanted would fade at any second when Mars realized her supposed mate was someone. . . someone that. . . well, someone who was like me, Lilith Chambers.

Being called a werewolf's mate would normally be enough to get someone committed to an asylum. And here my subby ass was asking dumb questions like, "Someone actually wants me?"

Dating as a trans woman typically consisted of get-togethers that might end with me feeling satisfied for a few hours before the crushing realization that I was alone in this world fell upon me like rubble on a Lannister. But it would more likely end with me walking away from a woman's house or car or the bar bathroom in tears. And THEN I'd be crushed by the realization that I was alone in the world. It was a fun coin toss, actually.

Now, here I was, sitting on a bed that belonged to a woman who made me feel like a million bucks (which, thanks to inflation, wasn't worth as much as it used to be). And not only was she refusing to rush me out the door, but she was actively telling me I was her mate. The partner of a werewolf. Lilith Chambers, the once and future monsterfucker.

Gratitude was a damn weird feeling in this scenario. But fuck was I lonely. So, maybe that explained a thing or two. If Bloody Mary climbed through my bathroom mirror and said I was now "cursed" to be her girlfriend for the next century, I'd probably have been pretty grateful for that as well. Transfemme touch starvation was real.

Of course, the other half of the equation was fear, fear that Mars would regret discovering her mate was a trans girl with a penchant for stripey socks, cheap skirts (that go spinney), and giant shark plushies.

"Okay, you're the expert here, Mars. Why don't you tell me what you're thinking about all this mate business?" I asked, looking up into her once-golden eyes.

She rubbed her chin for a second and then grinned, "Well, my initial thought is I mated you pretty damn good."

My cheeks flushed as I recalled the feeling of her hands on my hips, pulling me toward her with gentle but undeniable strength.

"Yes, well, that's not quite what I meant," I coughed, looking down at the fur blanket I sat on. "That said, I can't help but agree with you."

Mars walked over and grabbed my chin.

"You'll get used to that," she said, winking.

Her strong fingers grasping my chin sent all kinds of inappropriate thoughts shooting through my mind. I was almost panting again.

"I — I'll get used to what?" I stammered.

She smiled like she wanted to eat me whole.

"A great many things, most of all agreeing with me. I am not only your mate, but your alpha. And from how you smelled as I took you over the side of this very bed, I get the feeling you're inclined to enthusiastically agree with powerful women who give you commands. Is that about right?"

More memories of our time together raced through my mind like electricity running down a power pole. I squeezed my legs tighter together.

Mars pulled my head forward and buried her nose in my thick black hair, taking a huge whiff and then several smaller sniffs along the side of my noggin just above my ears. I couldn't help but giggle.

"Oh yes. You'll do just fine as my mate. I'm rather excited to see what other noises I can coax from you," Mars half-growled and half-whispered in my ear while she lumbered over me. "That is, assuming you consent to future fuckings."

I'm pretty sure I consent to all activities where you're concerned, ma'am, including repeatedly running me over with your pickup truck, I thought.

Mars moved her face down my neck and to my shoulders, pausing to lick the spot where she'd bit me. The werewolf lapped up the blood she drew while I shivered and moaned all over again.

"Why am I so horny for your tongue?" I asked with my eyes closed, leaning entirely into the alpha.

"You've just been awakened to your mate. Congratulations, Lilith. You're officially in heat for me. And you will be for the next week," Mars said.

I swallowed nervously.

"Wow, that is so hot and disturbing. What happens after the week is up?" I asked, almost pleading for her to lick that bitemark again.

She seemed to know what I wanted and obliged me as I softly moaned, falling entirely into her body as her tongue ran over the wound her teeth had opened.

"Nothing much. Your cravings for me drop from insatiably horny to mildly horny until the next month rolls around, and you go into heat for me all over again."

The room did feel hotter with Mars licking me.

When she finally showed me mercy and pulled away, I was still vibrating with giddiness at her touch.

"And when do you go into heat for me?" I asked, opening my eyes again.

She smiled.

"It doesn't work that way. I'm the dominant one here. I'll always want you, but your body is the one that calls out to mine."

I shrugged.

"Fine by me. I still have about a million questions, but the one at the top of the list is. . . do you regret that your mate, the one whose body calls out to yours, is trans? Fucking me for a night is one thing. Being metaphysically bound to someone like me seems like a much heavier commitment, one you didn't get a choice in."

My heart quivered asking this, but I figured there wouldn't be a "right" time to ask it later. We could sort out all the magical bullshit in the days ahead. But if I was going to be horny for this werewolf for one week out of every month for the foreseeable future, I needed to know how she felt about my body.

I braced myself for a noncommittal answer or a joke. That's what I'd be tempted to do in this situation. Sidestep. Dodge. Avoid. The harder questions always came with an urge to evade.

Tears welled up at the side of my eyes as I thought back to real things other women, both trans and cis, had told me through the years.

"Look, we had a fun night. Let's just leave it at that."

"Sorry, I'm not looking for anything serious."

"I'm not really about that at this point in my life. Are we cool?"

"Don't get me wrong. I just don't feel that way about you. It was just sex, ya know?"

"I just don't think we're all that. . . compatible. Look, it's getting late, and I gotta go. I'll text you later, okay?"

Mars would probably be in the same boat. Why wouldn't she? Fated or otherwise, how could someone be okay with reaching into the grabbag of mates and drawing me? No one else had wanted me beyond a night or two. Why should Mars be saddled with the girl everyone else said "no" to?

It was the difference between being served a hot bowl of made-from-scratch ramen at a restaurant and the stuff that masquerades as ramen in the package that costs 33 cents and needs a kettle of hot water and artificial flavoring to imitate the real thing.

While the werewolf considered her words, I started looking around for my gaff so I could get dressed and leave. Maybe there was a pill I could take to ease off the horniness for the next week. Or I could just skip my progesterone dose over the next seven nights.

As I stood up to better search for my gaff, Mars gently sat me back down on the bed. She cupped my cheeks with her firm hands and looked deeply into my eyes. I could have sworn I felt my pupils dilating, and the oxytocin ramping up in my brain the longer I remained in her gaze.

I blinked away the tiny drops that had been welling up at the edges of my vision but didn't break eye contact with the werewolf. With as soft a voice as she could manage, Mars said, "I'm sorry others have mistreated you, Little Cottontail. But you need to understand something. You're mine now. That bite you're so thirsty for me to lick will never fade. It marks you as the mate of Mars Dubois, alpha of the Dubois Pack."

". . . 'Kay," I muttered, still reeling from the amount of love chemicals sloshing through my noggin.

"Do not believe for a single second that I feel cheated or disappointed over my mate being trans. Your very soul is linked to mine. Fate wrote the name of 'Lilith Emily Chambers' on my heart before either of us knew it. And now that I see you, smell you, and taste you, I know what it feels like to be made whole. You are everything I've wanted since I first knew that I wanted someone to call my mate."

It was getting harder to form words as the gratitude finally kicked fear from my chest. Nobody made these kinds of declarations willy-nilly. If you said shit like this, it was because you damn well meant it.

"You want me?" I managed to squeak out.

"Want you? Lilith, I have you. The question you should be asking is if I'm ever going to let you go. And before you ask, understand that the answer is no. Unless, of course, you don't want me. . .. Do you want me?"

Nodding before she'd even finished the question, I felt my skin twitch where I'd been bitten. Desire came alive in a renewed way.

"This is wild shit," I said, panting. "Are you sure you didn't spike my beer?"

"No. But I'm willing to spike you again if you desire."

"Oh, I desire. I desire very much," I sighed as she kissed me.

And then, she took me again.

━━

I SHOWERED and threw on a pair of plaid pajama pants and an oversized gray t-shirt with the words "Mothra Slut" written across the chest.

Holy shit, I realized. *I'm the eepy girlfriend wearing my partner's oversized shirt and pajamas.*

Gender euphoria flooded through me as I grabbed my cheeks and relished every moment I could still feel the raw elation.

I walked out of the guest bathroom and into the hallway, heading back toward bed. Exhaustion and contentment filled every muscle in my body, and I felt loose and at ease for the first time in years.

Before I grabbed the doorknob, Mars' hand lightly took my wrist.

"Where are you going?"

"To. . . bed?" I asked.

Mars raised an eyebrow.

"Oh, no, the bed is for fucking. Along with many other

places we'll work our way through in time. But the den is for sleeping."

We sleep in the. . . living room? I thought, bemused.

Instead, Mars led me into the back of her farmhouse where an honest-to-god conversation pit big enough to hold a king mattress lay in waiting.

"Wow. I thought they got rid of these in the '50s," I mumbled.

"They're surprisingly popular with werewolves. In the Wolfout subreddit, at least half of the members have one, and another quarter are building them."

The pit must have descended into the floor about five feet, with all sides consisting of a fuzzy red sofa and cushions. Tons of large pillows covered couch cushions, along with a mess of fuzzy blankets.

I started to shiver as I stepped into the direct line of an A/C vent. While the bedroom was warm, I noticed the den was a fucking ice box. Blackout curtains covered all the windows. A long table with two antique lamps provided the only source of light. A ceiling fan spun at max speed above us. It swung back and forth as the blades rotated fast enough to propel a plane.

A large painting of a white wolf napping in a patch of sunlight covered one of the walls opposite the lamps.

This part of the farmhouse smelled a little older and a bit more musky. But I kind of liked that. Like, this was part of the original home's core.

Turning back to Mars, I asked, "Wait — did you say there's a subreddit for werewolves?"

She nodded.

"Yeah, it's a private community. But there are a few thousand of us posting on any given day from around the world. We talk about werewolf safety, custom home modifications, hunting techniques, and more."

My eyes widened.

"So if r/wolfout was ever exposed, all your fellow werewolves would have to. . . PACK up and leave?"

Mars rolled her eyes.

"And you thought being trans would be the biggest barrier to my accepting you as my mate. When in reality, you should have been much more worried about your awful jokes."

I bumped my hip into hers and said, "Hey, from girldick to puns, you're the one who said I completed you. So, are we sleeping on the cushions or . . .?"

Mars snorted and then started sniffing me again. I had to assume I'd get used to that since it came with the territory of having a werewolf mate. For now, it still gave me the giggles.

As I stifled a laugh, Mars said, "Oh, good. You used my cinnamon soap."

"That's good?" I asked, once again uncertain of her meaning.

"Mmmmhhhhmmm," she said, starting to rub her cheek against mine. "I want you to start smelling like me, and that's a solid start."

I closed my eyes while she continued to rub cheeks with me. Fuck. Even this was strangely comforting. What the hell happened to me in the three hours since I'd met Mars and left Wylde Night?

"I'm supposed to smell like you?" I asked.

"You're my mate, Little Cottontail. My scent will define yours so any other creatures thinking about making a tasty little snack out of you will think twice."

Cocking my head to the side, I asked, "And aside from you, there are how many other creatures in Pine Springs?"

She shrugged.

"Way more than you know. I'll teach you the basics

soon. For now, just focus on being mine. And be warned that werewolves can be extremely possessive of their mates. Is that going to bother you?"

She's going to be possessive of me? I thought. *That might be the hottest thing she's said so far.*

I let Mars continue to exchange scents with me until she finally led me toward the conversation pit.

"I'm still just over the moon that someone wants me, Mars. You wanna be possessive? Go for it. I don't think you'll have any problem with other people making moves on me. I'm not exactly F1NN5TER, you know."

My mate pulled me into a tight embrace and said, "Like I said, we'll go over the specifics later. But understand that your entire world is going to be different now. A werewolf's mate can get into all manner of monsters and mayhem. That's why I have to be possessive, to protect you."

As I drowsily took in her scent of cinnamon and dry leaves, I nodded. Go ham. Be possessive. It still sounded fucking hot to me.

"And no, we don't sleep on the cushions. The couch and pillows just form the outer walls of my den."

Mars walked down a small staircase on the left side of the conversation pit, and where I expected her feet to meet a floor, I was surprised to discover a large Japanese futon mattress. She pulled down a couple of the pillows and unfolded several large blankets before declaring her den complete for the night.

When I nestled down into the mass of blankets, futon, and pillows, I had to admit, this felt pretty damn cozy. With the couch walls all around us, this really did feel a bit like a den that a wolf might sleep in, just with the modern human comforts of air conditioning and a mattress.

Massive arms wrapped around my waist and pulled me

into a spooning position. I laughed as Mars moved me several inches closer with all the ease one might carry a stuffed animal.

"How fucking strong are you, anyway?"

Mars chuckled, and I felt it across my entire body.

"Why? Are you imagining me snapping you like a twig?"

"I've imagined all kinds of things you might do to me over the last hour."

I could almost hear her smiling.

"We'll have to make a checklist, then. I can't have an unsatisfied mate."

My body heat must have climbed a few degrees despite the frigid air outside the den. I think that's one thing neurotypicals failed to understand about the neurodivergent relationship with heat. We didn't want to be hot. We wanted to be cold and then made hot by a blanket. Or maybe a blanket and werewolf cuddles.

"So why am I automatically the little spoon?" I asked, yawning.

"Easy. Because you're submissive and breedable as fuck. Oh, and so I can do this," she said, nosing my hair out of the way and slowly licking the back of my neck.

Shivers of pleasure and familiarity to my mate ran down my spine as I sighed. Being a werewolf's mate was changing me in ways I couldn't even begin to comprehend. Maybe we'd go over that during breakfast tomorrow.

Just before my eyelids became too heavy to keep open, I asked, "Hey, Mars?"

"Yeah, Little Cottontail?"

"Where's the rest of your pack?"

Her arms tightened around me, and I could have sworn I started to feel the alpha shake behind me. Oh fuck! What did I just do?

But her shaking stopped after a few seconds, and she said, "That's a long story, Lilith. Ask me again when you can handle bitter things."

Somehow, Mars found a way to squeeze me even tighter. And I found myself imagining all kinds of answers to my question.

What happened to them? I thought. *Did they die? Did they kick her out? Did they join the Wolves of Thunderclap?*

But no answer seemed to fit right in the puzzle, so my restless mind found rest in the arms of my new mate and the promises of more answers to come. And, of course, given that I was now in heat and in the grasp of Mars, answers wouldn't be the only thing to come.

Chapter 4

The old pickup truck lumbered to a stop in front of the Pine Springs Public Library, an old brick building on the outskirts of downtown. She was old, but she was mine. Literally. I was the only one here to take care of her, one of five recipients of the Maine Rural Librarian Grant.

In an attempt to make sure small communities across the Pine Tree State had access to literature, public internet, and other community resources, a whopping $160,000 was awarded via grant by the Legislature each year. It paid the meager salary of small-town librarians like me.

For the promise of a musty building, old books, and a $32,000 salary, I traded my small hometown in eastern Colorado for Pine Springs. I couldn't afford to live alone, so I found a shitty spare bedroom in an old house and became roommates with a stranger named Alan.

I groaned inwardly thinking of facing him again.

"Hey, Earth to Cottontail. You good?"

Snapping back to reality at the voice of my mate (a word I still wasn't used to), I shook my head a few times.

"Sorry. I was just lost in my thoughts. What were we talking about?"

Mars rewarded me with the deep rumble of a chuckle and stroked the side of my head, pushing hair away from my face. I leaned into her touch and closed my eyes, grabbing her wrist.

"That's my good girl. You remember my touch. Keep the feeling of my flesh against yours in your mind all day."

"I will," I moaned, feeling her strong hand slide down to the side of my face. Her thumb rubbed against the bottom of my lip, and I bit it. Not hard, mind you. More like a love nibble.

Mars effortlessly pulled me into a deep kiss, finding yet another great use of her werewolf strength. I stifled another moan as her tongue met mine and pushed it down. Even here, I submitted to her.

When she finally pulled away, a small line of saliva bridging our lips, I paused. Mars grinned and then leaned back over, licking it up.

"Don't want to waste a drop of my mate's taste," she whispered before bumping her forehead to mine.

My cheeks flushed as heat rushed to my face.

"Do you remember everything we talked about at breakfast this morning?"

"I think so. Um, don't freak out if 'strange' things start happening around me. Being a werewolf's fated mate brings uncertain and unpredictable magic into my life since I'm just a regular human."

She nodded.

"If I feel threatened or scared by anything, you'll be able to sense it," I said, trying to recall the highlights of our conversation over waffles and bacon an hour ago.

"Good. And the other major thing?"

I closed my eyes to think, taking in the warm farm scents Mars brought into the truck after running through a couple of small outdoor chores while I did my makeup this morning.

"Ummmmm," I mumbled, struggling to focus.

Mars kissed the tip of my nose.

"Gods, you're cute. The last thing I need you to remember is to be careful around other people's dogs. They'll smell me on you, and depending on any number of factors will be inexplicably sweet or outright hostile to you. Werewolf scents don't seem to leave any middle ground in man's best friend. They either love us or hate us."

I nodded, still feeling like the moment I got out of this truck would end the pleasant dream I'd found myself in since Mars rescued me from that creep at the art gallery last night. My fingers hesitated on the worn metal door handle.

As I shifted uncomfortably in the patched leather bench seat of Mars' antique truck, I took in the smell of alfalfa and protein pellets that seemed to blanket her this morning.

Seeming to sense my hesitation, Mars grabbed my chin and turned my face to hers.

"Easy now, Little Cottontail. You'll see me again tonight for dinner. Remember? I've gotta drive out to Lubec to drop off a few things. But I can pick up some fresh lobster tails to grill tonight if you want."

My mouth was suddenly watering at the thought of, not just seafood, but seeing Mars in one of those cheesy, "kiss the cook" aprons while standing over a charcoal grill.

"Yes please," I said.

"Good. Bring your appetite. I'll never let my mate go hungry."

Without thinking, my voice spit out some words that left Mars momentarily stunned.

"I know firsthand how good you are at stuffing me."

My mate froze and then burst out a raucous belly laugh.

"Your puns are terrible, but your one-liners just make me want to drag you back to my bed and fuck you so hard that the only words you're left with are gibberish."

I leered at Mars until she kissed me again.

"See you tonight, my mate," she said as I climbed out of the truck. And it occurred to me that I'd never had someone looking forward to seeing me before. Certainly not this far in advance. Most of my hookups came in the moment when I drove out of town to hit up a bar. But here? I knew a pretty woman was not only excited to see me, but to welcome me into her home again.

Warm butterflies fluttered in my tummy, amidst the waffles I'd devoured. And for at least a minute or two, I stood there gaping on the sidewalk. Dumbfounded over my sudden smittenness, I shuffled around my purse awkwardly the key to the front door.

Walking inside the single-story library, I took a deep breath. The scent of old books and tired carpet greeted me.

There was nothing quite like the feeling of being surrounded by books. I didn't like to think of myself as some sort of cliche soul who romanticized the printed word, but the truth was, few things could seduce me faster than talking about what one was reading or how many books they had on their shelves at home.

And I wanted to hear about it all. Audiobooks, graphic novels, ebooks, what you bought at Narnes & Boble, your interlibrary loan orders, anything you were reading. I wanted people to have access to stories, biographies, reference material, comics, and anything they needed to let their minds escape the dull tedium of this world for even a few minutes. Heaven knows that's why I first started sticking my nose in books. It's harder for dysphoria to fuck you up when your mind is busy processing the words and images of an author.

When I was thirteen and lamenting the smells of a boyish body hitting puberty, I'd bury myself in lotions I stole from Mom and escape to Earthsea to travel on magical adventures with Ged and Tenar.

Sighing and shaking the old memories from my noggin, I flipped the lights on and watched three large chandeliers begin their daylong hum, bringing light to my sanctuary.

The front desk stood about ten feet from the main door, and I tried to keep it mostly clear. Only my laptop, a barcode scanner, and a basket for book returns covered the heavy oak furniture.

I booted up the laptop and waited for that familiar field of grass background to appear. It took several minutes as Windows was slow to wake some mornings.

"Yeah, yeah, I know," I mumbled, launching our checkout software as the hard drive clicked and whirred.

The old Dell computer was a leftover from the state that had been graciously awarded to this library a few years ago. Unfortunately, it was old even then. I'm pretty sure this laptop hit store shelves when Obama was still in office.

When the checkout system was finally open, I walked to a basket full of books that'd been dropped in the overnight return chute. Quite a few people who came to Wylde Night took the opportunity to drop their books off, seeing as they were already downtown.

I picked up a biography of Teddy Roosevelt, a couple of Louis L'Amour westerns, a self-help programming guide from a writer who simply published it under the pseudonym of "Soph," and a few volumes of Inuyasha.

Taking the titles to the front desk to check in, I found myself curious about the programmer and looked her up on Foogle. I found her website easily enough.

"Of course she's trans," I chuckled. "Statistically, eight out of ten programmers will find themselves dissatisfied with their gender and ascend to a new form."

After I got the books checked in, I added them to my trusty beige cart that squeaked like nobody's business and started reshelving books.

The library was broken into two wings when you walked in. The right side was divided between nonfiction and fiction sections. The left side was filled with children's books, bean bags, toys, and a cozy corner where a drag queen from Bangor drove in to read to kids once a month.

A few patrons had grumbled about it, but surprisingly, nobody had organized a protest yet. I didn't exactly make a big show of advertising it. Belinda Books randomly hopped into my inbox one day, offering to make the drive and read to any interested kids. She did it all on her own dime because the state sure as hell wasn't going to pay storytime readers to visit the Pine Springs Public Library.

She showed up after I spread news of the event by word of mouth to some chill parents who frequented the library. And to my surprise, Belinda always had a crowd of at least a dozen kids who loved to hear her silly voices and colorful stories. (Colorful, as in, the art on the pages had bright colors. Not colorful, as in, explicit).

The morning went on rather quietly, and I ate a quick lunch Mars had been sweet enough to pack me.

While the library was still closed for my lunch break, I unlocked the door to the basement and descended to our media storage section. We kept DVDs, CDs, and audiobooks on a bunch of dusty white shelves about half my size.

You never knew when a Boomer would wander in asking about checking out season four of *Everybody Loves Raymond* or the last season of *The Sopranos*. I pulled the drawstring and a pendant light clicked on, bathing the exposed stone walls in pale amber light. It swung back and forth while I shelved a DVD copy of *Star Trek: Nemesis* that'd been returned while I was eating my sandwich.

Turning to leave, I heard something crack to my right. My eyes focussed on a small brown mouse sliding out of a hole in the ancient wooden wall. It plopped to the dirty floor and bounced a few times before scurrying off into a dark corner.

"That thing probably needs to be inspected for stability," I mumbled before the crack grew longer and louder, spreading in two directions from floor to ceiling.

Oh shit! I thought before two wooden panels on the library's original wall fell loose, clattering to the ground.

I jumped and covered my ears, never a fan of loud noises.

A cloud of dust slowly cleared, and I wiped my eyes noticing some sort of room or chamber beyond the wooden wall.

"What the actual fuck?" I asked, daring to scoot a few feet closer. It was dark, but I could make out a table maybe?

This building had just celebrated its 200th birthday last year, and I knew it'd had very little restoration work done to keep the original structure as intact as possible. I'd worked here for a few years now and had never once noticed a second room in the basement.

I mean, the basement always seemed smaller than I expected. But a hidden chamber? Part of me expected Mr.

Barlow the vampire to come stumbling out. Actually, come to think of it, now that I knew werewolves were real, a vampire walking out of the secret room of my library's basement was at least 27% more likely.

"H — hello?" I called stupidly into the darkness.

And I flinched when a strange clattering noise greeted me. My heart rumbled like a jackhammer in my chest as adrenaline did its job and tried to convince me to fight or fly.

With a few deep (and dusty) breaths, I stepped toward the rattling noise. It sounded bigger and heavier than the mouse that climbed out of this decrepit wooden wall.

Placing a hand on the 18th-century lumber where the panels had collapsed, I was greeted with an old and chalky sensation, as though the very air in this room hadn't moved in a very long time.

The rattling grew louder as I turned on my phone and used the light to make sense of my surroundings.

A stone floor stretched out for at least 20 feet in all directions before me. The walls had no windows and a large candelabra stood on top of a shelf full of antique glass jars and powders to my left.

Slanted wooden beams held the ceiling up about five feet above my head. They appeared to be holding steady, unlike the piece of wall that collapsed to let me in here. The entire room smelled of dry lumber, ancient herbs, and chalk.

Ahead of me against another wall sat an honest-to-god caldron and some sort of an altar topped with long-ago melted candles, small metal tins of ingredients, and finger bones that appeared to be from someone's hand. The good thing about being From Away? I knew the skeletal hand belonged to nobody I knew.

"My bad. I didn't know we were opening a Spirit

Halloween in the basement. That shit really will spawn anywhere, won't it?" I said to no one, mostly to calm my nerves.

Did the historical society know about this? If not, they'd definitely want to. Fuck, a secret occult chamber found in the basement of the library would be the front page of the Pine Springs Gazette tomorrow. The Bangor TV station would probably send over a young reporter to do a story on it. And I say young because Bangor was a tiny-ass news market, and reporters who wanted to work in Portland typically had to cut their teeth in the Queen City first. At least, that's what a reporter I hooked up with at a club in Portland told me she had to do. It seemed kind of tedious to me. Books were simpler.

And speaking of books, that rattling noise had only grown louder as I stepped further into the room.

My eyes flew to a center table that appeared to be hand-carved from mahogany. And despite how old everything else in here seemed to be, the table looked as sturdy as the day it was chiseled and hammered together.

In the table's center, on a worn, loosely folded black cloth sat a book. Then again, "sat" probably wasn't a strong enough verb to describe the book's activity. It was shaking every few seconds like a phone on vibrate.

The leatherbound tome was the size of a college notebook and sealed shut with a buckle on the side. Gooseflesh crept over my arms as it continued to rattle and dance in my presence.

Every single lick of common sense I'd built over the years as a librarian was telling me to leave and call someone whose job it was to deal with hidden basement rooms. Then again, in some twisted way, wasn't this my job? I was the librarian. And here was a book. My entire career was built around books. Why should this one be any different? Intense shaking aside, I mean.

My hand seemed to stretch toward the book without my knowledge. And while I probably should have stopped it. . . I didn't. The past 24 hours had seen me become a werewolf's mate, and I was warned unpredictable magic and madness were to follow. Why bother trying to avoid it?

As my fingers traced the leather and iron buckle, the book suddenly sat stone still. The binding felt. . . warm, pulsing with life, even.

Aw shit. I'm gonna open this thing and wind up with a chainsaw for a hand, I thought, unlatching the book.

"Groovy," was the last thing I said before the tome spilled wide open. Without warning, an invisible force slapped me backward and sent my ass sliding across the dusty stone floor. Some arcane power burst forth with a near-deafening boom.

A queer static and blinding golden light seemed to fill the entire chamber afterward. Even grimacing with my eyes shut, I saw the powerful illumination.

It took a few tries to sit up and open my eyelids. Everything that had once been dark was now bathed in yellow light, all tracing back to a single source.

Hovering a few inches above the tome of fluttering pages stood a woman made of pure fire. Long blonde hair wafted around the book-bound entity, and her solid white eyes opened wide, searching the room around her.

Gradually, the flames died down a bit, revealing a more human flesh underneath. The woman, who appeared to be in her late 30s or early 40s stretched and yawned.

My jaw was practically on the floor as I gaped up at her fiery form.

When she finally noticed me, the hovering woman

spoke with a smoky voice that seemed to slide into my ears as easily as a cotton swab.

"Greetings. My name is Phenna. And it is about fucking time someone opened my book. I beseech you, good woman. Tell me the year of my freeing. And share with me your name."

I sat there dumbfounded, unable to even remember how speaking worked.

Chapter 5

I'm not sure how long we stared at each other, me on my ass and her hovering above the table of my library's newly-discovered basement chamber. She seemed patient enough to wait for my brain to come back together into a cohesive form.

And at last, when I found words, I gave them to her.

"Phenna, was it?"

"Indeed. That is what I am called. Who am I making the acquaintance of this fine day?"

I shook my head a little. Her speech was. . . antiquated, but only partially so. And her voice was so heavy with smoke and weighed with magic.

"L — Lilith, ma'am. My name is Lilith."

A finger stroked her chin as her smile grew.

"It's my pleasure to know you, Lilith. And ma'am? Goodness me. It's been centuries since I was called anything by a flesh-and-blood mortal, but even in my day it was rare that I be addressed with such language."

I just sat there and listened to her, not wanting to stop

the woman who'd previously been on fire before my very eyes.

"Only Lord Wylde addressed me in the manner I preferred. I don't suppose he was ever found, was he?"

For what felt like the millionth time, my jaw dropped to the floor.

"Lord Wylde? Lord Jameson Wylde? You knew him?"

Phenna's face flushed a little, and she giggled.

"Well, of course, I knew Jamie. And he knew me, the real me. He didn't call me Peter. He addressed me as Lady Phenna. As thanks for him being the only one to see me, I dedicated my life to Understanding to help him solve the mysteries that surrounded his new town. Lord help me, I was so distraught when he went marching into the woods and never returned. Was he ever found?"

Holy shit. How old was this book lady? I tried to remember back to last night, before being thoroughly assfucked by my werewolf mate. When did the historical society say Lord Wylde went missing? Like — the early 1800s? And Phenna knew him?

"I don't mean to sound rude, Lady Phenna, but. . . what are you? And I don't mean in a sense of sex. I mean — like, in the sense of fire and book imprisonment."

It was only just now occurring to me that Phenna said other people called her Peter. Did that mean what I thought it meant?

She cocked her head to the side and then laughed again. Her smoky chortle filled the basement room.

"Oh, no, you certainly don't have to call me Lady Phenna. Just Phenna is fine. Lady Phenna was what Jamie called me. And I certainly wasn't imprisoned in the Mágissa Biblia. It became my home when I shed mortal flesh to supersede my physical limitations and consume all manner of arcane thought."

I held up a finger, indicating that I'd be right back. Fucking a werewolf was one thing. But this shit was making my head hurt. I walked upstairs to the breakroom, pulled out an ice tray from the library's antique refrigerator, and poured a glass of water. Then, I downed it. I repeated the process, and all the while my brain was abuzz with Phenna's words.

Mágissa Biblia. Lord Wylde. Arcane thought. This was all too much.

Taking a deep breath, I returned to the basement with my third glass of ice water. Without thinking, I offered it to Phenna who politely declined with a simple gesture.

When I started sipping on this third glass, I nodded.

"Okay. So. . . you're a trans witch who lived in the 1800s. It's 2024 now, by the way. I'm sorry if that shocks you, but given all that I've seen and learned in the last 10 minutes, I think it's only fair to return some surprise."

Phenna's eyes drew wide.

"Oh my. So many days have passed. And you'll forgive me for wrinkling my nose at the term 'witch.' That terminology doesn't come close to describing what it means to truly Understand the arcane properties of the Five Realms."

She paused for a moment, seeming for the first time like she didn't understand part of what I'd said. Her eyes narrowed, and Phenna pursed her lips.

"What is trans?" she asked. "You used the word as an adjective, but I'm unfamiliar with how it further describes the term 'witch.'"

I scratched the back of my head.

"What is trans? Shit. I asked that exact question the first time my high school visited Denver to see the Nature and Science Museum. We passed a trans woman, and some classmates were snickering about it. But I couldn't stop staring at her. She had this confidence as she strode down the sidewalk like her ego was surrounded by a castle their jabs and laughter couldn't touch."

Phenna's confusion didn't abate.

"So trans is a modifier for witch and woman?"

I cleared my throat.

"Sorry. Your question brought back a memory from the day my egg cracked a little."

"Your. . . egg?"

Rubbing my forehead, I realized that my words weren't helping.

"Sorry. A phrase of modern culture. I'll order you a Blåhaj later. Um, trans is a modifier used to mean a person's gender identity doesn't quite match up with the sex a doctor assigned them at birth. It has roots in words like transsexual and even earlier transvestite."

At last, we cracked the language barrier of this one word, and understanding filled Phenna's expression. The floating woman nodded.

"Ah! Yes. I see. In my day, they just called us 'masqueraders' and other pejorative terms I've long since banished from my lips."

Phenna kept hovering there, and I found myself wanting to know so much more. It was as though her very vestige drew forth a hunger within that I'd not witnessed before. She had power. I felt it from the gooseflesh on my arms to the marrow in my bones.

I licked my lips, and she grinned wider, continuing to make eye contact. It was strange to see her so patient. There was almost something inhuman in the way she just waited for me to ask questions or make idiotic statements or terrible jokes. Time hadn't mattered to her for the last couple of centuries. Why should it start now? With no flesh to decay, what was time to a being whose only hunger was.

. . spellcraft? What she'd called arcane knowledge. Something about five realms?

Phenna's eyes glowed with confidence, in herself? In her knowledge? In her abilities? A part of my soul unhinged its jaw and ran to devour even a morsel of that same confidence. A shred of that power.

I spent so much time every day wondering what it'd be like to walk around without wondering if someone was going to haul off and smack me for no good reason. And how many headaches had I suffered through facedown on my bed as dysphoria sent lightning bolt after lightning bolt through my head carrying words like "not feminine enough" and "still a man"?

But Phenna? She didn't show any sign that these things were still a problem for her. As she floated in a veil of power, still anticipating my next sentence, I kept opening my mouth and then closing it.

Each time I did that, I swear her lip twitched upward.

I didn't feel like prey standing in her line of sight, nor did I feel like a wayward soul being graced by a guardian angel. It was more like. . . I'd opened the book and set her loose. And now she was plenty content to hang around until. . . until what? Did I get wishes? Was she here to guide me? Would Phenna become my fairy godmother?

"Are you scared?" I asked, stupidly. Of all the words to escape from my lips, I'd settled on those? C'mon, Lilith. You're smarter than that.

Phenna raised an eyebrow.

"Not particularly. Should I be? Do you have a hungry woman in a candy house waiting to devour children stashed around here?"

I smirked.

Hey, I understood that reference, I thought. *Cultural bridge constructed.*

"You seem pretty strong. I just wondered if you really feared anything when you had that much power."

"Understanding," she corrected.

Cocking my head to the side, I waited for her to explain why she kept using that word.

"You keep throwing around all these words. Confidence. Power. Magic. But it all boils down to Understanding, truly knowing how the Five Realms work. Arcane knowledge is what stripped away the fear I found myself so eager to shed when I was your age."

My tongue felt dry. The air in the basement seemed to be making me even thirstier, and not just for the dripping glass of ice water in my hand. Still, I downed the water and cleared my throat.

Without much prompting, my thoughts turned to Mars. She had power and confidence. It was what made it so easy to submit to her and fall headfirst into all this fated mate stuff. A pretty woman strolls up to me with biceps that could raise the Titanic and says I'm her one and true mate? Yup. I'm sold. No further evidence is needed, Your Honor. We, the jury, find the defendant fuckable in the most extreme sense.

Outside on the street above, a diesel truck roared by and rattled the concrete foundation of the library. I rolled my eyes.

Phenna didn't seem to pay it any mind.

"Is it possible for someone like me to become as powerful as you, Phenna? Half as powerful?"

The floating woman flashed me a look of annoyance, flicking her tongue with a sigh. And I realized I'd fucked up.

"Sorry — that was a dumb question."

No. . . it was poorly worded, I thought, eyes widening with an awakening thought.

I was starting to realize there might be rules to what the book woman could answer or how her sentences had to be formatted. Rules and structure could very well be key pieces of the foundations to her — whatever it was she had that I so desperately craved right now.

Setting my empty glass down on the table, I took a few steps back.

"How do I gain Understanding like you, Phenna?"

What cogs had to spin through my mind before I could possess and set figurative fingers to the secret knowledge she possessed? Because I wanted it. My soul was thirsty and ravenous for what Phenna had. And the longer I looked at her, the more difficult to ignore those cravings became.

I could have sworn I saw recognition in her eyes. She knew my hunger for power, to be sure that I'd find happiness one day that couldn't be stripped from me or maybe even a way to make my own.

"Now we're getting somewhere," Phenna said, throwing back her head and cackling. Then, without missing a beat, she stopped and stared at me with a deadpan expression. "Understanding does not come without time and sacrifice, good woman."

I squared my shoulders even as I felt my stomach drop at those words. Maybe if I looked unafraid, I would be.

"How long did it take you? What did you sacrifice?" I asked, crossing my arms.

"I believe your second question has an obvious answer judging by how you found me and the fact that I've yet to set foot on the ground, sweet thing."

It was uncanny how quickly her speech was changing or evolving to mimic a style closer to my own. I guess I'd have to attribute that to her Understanding as well.

My cheeks flushed. Something was seriously warped in

my mind the way my heart fluttered when an older woman called me some form of "sweetie."

And while Phenna was centuries old, she looked to be in her 40s. If I hadn't just found my mate and been marked by her (which was still so incredibly hot whenever I thought about her teeth imprints on my chest), I might have been fawning all over Phenna to drag me into that book of hers and do things to me with "magic."

I'd wager she could make me arrive at an understanding pretty fucking quick.

"As for your first question. . . there's only so much I'm allowed to say for one who has paid no price save for opening the Mágissa Biblia. Understanding begins by binding your soul to the Yggdrasil Tree and continues with forming a bridge to The Maiden, The Mother, and The Crone. It took me almost a decade to do those things. A year to figure out how to even read the Mágissa Biblia and another seven or eight to walk into the — well, in your tongue the place's name translates to Blood Valley."

Running my hands through my hair, I bristled at the options before me. Wait a fucking decade to even start learning magic? Even trans folks in the UK didn't have to wait that long to get access to HRT, which was its own form of magic.

I rubbed my chin.

Actually, with the way my dysphoria makes me feel some days, sacrificing my body to become a fiery cougar who floats through the air doesn't sound half bad, I thought, rolling my eyes.

"Sorry to sound extremely American here, but. . . is there a shortcut? Like — what if I want to microwave my magic instead of warming it up in the oven?" I asked, squinting even as I asked the question.

And where I expected more annoyance from Phenna,

she merely flashed me a look of what I could best describe as "morose caution."

"It is because I still remember having a beating heart in my chest that I give you this warning once and only once, Lilith."

I flinched at her words.

Well shit, I thought. *It seems we're done with "sweetie" this and "sweetie that."*

"You're hungry. I feel it rising from you like steam from a fresh loaf of bread. That hunger to learn, that craving to discover, that itch to snatch arcane knowledge. . . won't ever go away. In fact, once you taste the fruit of the Yggdrasil Tree and welcome the chilled embrace of The Maiden, The Mother, and The Crone, it will only grow worse. And there are only so many things you can give away before you're left with nothing."

A shiver ran from my heart straight to my toes, faster than a bullet train. But as her warning tempered my appetite for something I just discovered minutes ago, a dark question formed in the back of my mind.

"What. . . exactly could I do with Understanding? Could I. . . not sacrifice my flesh, but merely reshape it to my liking?"

Phenna leaned forward now, seemingly floating on her stomach. The book woman folded each arm, resting her chin on her wrists. Gone was the expression of warning. It'd been devoured by a face that I'd describe as "cat ate the canary."

What is WITH this woman? I thought. *She's all over the place.*

The way I couldn't get a solid read on her left me all the more unnerved. It was like one moment she wanted me to run screaming from the path she'd chosen and the next, Phenna was practically throwing wide the gate for me to enter her domain. Is that what being locked in a magical book for centuries did to your mind?

"I can't say what you'd be able to do with Understanding. But I can tell you from a purely historical note that the Mágissa Biblia contains 57 smaller books compiled by sorceresses through the ages. And one of them, written by a woman who lived 2,500 years ago, deals with advanced concepts of flesh made clay."

She's telling me "yes" without saying "yes," I thought. Looking down at my hands and sighing at the hours and days I'd lost wishing for different chromosomes, I made a snap decision right there and then.

"Fortuna iuvat," I muttered, clenching my hands into fists.

I was done wishing. It was time to roll up my sleeves and make something happen for once.

"Ooooooo, quoting Virgil. Oh, Lilian, you truly must be a librarian," Phenna giggled. "Which means nobody has moved this book since I forsook my flesh years and years ago."

I nodded.

"You remain within the Pine Springs Community Library, built by your own Jamie in 1823. Now, in exchange for that knowledge, I'd like you to grant me passage to the Blood Valley," I told Phenna as I crossed my arms and put on a stern face.

But she merely laughed.

"Bravo! You really took a swing there, you mortal doll. But I will not grant you something that took me eight years to learn for knowledge that took you eight minutes to gain. Where is the equivalent exchange?"

Probably with a short blond boy wearing a red coat and carrying a metal arm, I thought, bitterly.

I rubbed my hair again and looked around the altar of

this room given breath again for the first time in decades. Had Phenna studied down here trying to puzzle out how to alter hen flesh in the 1800s? What was her relationship to Lord Wylde that she called him "Jamie"? And what did she ultimately gain from sacrificing her flesh to live in that book?

Too many questions. Not enough knowledge. Not enough Understanding. I didn't need all the answers right away. I just. . . I required an on-ramp to speed down toward the interstate. What could I offer Phenna for her eight years of studies? I racked my brain, feeling like I was staring at a keyhole. Only, instead of looking for the key, I was trying to solve a riddle, as if riddles opened doors. Well, doors not made by dwarves, anyway.

For the life of me, the only thing I could hear in my head was music. Brass, woodwinds, strings, percussion, and me seated in the middle of it all holding my — my eyes snapped open. I knew what to offer Phenna for my bridge to the ultimate femme triumvirate.

"Eight years you studied the Mágissa Biblia to gain access to the Blood Valley, yes? Then eight years of study I offer you, Phenna."

The floating woman dreamily tilted her head to the right while she waited for me to explain.

"Oh?" she asked.

"In ninth grade, I started playing the trumpet in my high school's marching band. And it provided a music scholarship for me all through college until I'd earned my four-year degree. That's eight years of musical study I can offer you."

She didn't need to know that I hadn't touched my trumpet since I heard the magna cum laude give his speech in a basketball arena with a crowd of hundreds of other college grads.

"Clever. You're sure you won't miss that musical skill? Growing up, I knew girls who rehearsed for years to memorize their scales and sightread music. You'd trade all that away just to START your path to Understanding?"

I took a deep breath and nodded.

"Having the right body is more important to me than knowing the finger positions for B-flat. Getting a head-start on learning the arcane knowledge necessary to reshape my flesh is worth this sacrifice."

Phenna's expression spun back around to a stern warning before she spoke, and I felt my flesh itch under her glare.

"Simply eating fruit from the Yggdrasil Tree doesn't grant you a completed painting, Lilith. It merely gives you a few colors and a brush for your canvas. Everything else is up to you. And sacrifices for shortcuts only get more tempting as time goes on. Many a practitioner has grown impatient in their studies before convincing themselves they can live without something. Eight years of studies, eight years gone, young one."

As she said that, Phenna blew out a small cloud of smoke over her fingers. When it cleared, her hand grasped a polished champaign glass.

I just sat there blinking.

"A toast to my first bargain?" I laughed, nervously. Her glass was empty. She didn't smile.

"There's a legend about a wolf who bargains with a raven that I think you really should learn someday. Nonetheless, your price is paid."

"Will this hurt?" I asked, dread suddenly welling up in the pit of my guts like serpents made of tar and bile.

Phenna shook her head.

"Making the sacrifice is the easy part. Understanding what you actually gave away is the hard part. That comes later. It arrives in the long hours of the night when you'd give anything for your eyes to close and your mind to finally stop thinking."

Before I could retort, my eyes started to water. Only. . . I wasn't crying. I didn't feel like I was crying. But my vision grew blurry all the same. And I watched as bubbles leaked from my eyes like tears, growing the longer they floated through the air.

The fuck? I thought, blinking several times.

But each time I wiped my eyes, more bubbles leaked out and drifted lazily over toward Phenna's glass. When I focussed on the bubbles, I realized that each contained something. . . a narrow black form.

Only when the soft music struck my ears did I realize a single musical note bounced around inside each bubble as if they escaped the staff they were written on and hitched a ride in these bubbles to make their getaway.

And they just kept leaking from my eyes. I heard a trumpet performing different pieces of songs within each bubble. No. . . not A trumpet, but MY trumpet. These were songs I'd played!

"Holy shit! That's Gustav Holst's Second Suite in F!" I hissed, staring at four bubbles flying close together. "That's *March.* And that's *Song Without Words.* We played that at a regional competition. Oh! *Song of the Blacksmith!* And that's *Fantasia on the Dargason!*"

Memories of the hours and hours of rehearsal came rushing back as I sat between Regan and Tristen, second chair trumpet during most of my senior year.

Phenna's expression softened as each bubble popped over her glass and filled it a little more. She listened to me talk.

"We ended up taking. . . the. . . well, it doesn't matter. It'll come back to me. We won a big trophy."

The floating woman tilted her head to the other side as more tears became bubbles before my very eyes.

"Oh! I recognize that one, too! That's *In a Gentle Rain* by Robert W. Smith. Gods, I fucking loved that piece. I think we played it in. . . tenth grade? No, maybe my junior year? My brain is farting all over the place."

My joy faded a bit more with each song I recognized. My head felt lighter and lighter the more I tried to grasp at my memories. As my fingers twitched, trying to recall whether trumpets played in treble or bass clef, my heart sank.

Another bubble's music hit my ears as I recognized a song called *And the Fire Raged* by Ted Ricketts.

Before I knew it, Phenna's glass was full. And I. . . I couldn't recall a single marching formation, despite the many hours in the summer blistering sun I'd spent standing on tiny wooden tiles to memorize my movements for football games to come later that fall.

Phenna swirled the glass around, watching my memories and sold skill carefully. Then, she downed it one gulp, as though it were a moderately priced wine at a nice restaurant.

"I've never played a musical instrument before. This will be interesting to experiment with."

My shoulders drooped, and a feeling of further dread began to worm its way through my guts as her words about sacrifice came roaring back to my memory.

I started to shake and feel cold as Phenna ate her champagne glass like it was a candy bar, glass crunching on her teeth. Then, she swallowed it.

"You feel it now, yes? The weight of a bargain struck in haste?"

I nodded, glum and wanting to kick myself.

"Now imagine you have no flesh," she said, rising again to a standing position in the air.

Before I could ask about regaining those lost memories, Phenna's eyes lit anew.

"Oh, look at that, sweet thing. A doorway."

Turning to look behind me, I followed her gaze. My eyes fell upon a red door in the shape of a pentagon with a little gold knob in the center. It'd been fitted perfectly into the wall that collapsed to reveal this chamber.

"Better get moving, Lilith. You have mythical fruit to devour and ancient sorceresses to embrace. I truly hope what you find in the Blood Valley is what you were looking for. If you need me, I'll be practicing *Into the Storm*. Do you recall who arranged it?"

I shook my head without turning back to the floating woman.

"Robert W. Smith, of course. You just told me his name a couple of minutes ago."

Had I? Fuck.

If I felt this shitty now, how much worse would I feel in the long hours of the night when my mind refused to quiet no matter how tired I felt?

Well, speaking of sleep, I'd made my bed. Now, it was time to lie in it. Taking a step toward the weathered red door, I suddenly yearned for the den I'd woken up in this morning with Mars' warm arms wrapped tightly around me.

Double fuck, I thought. *I've been a werewolf's mate for a day, and I've already made a bargain with a witch imprisoned in a book for a little magic — sorry — Understanding.*

All that was left to do was taste this supposed fruit. I wondered how literal Phenna was being when she talked about the tree.

Only one way to find out.

Chapter 6

My green pickup truck carried me through several small Maine towns on the way to Lubec. Millinocket, Mattawamkeag, Topfield, Whiting, and more. The Chevy Apache I'd secretly named Brego rumbled around curves and over bridges, past woodlands I'd run through aplenty in my 30 years as a werewolf.

Inside me as outside Brego, rain fell. Something spectacular happened last night, a thing most werewolves spend their lives dreaming of. I found my mate. And she was lovely in all the right ways to my lonely heart.

Even now, driving southeast from Pine Springs and putting more distance between us, I felt her in my chest. And I longed to taste her again tonight.

But that was the future. The now, the current time, the present moment, demanded a somber soul. I was going to see my pack.

Chilly bands of rain ran along my windshield as thick curtains of fog draped the edges of my road in tones of faded blue and gray. The windshield wipers spread quietly over the glass a few feet in front of my face. The moment they'd start to squeak, I'd replace them, as I had every piece of my baby.

Brego's engine had been rebuilt three times since I owned her. And I'd done it all myself. I'd replaced broken windows, patched holes in the leather bench seat, and dropped in a new transmission when my old one coughed and sputtered into a well-earned grave.

My hand shook as I held onto the gear shift and worked the clutch, downshifting as I came upon a logging truck.

I smelled the lumber it was hauling to some mill that likely only had a decade or so of life left in it. Wet wood and diesel smoke.

Reaching up, I tuned the radio to KQIL 89.4 FM, the oldies but goodies station my father used to listen to when we rode Brego down into Bangor for shopping or took her up into Quebec for a camping trip. Even now, I still smelled his crappy pine air freshener hanging from the rearview mirror mixed with a small bit of Irish coffee he had with breakfast.

"Just a sip to warm the morning," he'd always say. I trusted him. Because he was my father and my alpha. The man could do no wrong. And on the off chance he did do wrong by Mom or another pack member, that just meant we'd throw a couple of fishing poles in the bed and ride over to the lake so they'd have the day to cool off.

And bonus: when we got back, there'd be plenty of trout for supper.

After almost four hours of driving, I pulled up to a small pier on the north side of Lubec. I parked Brego along Johnson Street and walked through the damp autumn air. Fog clung to the shoreline even thicker than before.

Across the bay, I could make out the shapes of several

small boats, anchored and waiting for a trip out into deeper waters.

"Damn. Lovely day for a pack visit," I mumbled, pulling my leather jacket from the passenger seat and sliding it over my buttoned-down flannel. I pulled out a large hair clip from the glovebox and ran my hands over the top of my head, pulling everything back into a large bun.

My wavy hair remained soft and loose with nary a bit of frizz to be found. Werewolves. We've got perks.

Walking down to the pier, the smell of salt water and seaweed ran through my nostrils. I liked the coast just fine, but I couldn't imagine why anyone would want to live on it, aside from the y'know, stunning beauty of it all.

I continued toward a sign that said, "Downeast Boat Rentals."

By now, the rain had stopped. But there was enough mist to keep me from seeing the Mulholland Point Lighthouse.

A tall, rail-thin man was fussing with a tangled piece of boat rope when I approached. His hair was cut neatly and rested beneath an old blue ballcap. The boatman looked to be in his 60s, but I knew from experience he was much older. His eyes glowed an emerald green as they met mine, and I smelled a fishier odor to him than any other red-blooded human carried.

He dropped the rope and held his arms wide as I approached.

"Well, well! The little pup comes to visit her favorite uncle," the man said with a heavy Québécois accent. Most folks would say he sounded French. But people who actually came from France would be thoroughly disgusted with that label being given to someone from Quebec.

I huffed and walked into a deceptively powerful hug.

"Hey there, Pierre. Good fishing today?" I asked.

The man wasn't actually my uncle. He was just a long-time friend of the pack and one of the few people still breathing who knew me as a kid.

"Non," he said, shaking his head. "I think the fish are sleeping, which is what I'd like to be doing right now. . . but I suspect you're going to ask for a lift out to the island, ah?"

My smile faded. He knew me all too well.

"Uh-huh! That's what I suspected," he said, pulling out a box of cigarettes and sticking one between his lips. Lighting it, he continued, "Why else would you be in Lubec?"

I sighed. Pierre wasn't trying to make me feel shitty. But he was right. I only came up here to see the pack. And he rarely made it too far inland, certainly nowhere near Pine Springs. The man loved his boats and shoreline. He had more salt in his blood than any human I knew.

"Sorry, Pierre. I've just got some important updates to give Mom and Dad."

He rubbed his chin and took a drag from the cigarette. As the tip glowed a dim orange, he grinned.

"Oh yeah? Big news out on the farm? You get a new tractor or something?" he asked.

I snickered.

"No. I uh. . . found my mate," I said, feeling my heart sort of pause as I waited for his reaction.

The Québécois blew smoke to the right and then smiled big when he turned back to me.

"Hey! That's great. Tell me about her," he said, putting his hands in his jacket pocket.

"Well, she's——"

He held up a hand, interrupting me.

"Ho, ho, hold up. Before you say anything more. Tell me. Did you have the sense to find a Canuck?"

I shook my head.

He scoffed and turned around, walking toward a boat tied up at the edge of the pier, bobbing gently with the rising tide.

"Never mind. I don't care."

I walked after him.

"I didn't even tell you her name. It's very pretty like she is," I said, stepping onto squeaking old boards to follow Uncle Pierre.

He stopped abruptly and turned back.

"Does she at least speak French?"

I shrugged.

"My mate was a little too busy moaning to reveal if she was bilingual. But I'll be sure to ask her tonight."

Pierre scoffed and turned again toward his boat.

"I see a lack of good taste runs in your family bloodline. You know, I was once in the running for your mother's heart," Pierre said, proud and beaming as if he hadn't told me this 1,000 times already. "We were to be married, and I was going to take her up north into more civilized lands."

Finishing the story for him, I place a hand on his shoulder.

"But then she met Dad and found her fated mate. They got married instead," I said.

He kicked an empty beer can in mock outrage as though hearing my mother's answer for the first time. Then, he shrugged and started to untie his boat.

"Like I said — no real taste. A classy woman like Adeline deserved a literal salt-of-the-earth man like me. Not that silly goofball Roger Lee. Ugh. Even his name. . . ridiculous."

If I caught anyone else trash-talking my old man and alpha, I'd smash their head into the nearest fire hydrant. But even now as he talked, I remembered Pierre standing in front of Dad's body and promising to do right by me. A young and sobbing werewolf with only a few transformations under her belt clung tightly to the man who smelled like seaweed and low tide no matter how often he showered.

To this day, I remembered his words and sometimes caught myself reciting them.

"You're a good man, Roger Lee. You toed the line and did what was right, even when it cost you and your pack everything. And I'll ensure your daughter has whatever she needs until you return. I swear it by the scales of my very flesh," he'd said on the island.

And he'd kept his word. I moved in with him for several years until I was ready to return home to Pine Springs and start my farm.

We were on the way to Treat Island when I plopped down in a seat next to Pierre and lightly kicked his leg.

"Hey now! Easy on the captain. You don't want the ship to sink, do you?"

"You can breathe underwater, and you made sure I could swim laps from Lubec to Dudley Island before I turned 13. I think we'll be fine."

The captain rolled his eyes.

"The things Uncle Pierre must endure. If I knew how much of a pain his pup was going to be over the next three decades of my life, I wouldn't have made that silly promise to Roger Lee," he said.

I leaned over and kissed him lightly on the cheek.

"Yeah, but you'd be so much lonelier sitting in that shack you call a home if I didn't stop by now and again."

"I hope your mate enjoys the arrogance you mistake for charm, little pup," he laughed.

"Oh, she was putty in my fingers within five minutes of our meeting," I chuckled.

I wouldn't be surprised if she asked to be clicker trained before the week ended, I thought, shaking my head and snickering.

The fog decided to stick to us like student loans to a college dropout as Pierre approached the dock. A patch of evergreens ran north to south over most of the island.

A "No Trespassing" sign was posted on the edge of the island's small dock. Above us, a pair of seagulls flew over the island, screeching before vanishing into the mist.

"How's that PFAS contamination story still holding up? Keeping folks off the island?"

Pierre nodded and brought the boat's engine down to idle as we drifted closer to the dock.

"Sure is. Most folks here know somebody who was made sick by those fucking chemicals. So, it's not a far stretch to imagine the island got polluted some years back in a spill. Keeps campers and kayakers away from your pack."

Hopping out of the boat and landing on the island, I felt a pang of dread in the pit of my gut. My legs turned to jelly as my body remembered where it was.

Turning back to Pierre with renewed weariness, I tried to sound cocky and undisturbed.

"Keep the meter running, yeah?"

He cut the power and pulled out a small paperback novel. I had to squint to read the title, but in small print, I could barely register the words, *The Ties That Bind.*

What the fuck is my uncle reading? I thought, turning to walk onto solid ground.

Somehow, the air around me grew colder as I worked my way between trees to the center of Treat Island. I stepped through a patch of tall grass and came into view of the pack.

The smell of frozen flesh and familiar blood washed

over me as I stepped into a circle of petrified bodies standing in various poses of defiance.

My father stood baring fangs and ready to attack after the wraith's appearance. He'd barely had time to push his mate behind him when everyone was struck with a powerful wave of shrieking sorcery. Magic that chilled the marrow in your bones no matter how deep it burrowed. It stole the strength in your limbs, the breath from your lungs, and the balance in your mind. Only chilled horror remained afterward.

My father stood wearing a tank top and stained jeans, forever looking up in the sky at the specter of my nightmares that took everything from me. An otherworldly fucker who strolled right in and stole my family with the snap of her fingers.

All six werewolves were awash in bespelled glaciers before they could even react, and only their little pup remained. Even now, I heard her hiss of a voice.

"But you, tiny wolf, will remain to remember what happens when mortals deny me what is rightfully mine. Their memory of misfortune and poor choices will live on in you. . . for as long as you can stand the pain, anyway," she'd said before descending into the shadows and leaving me alone with my pack. . . my imprisoned, frozen-solid pack.

Dad's shaggy brown hair was flared and ready to attack. How could he have known the scale of what was coming? Mom's sandy blonde hair was pulled back into a long braid with a silver ring embedded in the bottom. Her amber eyes were wide with rage, staring at the same sky Dad was.

From her black leggings to her floral sundress and beaded necklaces, my mother, Adaline, was every bit the hippy she appeared to be. The mother who named me after her favorite planet stood trapped in frigid crystal, unable to see how her daughter grew up, even though I came out here several times a year.

My heart sank as it often did, and memories of our family ran full steam through my brain, tearing my heart to pieces. I choked back a sob. Blueberry hikes, salmon fishing, camping with the eager little werewolf who just wanted "one more" of everything. One more wagon ride. One more scoop of ice cream. One more bedtime story.

And because Dad was a helpless and loveable sap wrapped around my finger, I often got what I asked for.

That all came to an end the day shadow descended upon our pack, and eternal winter came to my loved ones, taking them with all the violence of a sudden nor'easter.

"Hey, Dad. Hi, Mom," I said, pausing for a greeting I knew wouldn't come.

My feet wanted to rush back to the boat and grab a pickaxe or a flamethrower. But I knew from years of painful lessons and tear-filled study that this curse ran deeper than any mortal tool could dig.

"It's been a few months, but I had some pretty big news that I couldn't wait to share with you."

Their expressions didn't change, but the level of nausea in my gut did.

"I found her," I started after clearing my throat five times. It kept wanting to close on me. "My mate. She's. . . perfect. And it was exactly like you both described! The way I had to keep nosing her hair and tasting her skin. It was like she was a bottomless well, and I couldn't drink her fast enough. All those stories you told me about how your heart feels like it's soaring high into the sky couldn't have prepared me for the ecstasy of hearing her name. . . Lilith. Gods, I had the best night with her."

I continued to vomit words as I remembered what it

felt like to take that small girl with long dark hair into my arms and refuse to release her for any treasure this world had to offer.

"The lightning that hit my brain and raced straight to my toes after our first dance was stronger than anything I could imagine. And as powerful as I was. . . Lilith toppled me.

"No desire can I recall such as the feel of her breath upon me. And no protection I'd offer as her mate ever feels enough. How can I possibly explain to this human girl that I would rip the tongue from any who would dare besmirch her name or character? These feelings are fucking Shakespearean, and while you both warned me repeatedly. . . I feel as though I didn't pay close enough attention."

I sat down upon the earth between Mom and Dad and alternated looks between them.

"Something's changed in the air, Mom. And, Dad, I know this sounds crazy, but I feel gears churning like never before. After years of rotten loneliness and coming nowhere near breaking this curse, I feel, inexplicably, like my fortune has finally begun to shift, as one phase of the moon morphs into another."

And it was true. Amidst the sadness of seeing my pack in their imprisonment, hope remained lit like a single candle despite the darkness around it. As my mate, Lilith had become my hope.

Wind blew through the trees, and the mist thinned a little around Treat Island. In the woods around me, I smelled rabbits and squirrels stirring as though they sensed a subtle change in the weather.

Turning back to my folks, I bit my bottom lip to keep it from trembling.

"I miss you," I whispered, fearful that if I spoke the words any louder, I might shatter into pieces. "I miss our full-moon hunts. I miss Christmas mornings in front of the fireplace with bacon jerky and instant coffee. I miss birthday steaks, Dad. And I miss making jewelry with you, Mom. I know most of the shit I put together was horrid, but you wore it in front of the pack anyway."

Tears leaked down my cheeks, and I could no longer keep the river inside dammed up.

"I don't want you to think I've forgotten the pack. It's all I think about, setting you free. But I think Lilith is a sign that things will change soon. I don't have to be alone. And you don't have to stay cursed."

Slowly, I lowered myself to the ground and lay on my side between Mom and Dad. My bottom lip was trembling now.

"You taught me to be strong, and I will be. But right now, I just need to be a pup nestled between her parents. That's okay, right?"

More tears.

". . . Right?"

I quietly shifted into my wolf form and curled up tight between Mom and Dad, imagining that they heard every word I said and were whispering soft, loving affirmations in my ears.

For a while, nothing mattered. And I was just content to be in their presence, even if they weren't looking at me and hadn't for years.

I'll free you, I swore, as I had in this very spot nearly every time I visited the pack. *Telsyn will burn. I'll tear her to shreds and reduce the pieces to ash.*

━━━

DRIVING OUT OF LUBEC, I had the radio on again to

Dad's favorite station, and the DJ started up "Long Black Veil" by Johnny Cash.

One moment, everything was fine. I was staring at an ice cooler in my passenger seat filled with packages of lobster tail. I imagined how they'd smell as I cooked them on the grill tonight for Lilith and me.

And that's when panic surged through my chest. Ever since I'd marked my mate, I could feel her heartbeat in the right side of my chest, a complement to my own. This was the way all mates felt each other, to know whether they were safe or in danger.

I clutched Brego's steering wheel so tight that my nails shredded some of the leather. Taking shallow breaths, I searched inside my chest for Lilith's heartbeat. But it had vanished. Not stopped. Simply disappeared.

That'd never happened before, not to any werewolf mate I'd heard of. Even in death, a werewolf felt their mate's heart slow and sputter. But to go suddenly quiet?

I braked hard and pulled Brego off the road. What the fuck was happening? Pulling out my phone and calling Lilith, I was greeted with her voicemail.

"Hi, you've reached Lilith. I can't come to the phone right now because I'm in the bath reading, playing DnD, or actively being abducted by aliens. Please leave a message, and I'll return your call when I re-enter Earth's atmosphere. BEEP."

Bitch, you better be abducted by aliens because that is the only excuse I'll accept for your heartbeat going radio silent on me, I thought.

Running my hands through my hair, I took a breath. Lilith was in danger. Something inexplicable had happened to her. I needed to be back in Pine Springs immediately. That was another three hours down the road.

"But I could run it in half the time," I growled, hopping out of the truck.

Walking into the tree line, I threw back my head and let forth a howl that said, "Get the fuck out of my way," to any creatures in the area. And according to my heightened hearing, they took my advice.

Feeling the raw power of the wolf within me snarl forth, I shifted for the second time today. Mahogany-colored hair sprouted from beneath my flesh. Bones and ligaments contorted in an Olympic gymnastics competition as my body transformed into a fierce canine. My fangs extended at the same time my claws did, and I fell to all fours, hands, and feet becoming paws in the blink of an eye.

My vision sank into a world of movement and dulled colors as raw instincts replaced my human intellect.

Find Lilith, my brain thought.

It became my sole piercing cry as I rocketed through the woods I knew like the back of my paw. Charting a course for my mate, I willed her safety into being with every hair on my body. And if someone else was responsible for her vanishing, no god, no hiding place, no weapon would keep them from my wrath.

Chapter 7

From the moment I passed through the Red Door that my bargain conjured, I was blanketed in an otherworldly miasma. A thick purple mist floated into my throat, and where I expected to hack and cough, I instead felt my senses heighten.

My vision briefly swam before everything appeared sharper, as though reality had been rubbed raw with crystalline shards.

In my chest, the heart that worked every second to keep me alive slowed. My feet met crunchy leaves and twigs scattered either minutes or millennia ago.

Things moved in the mist, and my ears twitched with every crunch of discarded pine needles and fallen branches.

A trail, if it could be called that, spread before me just as my mind started to ask, *Well, what now?*

I didn't ask the question out loud, though, because I knew what came next. I'd paid a price, and it was time to collect my prize, the start of my Understanding.

"That's one small step for trannies, one giant leap for

trankind," I mumbled, placing one foot in front of the other and folding myself deeper into the mysterious forest.

My brain told me none of this was possible, but my soul wholly accepted that I'd left Earth behind. The air was heavier, the ground far less dense, and everything seemed to cling to an unspoken sense of agelessness.

So, I steeled myself, packed what little courage I possessed into a Tupperware container so it'd stay fresh, and strolled forth into the unseen beyond.

It wouldn't be accurate to say magic permeated the air. What I felt on a deeper level was that this entire world was comprised of magic, as though it were a natural element like carbon or helium.

The energy of this world greeted my soul as a ball of yarn and started to unspool it like a basket of kittens. Yet, I did not falter. I continued on across bone-covered hills, over streams of licorice-colored water, and between trees reaching toward an ever-orange sky.

Snark faded (which was extremely rare for me), and I gave my thoughts over to the whispers of spirits I didn't know.

"She calls for power," one said.

"The new sorceress pays more than she knows to Understand," another cackled.

"Another girl seeks divine triumph and blessings, but will she join us in the mist?" one asked.

Their voices called to me in tongues that should have made no sense. But I knew what they spoke in the same way I knew to keep walking down the path. Something deeper than instinct drove me forward. It was raw desire. The desire for power, the desire to set things right, and the desire to become what I knew I should have been when I first came into this world.

The ground gave way, and my steps betrayed me as I

tumbled down a sharp ridge hidden by violet fog. In the movies, one simply rolled down a hill and stood up dizzy at the end. But in reality, my shoulders slammed into tree trunks, roots clawed at my face, and fallen leaves did their damned best to choke me when I remembered to breathe in all the chaos of gravity and pain.

Suddenly, there was no more ground. My stomach heaved as I opened my eyes and searched for hard earth to fall upon. And just when I expected to crash back down into packed soil, I instead found my weight ensnared in something sticky that made my flesh crawl.

Pulling my arms and legs, I discovered them stuck firmly to whatever had captured me. When the room (or — wait, I was in a dense forest, right?) stopped spinning, my eyes tried to make sense of where I'd landed.

And just before a horrified moan could pass from my lips, a large form emerged silently from the side of my vision. Eight legs, a segmented body, and several shimmering eyes crawled toward me. Wrapped around the spider's. . . neck (what the fuck was that part called?) hung what appeared to be a scarf made of gray woven webbing.

"A web! I'm stuck in a giant web," I managed to choke out.

The black and white striped spider, which was three times my size, approached before rearing up on hind legs and. . . not immediately devouring my blood. Nor did it cocoon me in webbing.

"Um, greetings?" I asked, watching its eyes judge me.

The surprises kept coming when the spider's mouth opened, and a thick Parisian accent scuttled out. The spider sounded like a woman lying on a piano, smoking cigarettes in between downing glasses of wine.

"Tell me. Which greetings do you bring? For I have heard many, and many more I do not care for."

My eyes widened while hers stayed the same.

"What greetings do I bring?" I sputtered, wondering if I'd been given a riddle that would determine my fate. "Good ones, I suppose?"

The spider rubbed the side of its head.

"Who determined that these greetings of yours were good?"

Was there a bite of humor in her tone, or was all the blood just rushing to my head from hanging in this web?

"Well, I checked the expiration date, and the greetings still had a few days left when I packed them," I said with a weak smile.

To my immediate relief, the giant spider threw back her head and cackled.

"Not only greetings do you bring me but jokes as well? It must be my lucky day. Tell me, who tumbles into my web?"

"Um. . . my name is Lilith Chambers, ma'am," I said, feeling like I might not be devoured after all. Or maybe the spider just liked to set her prey at ease before sucking them dry of life juices.

"Ma'am? You may address me as Maiden."

Well, I certainly prefer Maiden to Madame Web, I thought, fighting an eye-roll. Oh good, my snark was returning. That would help me survive this encounter.

One had to choose their words carefully when they found all limbs bound in a web. It was just the unspoken rule of such things.

"Wait — you said your name is Maiden? As in, part of The Maiden, The Mother, and The Crone?" I asked, trying to recall everything Phenna had told me about starting the path to Understanding.

"I am the first of three questions, the starting gate on the path to Yggdrasil, and the youngest of three in the ring of Understanding. If you seek the Sacred Tree, your words must first satisfy me."

I swallowed nervously, recalculating the odds that I was about to be devoured. The way the Maiden switched between easily humored and threatening made my guts rile with uneasiness.

"So. . . you're here to judge my intentions and determine if I'm good or evil before I can see the tree?"

The spider lowered herself flat against her web and sighed, bumping my shoe with one of her massive legs. It felt like being tapped by a fallen tree.

"No, Lilith Chambers. Many would-be sorceresses fall into my web. And some leave to continue their journey. Of those who leave, I have counted murderers and thieves alike. Your intentions do not hold my interest. I take no pleasure in knowing your moral code."

I shook my head.

"Then what, Maiden? What will you ask of me?"

"Careful, Lilith Chambers, she named for the First Wife. An ant caught in a spider's web does not control the hands on the clock. You will know what I want of you when I say it and not a moment before."

My blood was suddenly frigid at her words. Polar bears could have set up a den in my veins and been perfectly at home, drinking Coke every Christmas without complaint.

Nodding, I acknowledged my fate was now in her hands.

Was it truly worth it to trade my trumpeting skills away for this? I thought. *Phenna did not warn me the path to Understanding would be so perilous.*

Or perhaps she did. She said I had to welcome the chilled embrace of The Maiden, The Mother, and The Crone. Being trapped in a spider's web could technically fall under the umbrella of a "chilled embrace," I suppose.

There was plenty of wiggle room. I mean — I was pretty chilled at the moment. Certainly, I was shivering.

"Ah, silence sounds sweetest in the cup of powerlessness. The realization that you can do nothing without my leave, it hits hard, no?"

She thumped my foot again with one of her legs. Another tree trunk of a wack that left my ankle tingling.

"Truly, you hold all the cards," I said.

The Maiden nodded.

"And it's with that realization now settled on your shoulders that I say this. Many in the realm of your birth want power. Some even need it. Speak to me of your need, for I sense it screaming within you, and I wish to know the quality of those shrieks."

What kind of question is that? I thought.

The only part that made sense was the knowledge that I'd be fucked if I didn't take the time to carefully consider The Maiden's query.

How did I describe my quest for Understanding? Well, I certainly wanted it. I wanted it bad enough to trade Phenna something I spent eight years of my life learning just to open the Red Door.

No, that wasn't right. I didn't just want to Understand. One didn't hand over such a big chunk of their lives simply for something they wanted.

Deep down, I believed there was something fundamentally wrong with me. I'd come out of the oven baked in the wrong shape, as though the wrong cookie cutter had been used on my dough. I'd never had the chance to change that before now. And it burned hot within, the need to correct this mistake the universe had thrust upon me without my asking.

I clenched my fists and glared up at The Maiden. This went far beyond any want. One might want Understanding for parlor tricks or for petty reasons, but I needed it to fix me. And that was the only answer I had for the giant spider.

"I need it," I said.

She cocked her head to the side.

"Truly?" she asked.

Nodding, I took a deep breath and prepared to stake my life and the success of this quest on a scalding truth that scorched the inside of my furnace every day.

"I go through life knowing things could have been different, SHOULD have been different. Every day I wake up with the unerasable knowledge that the wheel which determined my shape stopped just short of where it should have. And my desire to correct that grand fuckup by the universe has driven me here, into your web. It will drive me past you and by The Mother and beyond The Crone until I've tasted the fruit of Yggdrasil."

A gust of wind rustled the web, and I felt it quiver beneath me as my limbs tightened without letting go.

"You're sure of this?"

"As sure as I am that you'd be doing the exact same thing if you'd been born without your spinnerets," I said.

That earned me a small grin, and I quivered a little. I'd never seen someone with fangs smile before, and I wasn't sure I liked the sight of it.

"I was scarred in the womb, Maiden, a spider who hatched with seven legs instead of eight. My flesh is wrong, and that realization moves me to terrible places. I paid a price to be here, surrendered something precious. That decision was fueled by need, need to heal myself from the grievous wrong that was done to me."

Without flinching, I locked eyes with The Maiden and glared as though I could set her very web on fire with determination and lifelong frustration with my chromosomes.

And when she climbed over top of me, still, I did not flinch. The Maiden lowered her massive self until the hairs of her abdomen brushed against my skin. Even then, I glared, her massive fangs inches from my own canines.

"You paid a steep price to open the door, Lilith Chambers. I don't care why. I just needed to know you understood that second-guessing your sacrifice is, perhaps, the greatest sin a sorceress can make, short of cursing our name."

My glare softened a degree.

The Maiden continued, the breath from her words striking me with a horrifying hiss, "Sorceresses aren't worthy of their power because of deeds or ethics. The worth comes from recognizing a dire need and doing whatever it takes to meet it. Understanding isn't about good or evil. Arcane knowledge doesn't recognize mortal laws. Sorceresses make choices and live with the consequences. It's as simple as that. You wanted power. You traded away something for a chance to have it."

I gulped nervously thinking back to lost thoughts and emotions from band class I'd traded to open the door. And then I pictured Phenna, floating above the book in all her power and Understanding. She didn't seem to regret her sacrifices. I shouldn't regret mine, either.

This was the key to getting what I wanted in the long run. Making an omelet without breaking eggs, and so forth. That's what The Maiden was trying to teach me.

I dishonored myself if I started to regret my trade. And I dishonored the Understanding that would come once I'd eaten from the Yggdrasil Tree.

"I won't regret my bargain," I said with a louder voice than I thought possible in the wake of a giant spider.

The Maiden paused, her eight eyes scanning every inch of my face for wavering thoughts or indecision. After what felt like a decade, she nodded slightly and climbed off of me.

"Good. Now go and face The Mother. Keep my words fresh in your mind. But do not expect her question to be the same as mine."

I sighed with relief and realized I was still stuck to the web.

"Um. . . how do I—" I was interrupted by the web around me rotting in an instant, giving way to my weight and sending me plummeting into depths I didn't know were beneath me.

Screaming all the way down, I tried to flip myself over and couldn't. How much longer did I have? How long had I been falling?

Wind whipped my long black hair all around my face until I at last landed. Wait — no. That wasn't right. It would be more accurate to say I was snatched from the air just before the ground reunited with my spine in a violent fashion.

Looking to my left and waiting for my vision to clear, I realized what'd caught me. I sat in the jaws of a massive wolf, and amber eyes the size of basketballs looked me over with irritation.

Slobber dampened my clothes, and I realized with renewed alarm that I was now buried in closed jaws. Teeth and tongue were my new companions where webbing had ended our relationship.

I was snared at the halfway point, the wolf's jaws closed over my waist.

"You're certainly a noisy power-seeker," the wolf growled.

Turning my head in the opposite direction, I saw two

pups that were closer to my size playing beneath the legs of my captor.

Her fur was the color of steel with splotches of white mixed here and there. And the wolf's whiskers were as long as me.

I looked back to see the giant canine hadn't taken her eyes off me.

"Th — The Mother, I presume?" I chanced.

The wolf huffed, and a warm blast of air that smelled like old meat and rotten berries whiffed around my body.

"It seems The Maiden has sent another would-be sorceress into my jaws. Come. Let me see how you fare in The Mother's den."

And I didn't get a choice in the matter as the massive wolf turned and carried me into the mouth of a large cave. Down, we descended into the darkness. Damp, cool air washed over me as I listened to the pitter-patter of the wolf pups running behind us, barking and playing together.

The Mother took her time, never unsure about a step or foothold.

At last, she arrived at the end of her den and slowly hung her head to the right. Before I could react, she snapped her head back and tossed me into a pile of old bones.

Disoriented and greeted by the smell of dusty decay, I took my time rising to my feet and finding a place to stand in the darkness. Above me, the massive golden eyes of The Mother stared down. At her feet, two sets of smaller amber eyes watched me, eager to play or pounce or kill me.

My eyes slowly adjusted to glowing blue stones projecting a hazy light above. They took mercy upon my disorientation and provided, at least, some measure of visual clarity.

"I have pups to nurse, so I will make my question quick. I am no spider toying with prey caught in my web."

Hunching my shoulders together and trying not to shake too visibly, I nodded.

"The Maiden determined you've realized the true scale of your need and that you lack any regret over decisions that led you here. Now I will ask you, oh she named for the First Wife, what does power taste like? If you want to seek Understanding, you'd best present me with a satisfactory answer."

What does power taste like? I thought. *Is Moro here looking for a flavor? Um, gee, Mother, I think it tastes like chicken. Do I win?*

The Mother's impatience wore on me as I resisted the urge to pound my head. How the fuck would I know what power tasted like? I'd never had it before!

Growing up in far east Colorado, I was constantly reminded of how powerless I was. I didn't have the power to force others to call me Lilith or treat me like a girl. I didn't have the strength to stop bullies from smashing my head into whatever locker happened to be nearest when they found me in the hall. And I certainly didn't have the influence needed to earn any respect in my hometown. Outside of my parents, most everyone treated me like shit. Even Mom and Dad were powerless to help when it came to dealing with the assholes of Piper's Ridge.

So, how on Earth did The Mother expect me to know what power tasted like?

Taking another deep breath and wrapping my heart with hope that blunt truth would save me from The Mother as it did The Maiden, I took one step forward. My neck arched up, and I glared at the massive canine above me.

"I've spent my entire life being bullied and pushed around by others. I seek Understanding to finally have some measure of power to transform my life and fix my flesh. At no point have I held power over another and savored its taste. And I will not know the taste of power until I eat of the Yggdrasil. You were born mighty. I was born broken. So my answer is this: You asking me about the taste of power is akin to me asking you about the taste of octopus or shark."

With another mighty huff, The Mother scoffed and lowered her massive face closer to mine. I did my best not to shrink in its presence. But it was difficult.

"What a lazy and foolish answer you've given me! You claim to have held no power all your days, but I do not believe for a second you've never stepped on a beetle or swatted a fly from the air. In those moments, you held power of those creatures. And yet, you did not think to tell me how it tasted," she barked. "These are things you've done many times in your life. So tell me, Lilith Chambers, what do you fault for your lackluster words? Poor memory? The lack of a tongue for tasting? What excuse do you offer me for this pathetic response?"

This time, I did shrink toward the pile of bones. And when the wolf slammed her right paw into the cave floor, I fell backward.

Her snout moved closer to me, nose wrinkled, fangs glistening, and accompanied by a growl that would blow the speakers out of any car.

My heart shot up into my throat. Had I truly escaped the spider's web only to be devoured in the wolf's den? Fuck. As my hands twitched, unsure of what they should be doing in the face of this massive threat, I froze.

"I should tear off one of your legs and let you be fresh meat for my pups. Maybe they're ready and don't need to be nursed by me tonight after all," she growled.

I tried to reach for words and failed to produce any.

Time seemed to freeze until, at last, The Mother closed her jaws and ceased rattling rock with her snarls.

The Mother heaved a massive sigh, sending some of the smaller bones scattering around the den. Her pups took to playing with them, ignoring her previous threats toward me.

"I would like nothing more than to add your sorry hide to my belly as I have many fools who sought Understanding, yet lacked the capacity to realize what power they'd already possessed in their lives. None of the ones I've eaten realized that without a sound mind, they would have become slaves to the power they sought, reduced to drooling beasts ever seeking more without giving a single thought to why. It was mercy that saw me end them before they could ruin themselves. And yet, for you, a different protection spares my wrath."

My eyes widened as I tried to understand the words that'd just been hurled at me from The Mother's snout. Did she say mercy? Or. . . protection?

"I smell on you the mark of another wolf. She has claimed you as her mate. Though her power is insignificant compared to mine, wolf custom forbids the killing of mates. It has been this way since long before either of you walked the realm of your birth. By her mark and scent, you are spared my fangs. Onward, you go, to The Crone. Though, I warn you, being a wolf's mate offers you no protection against her. May your words fare better in her grasp than they did mine."

Before I could ask any more questions, The Mother snatched me in her jaws again, this time with my belly down and against her tongue.

I didn't even have time to yell "Eep!" as she walked over to a hole in her den's wall and flung me into shadow.

Deeper I fell into the ground, until, at last, I crashed

into a frigid stream. Bubbles of air yelled from my lungs as I swam for what I hoped was the surface. It was dark, but the current seemed to know where it wanted to go, regardless of the lackluster light.

I sputtered and kicked being tossed here and there until my arms at last collided with a broken piece of a log. It clung to the surface far more easily than I did, so I wrapped it tight within my grip and prayed to The Maiden that I might not drown. She seemed far more kind than The Mother had been to me.

I'm not sure how long the current carried me forward, but my arms grew tired of clinging to the log lost in the underground stream. And just before they gave out, I found myself bathed in light again.

Out of the cavern and into another patch of misty forest, I thanked whoever was watching over me that I could see again. Moonlight filtered down through the tree tops and purple miasma as I washed forward in the river.

But the light did not sustain my joy long as exhaustion and chill crept through me, starting with my extremities. Yet even here, mercy was no stranger to me. For I was snatched from the water by my knees.

Coughing and gasping, I felt something tighten and coil around the middle of my legs. Feeling was slow to return, and my vision beat it in a race to restore senses. I was still by the stream. I heard running water to my right.

Below me, my arms dangled over a sandy nest full of massive white rocks. No, wait, not rocks. . . eggs! Those eggs were bigger than me!

When I turned to see what held me in its grasp, my jaw dropped (or rose, since I was upside down). A massive silver-scaled serpent squeezed my knees tight together with a tail that possessed more strength than I could imagine. It might shatter my bones if it wanted to. And every second the serpent didn't, I found myself grateful for intact kneecaps.

"Sssssssoooooooo, The Mother throws another would-be sorceress to the stream. Oh, goodnessssss me, how she amuses my old scales."

The serpent's tone was surprisingly cheerful, even more so than The Maiden. And her words didn't sound all that different to me than a Midwestern grandmother. I couldn't begin to imagine how that was possible.

"Tell me, girl. What are you called?"

"Um, Lilith Chambers. And by brilliant powers of deduction, I'm going to assume you're The Crone?"

With a thoughtful laugh, she nodded.

"Yessssss indeed. Many would-be sorceresses I've fished from the stream and dangled over my nest. Some I squeeze until they turn blue and stop moving. Others, I release to see the Yggdrasil Tree. My question, she named for the First Wife, is which of those will you be?"

"Jelly or set free?" I asked, making sure I knew my options.

Her threats were 20 times more terrifying when she delivered them like a granny about to offer me a tray of cookies. And there was also the fact that she was big enough to break one of Godzilla's legs.

For the second time, the serpent nodded, decidedly offering me no further hints.

Is this a trick question? I thought. *The Maiden asked about the need of power. And The Mother asked about the taste of power. Why is The Crone's question so different?*

Water droplets fell from my clothes as I dangled about 20 feet in the air. They dropped down onto the eggshells beneath me and dotted the sand.

With blood rushing to my head, it was getting more

difficult to think. Maybe that was part of her question. I shouldn't overthink things.

But what was the right answer? There were only two, right? I'm in the group that moves onward to Yggdrasil's fruit, or I'm in the group reduced to a stress doll that can be used exactly once while I'm still breathing.

Fuck me, I thought. *I'm so over these witchy kaiju.*

The serpent waited patiently for me to answer. And why shouldn't she? She was The Crone. I'd be willing to bet she was older than any who had achieved Understanding before me. Her tired voice certainly sounded like it.

Why didn't she ask me about power? I thought. *The other two did.*

Wait a second — what had The Maiden tried to get me to realize? What did the spider say? Silence sounds sweetest in the cup of powerlessness? What if that was a hint?

Maybe The Crone had asked me a question about power without using that exact word. Which will I be, squeezed until I'm blue and dead or set free? If I pick one or the other, she'd kill me. Because that wasn't actually the question she was asking.

The Crone was actually asking me, "Before I set you loose to claim your power, tell me what you are right now, what you have been since opening the Red Door."

And the answer was powerless. I was powerless in The Maiden's web. I was powerless in The Mother's jaws. I remained powerless wrapped in The Crone's tail. This entire quest to claim fruit from the Yggdrasil Tree was about realizing that the first step to Understanding power was admitting that I was powerless, at least, in terms of magic.

So, I placed my arms around the serpent's scales and

closed my eyes, willing nothing but surrender. My dizziness grew, but I didn't shake or quiver anymore. I was confident in my answer of silence.

The Crone was merciful after a few minutes and chuckled.

"A fine ansssssswer, Lilith Chambers. You have embraced The Maiden, The Mother, and The Crone. And now you will go on to Understand as sorceresses have before you."

"Truth be told, I feel more like I was the one who was embraced by all of you. I'm not sure I did any embracing."

The Crone laughed, and the warmth of her chortle seemed to finally chase any remnants of the stream's chill.

"Well, you certainly already Understand a good joke. Be on your way now. I have other potential sorceresses to fish from the water."

And before I could ask where to go, her tail pulled back and snapped upward, thrusting me into the air as I soared through tree branches and leaves.

"Fuuuuucccckkkk meeeeeeee," I hollered as gravity slowly claimed me as one of her own again.

A twig scraped across my jawline, drawing a small bit of blood as I crashed down into a massive pile of leaves. My world spun, but at least I was finally right-side up.

Crawling forward and stepping out from the leaves, I picked a few dead caterpillars off my shoulders and looked up at the towering pile of foliage.

"Shit. I bet the person who raked that thing probably walks around talking about smelling the blood of an Englishman."

It was only after I'd finished my millionth snark of the day that I noticed the stillness around me. Nothing moved save for my beating heart. Silence filled my ears. Mist thinned, and I slowly turned to find myself in the presence of a tree so massive that it probably shit out things bigger than the redwoods in California.

My skin tingled with what I could only assume was raw magic in the air. Moss crept up and down the bark, and five gargantuan branches spread out at different angles above me. Golden foliage hung still as if frozen in a vacuum.

The tingle grew stronger in my flesh as I found myself looking down at three different spots on my body.

The fuck? I thought, pulling aside my clothes and finding various tattoos on my skin I'd never seen before. A black spider outline marked my right ankle. A gray wolf marked my belly. And a long silver serpent wrapped around my left knee. All of these markings pulsed in front of the tree, and I nearly collapsed from the vibrations.

Hang on. . . I thought. These are where. . . The Maiden tapped my foot with her leg, The Mother held my waist in her jaws, and The Crone wrapped her tail around my knees.

They all left their marks. Was this what Phenna had meant by I had to embrace them all? Did she have similar markings somewhere on her body?

As they continued to pulse, I heard a groaning noise as the wood of the Yggdrasil Tree before me shifted. A smaller piece of a branch gradually leaned down toward me until a string of yellow grapes hung before my eyes.

"Is that. . . are you offering me your fruit?" I asked the tree.

When I got no response, I slowly reached out my hand toward the cluster of grapes — er, things that looked like grapes. I'm sure they had some magical name here.

"Okay then. . . I'm going to take them if that's fine with you?" I asked, touching the frigid fruits.

The tree made no move to stop me.

With a gentle tug, I freed the cluster of grapes and

brought them toward my nose. They smelled like fermented wine. It honestly seemed kind of noxious. But when I waited a few minutes for a forest ranger or even Boo Boo to come bursting out of the fog, telling me not to eat that, nothing happened.

Slowly, the small piece of a branch rose toward the sky as the wood groaned again.

Pausing to breathe deeply, I started to sweat. This is what I wanted, right? I braved The Maiden, The Mother, and The Crone to hold this fruit in my hands. It couldn't kill me, right? . . . Right?

I passed all the tests. I'd solved all the riddles. I'd made the sacrifice. This was my reward, the beginning of Understanding.

Raising the cluster of five small grapes, I opened my mouth wide and thrust them inside.

Down the hatch, I thought.

I didn't even have time to notice any flavors before my entire jaw started to burst like I'd just chugged a massive pack of Pop Rocks. My tongue and teeth felt like they were having a tennis match. But instead of a ball bouncing back and forth, it was a bolt of lightning.

My entire body twitched with energy, and I wasn't even sure I'd swallowed the fruit. It felt like my head was spinning in every direction.

An expansion of raw knowledge exploded in my mind like an atom bomb. It carved outward in my skull for an impossible number of miles. I didn't even think I had that much space in my head. But swirls and strings of Understanding continued to grow.

The last thing I noticed was a garbled scream tearing from my lips like the noise couldn't get away from my throat fast enough. A bright yellow light burned forth from my open mouth, my nostrils, and my eyes as everything opened wide.

And then. . . darkness. I ceased to know or realize anything.

———

CONSCIOUSNESS WAS SLOW TO RETURN. I think I felt the hard ground under me. Maybe my head was propped up on something? Someone was talking, I think. And I knew their voice. I craved it like a bear tearing into a beehive for honey.

My eyes fluttered open to the first welcome sight I'd had in hours. It wasn't a giant spider or a 20-ton canine or even a giant serpent. It was my mate. Her hazel eyes drilled down into mine. My head rested in her lap.

And in that moment of realization that I'd awoken, Mars looked torn between relief and frustration. Uh oh.

Raspy, my voice asked, "Why are you naked?"

The goddess of a woman cradling my head frowned.

"No, no, Little Cottontail. I'll be asking the questions now. All you need to know is you've officially lost your alone privileges."

As my eyelids drooped, I mumbled, "Yeah, that's fair."

Chapter 8

"So, just to make sure I have this right. I left my mate alone for a day, and she managed to sacrifice a piece of herself to a glowing woman trapped in a book, travel to one of the Five Realms, risked her life with The Maiden, The Mother, and The Crone, and ate from the Yggdrasil Tree. Is that it?"

Mars stood over me with her arms crossed, obscuring her healthy breasts that my eyes kept finding their way down to. They were so full and ready to be nibbled on. And the abs underneath them? My fingers longed to explore every single one.

Fuck, what's wrong with me? I thought. *I've never been this horny before, even at the height of starting prog.*

But the way Mars towered over me while I sat in an old wooden chair left me feeling like I was being scolded by one of my college professors. And I fucking loved it.

Wait, did I? Let me check my updated horny drive, and see if the new kernel I'd flashed it with was hot for teacher. Booting the drive. . . files loading. . . password entered. . . yup. I was now horny for teacher. I just needed Mars to have a fake pair of glasses and a tight bun, both of which would get messed up when I pounced on her.

"Lilith, are you still with me?"

I nodded unconvincingly.

"Yes. Sorry. I'm having a hard time focusing, what with you lecturing me while naked."

She grinned something fierce and wicked, somehow rising even further over me.

"Did you already forget? You're in heat."

Her bitemark between my neck and shoulder started to warm, and I grew even hungrier for the werewolf locking eyes with me.

"Right! How could I forget? Sorry. I've been through a lot of magical shit today. That nugget must have fallen out of my head somewhere between being caught in a giant spider web and washed out of an underground stream," I mumbled.

My desire for Mars spread further, from my heart right down to my groin. And suddenly, I needed to know just how strong this chair was.

"Sweetie, your pupils are dilated," Mars chuckled.

"I don't think I'm going to last until we get back to your farm," I said, feeling warmer all the time. "The library —"

Mars interrupted me.

"I flipped the sign and locked the front door when I got here. We're alone."

Was I really about to do this? At work? There were no security cameras in the basement. Our budget only allowed for two, at the book drop and the side door.

It should have disturbed me how quick I was to toss away conduct and rules that I'd honored since I got this job. But the fever I burned with could only be quenched by fluids from Mars. I needed her to smother me before I sank into a frenzy that hardly felt human.

And I had magic now, right? So who knows what kind of additional sparks would fly if Mars didn't sate me right. this. moment.

It's for the safety of Mars and this library that I engage in these explicit acts, I thought, breathing heavily and watching tunnel vision form around the werewolf standing before me with inhuman golden eyes.

She licked her lips and inched closer.

And just before the werewolf jumped my bones, she whispered, "I'm calling a timeout on the lecture for now. But I meant what I said about you losing your alone privileges. You gave me a fucking heart attack today, and I had to leave my truck behind to race here."

I nodded, barely able to focus.

"So, I'm going to expect a promise from you before this is all over. Got it? You've got magic now, and that comes with consequences."

Rolling my eyes, I muttered, "Everything in my life has come with consequences from transitioning to leaving home to becoming a werewolf's mate. Why should becoming a sorceress and gaining Understanding be any different?"

And while I still needed to determine *exactly* what I Understood now, magical exploration would have to come later. I was the one that needed to come now and by Mars' hands. My body called to hers in a way I'd never felt before. I suddenly understood why they made those tacky charms that were two pieces of a heart fitting together. My flesh needed to fit together with Mars'.

This was madness. I'd known the woman for two days, and my hunger for her touch, her commands, was out of this world.

"Stand up," she ordered, and I obeyed.

"The basement door —" I started before Mars interrupted.

"Locked. Now get over here so I can examine your jaw with my tongue."

Flooded with a foundation of carnal need and lust, I licked my lips and obeyed Mars' words, throwing myself into her arms. She didn't even flinch. I felt all the strength in her biceps as one arm snaked around me to squeeze my ass and the other moved so she could lightly grab my hair.

"Call me the Princess of Ida," I muttered, and Mars leaned down to unite our lips.

Her warm breath lit a fuse in me that went racing toward some bomb tucked away in the back of my skull.

Mars' tongue raced over mine and explored every single nook and cranny of my mouth, as though she expected it to have changed shape after what I went through. A light moan escaped my lips as she broke away to breathe.

"You're going to do exactly what I tell you, understand?"

And I went weak in the knees at this new sense of authority from her. Her eyes drilled into mine, and I acknowledged all at once how much power and influence over me the alpha had.

"Do you trust me?" she whispered.

I nodded.

"If you tell me to stop at any time, I'll stop," she said. "Do you consent to being ridden like a mare in the basement of your workplace?"

"I consent," I said, feeling her raw power wash over me and realizing my stresses from earlier were retreating like Napoleon from a Russian winter.

Mars ran her tongue down my neck, and I shivered,

gooseflesh racing down my arms. She pulled me tight against her and inhaled deeply, taking in the scents of my hair and my flesh.

"The magic within you makes you smell different, my mate," she hissed, inhaling deeply again. "I smell bitter strands from The Maiden's web, the warm breath of The Mother's den, and the worn scales of The Crone's tail that gripped you tight. And your magic carries its smell, hints of tree sap and acorns. It's intoxicating to a wolf's nose."

She motioned for me to lift off my shirt, and seconds after I did so, Mars unhooked my bra. The feeling of her fingers freeing my tits elicited a small gasp from me.

"You'll make more noise yet, Little Cottontail."

Mars pushed me down into the chair with one arm and thread spread her legs wide before sitting in my lap. I had never been more thankful this particular chair didn't have arms to it. Her weight settled on me, and the werewolf lightly bit the tip of my nose before joining our lips again.

And while our tongues danced, Mars' hands fondled my breasts, squeezing the nipples just to feel me jump and moan louder. Sparks of passion radiated through my chest with every movement as her fingers massaged my tits.

I broke the kiss.

"Mars. . . I. . . I need you," I said, struggling to make words.

"I'm right here, my mate. And I will see to your pleasure. Have no fear."

She continued to fondle my breasts as I sighed in the throes of passion. Hormones flooded my brain with every noise she coaxed from me.

And with every moan, the werewolf straddled me a bit tighter, growing increasingly wet. Her juices dripped down onto me. She ran a finger inside of herself and offered it to me, shimmering with her wetness.

I licked and sucked on her fingers while Mars watched with a smile. When I'd finished, she licked her fingers while my eyes fluttered.

When I was panting, Mars switched places with me after practically ripping off my pants and gaff.

She brought me down into her lap, and I felt her fingers move from my stomach down to the girldick I'd warned her not to touch the other night.

I flinched as warning bells sounded in my mind, dysphoria rearing its ugly head.

"Nnnnnuh," I hissed, startled.

Mars' fingers froze at my waist.

"Hey, it's me. And I remember your rule. I'm not going to touch it, I promise."

I remained frozen, unable to even breathe.

"Do you trust me?" my mate asked. "Because I swear, we can stop right now if you want. I only want to make you feel good. But I won't move another inch without your say-so."

Taking a few shaky breaths, I settled back into Mars' lap.

"I trust you."

"Good. Now, be calm, and let Mommy treat you right," the werewolf said, sinking her teeth into my neck just short of drawing blood.

"Ugh!" I buckled as her raw energy sank into me.

Melting into her embrace, I felt Mars move her fingers further down, pausing to listen to my breathing and heart rate. I took a deep breath as Mars' fingers moved to the base of my girldick and felt around gently.

My breath hitched when the werewolf found the nerve clusters she was looking for.

"There?" she asked as I shivered.

"Y — yeah."

Mars started slow with her strokes, applying pressure until I was as hard as going to get. Lightning chased waves of pleasure upward into my core, and I grunted.

"That's it," she said, continuing to run her fingers above the shaft of my gock.

And just when I thought Mars couldn't surprise me anymore, my mate adjusted her fingers again, delicate in exploration.

She avoided the girldick, instead moving her hands to my scrotum and feeling around for a pair of inner canals I couldn't believe she knew about.

"Doing okay, Little Cottontail?" she asked as I closed my eyes and sank deeper into the werewolf's lap.

"Yup," I hissed. "Keep going."

After more exploration, Mars found my inguinal canals and gradually penetrated them. Fireworks exploded all through me as her fingers pushed a little deeper inside.

"H — how did you know about those?" I gasped.

She continued to finger-fuck my canals as I shook, and ripples of pleasure raced from my core to my spine.

"Fuck!" I hissed.

Mars applied a little more pressure and gave me her most nasty laugh yet.

"Do you like having your trans cunts fingered, Lilith?"

I was shaking too hard to make anything but an animalistic noise.

"I'll take that as a yes, you sweet thing," she giggled, again. "How do I know about muffing? I dated a gorgeous transfemme up in Quebec City for a few months. Krystal taught me a few things about how to bring her to ecstasy."

On the verge of orgasm, I moaned and quivered.

"Mars, I'm about to. . .," I managed to start before pleasure robbed me of any further words.

Carefully, the werewolf stood us up. She began to grind

against me from behind, pulling tighter and applying more pressure in her muffing.

"Ugh!" I hissed. "Mars, I'm going to come."

With all the firm control of my alpha mate, Mars lowered her lips to my ears and whispered, "Be a good girl and swear on your magic that you'll never again strike a bargain without telling me first."

My brain was swimming in ecstasy, so her words didn't get much thought from me. I was putty in her fingers at this point and willing to give Mars anything she asked for.

So, I struggled through the storm of horniness and bliss to spit out that sentence.

"I swear on my magic not to strike another bargain without telling you first," I whispered as she thrust against me. I was suddenly reminded of when she took me against her bed, kicking my enjoyment up yet another notch.

With my body shaking uncontrollably from holding back, I felt the dam inside shatter. I came as Mars continued to grind on me. It wasn't long until she moaned and came against me, a unified contentment washing over both of us.

"Fuck!" I said as Mars guided me back to the chair. I once again sat on her lap as she delivered soft kisses up and down my back.

While we both basked in the afterglow of our sexed-up afternoon, I remembered what she told me to say in the throes of passion and scoffed.

"You. . . you tricked me!" I stammered, not entirely upset, more shocked than anything.

"And you risked my mate's life today without warning," Mars said, in between kissing my back. "But I didn't trick you. It'd be more accurate to say I coaxed you."

I pictured Mars panicking as I stepped through the red

door and realized for the first time how that must have left her feeling numb and raw with worry.

"Your heartbeat vanished, Lilith. It fucking vanished. One minute, I felt you in my chest. The next, you went silent. I was beside myself with dread, hours away from you, powerless to help."

I opened my mouth to speak and fell silent. I wasn't even sure what I was going to say.

"You were just. . . gone. And I wasn't here to — shit, Lilith. You found an old book in a dusty cult chamber and surrendered part of yourself to a thing trapped inside. How can you not realize how much danger you put yourself in?"

Mars' arms wrapped around me tighter as she shook on the verge of tears.

"I've already lost too much. If I lost my mate right after finding her, I'd go mad. Before you get angry with me for ensuring you have to speak up before doing something dumb next time, try to understand where I'm coming from," she said.

How were we having this conversation? We'd fucked twice, and suddenly it felt like our souls had been intertwined for years. Then again, they probably were. We just weren't aware of it until Mars and I found each other.

"Why does it feel like we've already been together for years, Mars? To be having a conversation of this magnitude after two days. . . it's nuts. And yet, I can't feel any more impacted by your words than I do right now. My heart is shaking as I hear you about to cry, as you confess your fear to me. And it's all. . . it's just. . . ugh," I said, clutching my chest. "Fuck."

Mars rested her chin in the crook of my neck and sighed.

"Welcome to being a werewolf's mate, Little Cottontail. Why you went and decided to become a sorceress on top of that is beyond me. But you won't do anything like that again without my knowledge from now on."

Deep inside my being, I felt an acknowledgment that she was right. My brain was buzzing with the feeling of a lock clicking shut. I'd sworn on magic I chanced everything to get. And while Mars may not yet know why I took those risks, I certainly did.

I was going to fix things. I was going to become the mate Mars deserved. And I was going to Understand every scrap of arcane knowledge that I could get my hands on. It'd just be without secret bargains going forward.

"Just. . . catch your breath, sweet thing. We'll clean up, and I'll call Buckie to give us a ride out to the farm."

And suddenly, catching my breath felt like the only thing left I had the strength to accomplish today. So, I set to it.

Chapter 9

We rode back to the farm together in awkward silence. Mars and I had cleaned the library basement and changed clothes, but we still very clearly smelled like sex.

The old truck rattled as we approached a corner on the shittily-paved two-lane highway that led out of Pine Springs.

Buckie, I learned, was Mars' stablehand and partner on the farm. He sat to my left wearing a denim vest and rocking shortcut ginger hair with a braided beard. His jeans had holes in them at the knees, and Buckie's work boots looked old enough that the leather must have come from a cow in the Viking Era.

His eyes, though, clearly weren't human. They were brownish-black, the color of mud pooling between two trees. And I could feel something stirring within me, an egg that wasn't ready to hatch yet. That something told me he was both like Mars and unlike her.

Buckie smelled of pipe tobacco and corn. The stable-hand wore his sleeves rolled up to his elbows, revealing olive skin and a few freckles on his right arm.

I widened my legs as he reached over delicately to upshift into third gear.

"I'm sorry, Lilith. I know riding in the middle is uncomfortable," he said. He spoke to me but kept his eyes on the winding road lit by a half moon and a sky full of stars you could only see outside of town. Large oak trees lined the highway we drove on.

"Bench seats and old trucks will do that. It's no trouble," I said, leaning my head on Mars' shoulder. "So, how long have you worked with Mars?"

Buckie scratched his head.

"Well, quite a while, bub. I'll tell ya that. Ever since she moved out of her Uncle Pierre's house on the coast and decided she wanted to live right in the middle of her family's territory."

Mars chuckled and scratched me lightly under the chin, which left me a bit dizzy with pleasure. The touch of your mate was a hell of a drug.

"That feels like so long ago," Mars said.

"Ahhhhhh, it wasn't that long ago you found me in the woods," Buckie said, clearing his throat.

We came around a curve, and I spotted a possum carrying her babies along the side of the road before she was swept into darkness again.

"How did you two meet?" I asked.

Buckie lifted the side of his shirt, revealing a jagged scar that ran alongside his ribs.

"Mars! You did that to him?!" I gasped, bolting upright.

They both just laughed, and I felt my cheeks heat.

"Goodness no, Little Cottontail. If I'd done that to him, he'd be dead. As it happened, Buckie was just NEARLY dead when I found him."

My eyes widened, thirsty for a story to fill the rest of the time before we arrived at the farm.

Buckie wiped his forehead and put the high beams on for a second before muttering something and switching them back off.

Then, he turned to Mars and flashed her a smile that carried years of familiarity. Because, somehow, these two were family, even if Buckie wasn't quite the same as my mate.

What is he? I thought. *A fifty-year-old. . . what?*

My Understanding was taking its sweet time to hatch, but it kept a slight buzzing in my noggin to let me know it was booting up.

Let's just hope it boots up like Windows 10 instead of Windows ME, I thought.

Without warning, my girlfriend picked up my wrist and began to nibble on it. Her teeth ran lightly over my skin, and even this touch sent goosebumps down my arms. I couldn't get enough of her wanting my body, my broken flesh.

Flesh that I'll reshape I thought. *She deserves a mate that she doesn't have to handle like a goddamn explosive.*

But how long would it take? How much studying of the Mágissa Biblia would be required before I learned the spell necessary to reshape my flesh?

The buzzing in my head grew in response to my questions, but I didn't feel a solid answer.

Buckie interrupted my thoughts by saying, "Must have been right around this spot. I'd been shot by a hunter in the woods. He was getting ready to put me down for good when Mars showed up. I remember seeing her on four legs first and knowing immediately that a werewolf from the Dubois Pack had returned to their territory after years of canine silence."

My eyes drifted back over to Buckie, enthralled with his story. He told it like a grandfather entertaining a kid sick in bed with a book of adventure and romance.

"The hunter had his shotgun pointed down at my head, and she just sort of appeared from behind a tree. She snapped a twig to get his attention. And in the time it took the hunter to look behind him, Mars shifted from four legs to two."

I looked back over at my mate, trying to imagine how fast of a shift that had to be. My brain couldn't picture it.

"Once the hunter was dealt with, I found myself staring up into her golden eyes and wondering if I'd become dinner. I asked her, 'Have I been spared the gun only to meet a pair of fangs?'"

Headlights lit the cabin of Buckie's truck as a red van drove past us.

I found myself asking the werewolf sitting next to me, "So, what did you do?" As if it wasn't obvious. She spared him, or we wouldn't be riding in his truck right now.

Mars' inhuman eyes stared at me as she picked up the story.

"He didn't have long. If I didn't make a choice soon, nature would make it for me. I told Buckie, 'If we didn't kill it, we don't eat it.' Pack law. You don't take kills from other hunters for yourself."

Pack law? Right. I kept forgetting she's part of a were-wolf pack. Or — at least, she used to be. I still wasn't clear on where they were or what happened to them. Mars told me I'd find out later, and I didn't want to push it.

"Your mate picked me up off the forest floor and said, 'No use leaving you for some useless coyotes to come along and devour.' See, bub, she was acting grumpy about it all like I'd inconvenienced her in the worst possible way. But she hauled me back to her car and patched me up anyway," Buckie said, chuckling.

Looking between the two of them, I kept eagerly waiting for the next part of the story.

"And then what?" I finally blurted out, impatient.

Buckie laughed all the louder and ruffled my hair.

"You're a good match for this here alpha, all right," the driver said, shaking his head. "Then again, mates chosen by fate are never wrong, are they?"

Mars lowered her voice before speaking.

"No. They aren't."

With a loud cough, Buckie cleared his throat again and rolled down the crank window. It squeaked something awful, causing Mars and me to cover our ears. The driver hawked a loogie out into the darkness. I felt sorry for whatever patch of asphalt the giant ball of phlegm landed on.

After rolling the window back up, Buckie said, "I asked Mars what she was doing here. She was younger then than you are now, little sorceress," The driver looked at me as he said that.

My mind itched after Buckie spoke those words. The driver downshifted as we came up to the gravel driveway.

"Mars told you?" I asked.

"She didn't have to. I smell it on you, the fruit of Yggdrasil. You sorceresses all smell the same, like acorns and tree sap."

I shook my head as the truck bounced up the driveway.

"What ARE you?" I asked, flabbergasted and at my wit's end trying to figure it out. When was my Understanding supposed to kick on? Was it like the water bill? Did I need to pay a deposit first?

The driver snorted.

"One answer at a time. I haven't finished telling you about how we met," Buckie said. "Anyway, Mars told me she was looking for land to buy, and said she was thinking about starting a farm. That would tie her to the territory for a long time. I asked her what kind of farm she wanted to run, and she had no clue. I asked her how she intended to pay for it, and she again had no clue."

I snickered.

"Not having a clue about the finer details? That sounds like Mars."

Mars snatched me close without warning and whispered hot and heavy in my ear.

"Funny. And yet. . . I seem to vividly recall the finer details of ravishing you, my mate," she said before licking the side of my neck and biting my ear for good measure.

I melted in her touch.

"Touché," I mumbled.

"Don't be a brat, Little Cottontail. You're not very good at it," Mars whispered before smelling my hair for the 50th time. "How many times did you come before we left the library?"

I shivered. How was I hot and cold at the same time? Goddamn werewolf mates defying the laws of physics.

"Thrice," I mumbled again.

"And I don't intend to let you forget it," Mars said.

"I couldn't if I wanted to," I said, shrugging my shoulders.

We reached the end of the driveway, and Buckie continued his story when we were finished flirting.

"As thanks for saving my life, I offered to help Mars find a place and get her started. We found this property a few months later. And by that time, I'd convinced Mars to try out deer farming."

The truck's headlights washed over several deer. I caught a few reflective eyes staring back at us.

"What do you get when you farm deer?" I asked,

feeling stupid for not knowing. But in my defense, when I was learning "Old MacDonald Had a Farm" in kindergarten, we didn't exactly get a verse about him having deer. E-I-E-I-O.

Mars put a hand in my lap as Buckie killed the engine, and the lights shut off.

"Meat and antlers for velvet," my mate said.

"Oh. . . I feel like that should have been more obvious," I said.

Buckie got out of the truck and closed his door. In the background, I could hear crickets and bullfrogs.

Looking over the farm for the first time in great detail, I spotted several pens with high fences and a few trees. Livestock were separated based on herds, Mars later explained.

On the back side of the property against the tree line, a second house stood. And where Mars' house was mostly brick, the one tucked away in the back was mostly log siding.

"After we purchased the farm, Buckie taught me everything he knew about deer. We bought our first stock, and he got the animals used to being raised and protected by a wolf. None of them bat an eye at me anymore, regardless of what form I'm in. After a few months, I offered Buckie a house here, and decided to keep the farm split 50/50 with him ever since."

I leaned against the hood of the truck.

"Because we're partners, right?" Mars asked, holding out her first.

Buckie chuckled and bumped his knuckles into my mates'.

"Yeah, she-wolf. We're partners," he chuckled.

I scratched my head while watching Mars saunter

toward her single-story house. It was covered with an old brown roof dotted with antique shingles and patches of ivy.

"Hey. . . how did you learn so much about deer?" I asked without looking over at Buckie as he walked toward his house.

Our driver didn't answer, and I felt a wave of magic shimmer through the air akin to Mars' when she shifted. I slowly turned my head toward the old man.

Standing in his place was a massive albino stag with thin white fur and antlers that looked strong enough to take out one of King Kong's knees.

"Oh, damn," I said, standing there with my jaw agape. "Wait. . . Buckie? As in — oh, that's some funny shit."

While I giggled, Mars rolled her eyes and said, "Come on. Let's get a fire going out behind the house so I can cook supper. Actually — belay that. There are a couple of folks I want to introduce you to."

My stomach growled, almost as if in response to the "delay in food" announcement.

"It won't take long," Mars laughed, peering across the farm's darkness. "They're always quick to come when I call."

Without warning, Mars threw back her head and howled. A beautiful, melodious note shot up into the night sky. It said, "I'm here! Where are you?"

Seconds later, two other howls climbed up toward the stars from somewhere out in the woods. I heard the snapping of twigs and grass before I saw silvery eyes reflecting light from the windows of Mars' house.

A rush of furry bodies rocketed from the darkness and spilled into view of the porch light. Massive shaggy dogs barked and leaped towards Mars.

Wolves! I thought, shaking my head. *My mate keeps wolves on her farm!*

"Hey there! Hi. Yes, I'm home. Calm down," Mars laughed. "Down!"

The wolves immediately lowered themselves to the ground.

"Good boys. Now listen. I'm here to introduce you to my mate. See that hot piece of ass over there? Smells like the world's most tasty tree? Go get her!"

"Wait — what?" I gasped.

Before I could react, the pair of wolves darted my way, one covered in shaggy brown fur and the other covered in dense black fur.

The brown wolf was faster and leaner, tackling me to the grass and sniffing my face while I laughed uncontrollably. Meanwhile, the black wolf was sniffing my jeans and starting to lick one of my knees for some reason.

"Okay! Hahaha, you win. You win! I'm down," I giggled as the brown wolf started to sniff my hair and neck. His sniffing in my ear was about all I could hear.

This continued for a few minutes before Mars knelt next to me and started to pat the black wolf on the back.

BAP BAP BAP. Nice loud pats.

"That black one sniffing your shoes is Chocolate. And the brown dog that currently has you pinned to the ground is Chip."

"Glorious," I said, scratching Chip behind the ears. "Where did you get two wolves for your farm? Do they sell them as pups down at the feed store?"

Mars pulled the beasts off me and helped me stand. But the moment I was up, I immediately kneeled to play with Chocolate, who quickly showed me his belly. As I scratched his tummy, I chortled in glee. They were so big and fluffy! Holy shit.

"Well, they're not pure wolves. They're technically wolf dogs. Each of them is about five percent German Shepherd," my mate said. "I found them when I was camping in New Brunswick a few years back. They'd been abandoned on a logging road and were malnourished. So, of course, I took 'em home."

I stood up, now covered in dog hair.

"Well, they're perfect," I said.

Mars patted Chip on the head and smiled. Then, when I frowned and cleared my throat loudly, Mars rolled her eyes and patted me on the head as well.

"Good girl," she sighed, smirking.

"THANK you," I snapped. "I AM a good girl."

The werewolf scratched my hair ferociously while I shut my eyes and let my thoughts go fuzzy.

"Okay, you two. Listen up. Your job from here on out is to watch my mate when she's on the farm. Make sure she doesn't make any bargains or do anything stupid when I'm not around. Got it?"

The puppers barked and then turned a unified razor-sharp stare on me.

"Don't I get to give them orders as your mate?" I asked, raising an eyebrow.

"Nope!" Mars beamed. "Now come on. Let's wrestle up some grub. I'm starving."

We walked through the house, Chip practically glued to my side, and Chocolate panting behind us excitedly.

Half an hour later, Mars had a campfire going in the pit on her back deck. Small embers would fly up now and again while we cuddled on a wooden bench with a nest of blue outdoor pillows.

The smell of smoke and cooking meat filled the air. I looked down at the pile of metal skewers with sausages on the end, roasting over the fire at our feet.

I sat in the middle of the bench while Mars perched on my right. Chip was curled up in a ball of fur with his head in my lap. I just shook my head and scratched his ears now and again.

Chocolate sat at Mars' feat. My mate was snacking on a package of pepperonis while we waited for the sausages to cook. Once in a while, she'd "drop" one for Chocolate or give one to me for Chip.

My phone buzzed, and I pulled it out to an annoyed text from Alan.

"Do you still live here?? You haven't been home in two days," his text read with a scowling emoji.

I sighed and put the phone away. If Alan was getting snippy again, it was probably because his girlfriend broke up with him.

Fuck, I don't want to deal with that bullshit again, I thought.

"Hey, Little Cottontail, what's the matter?"

"Just my roommate being stupid. It's nothing."

I muted my phone and turned my attention back to the goddess sitting beside me on the bench.

Mars raised an eyebrow.

"He's harmless. Just being a manchild. Nothing new," I said.

My stomach growled again.

"I think they're ready," Mars said, turning back toward the fire. "And just in time."

I picked up a skewer and tried waiting for it to cool before taking a bite. I failed, of course.

Did I burn the hell out of my tongue? Yes. Was it delicious and worth it in every way? Also yes.

While waiting for the feeling to return to my tongue, I watched Mars toss a couple of cooked sausages to Chocolate and Chip.

At last, I asked, "What did you mean when you said 'just in time'?"

Mars flashed me a wicked grin as I took another bite of my food.

"Oh, nothing much. I was just worried that I might not get to eat ANY sausage today," she said as I hacked and choked on my dinner.

Chapter 10

The black void of slumber draped my vision like curtains of night. Except. . . I wasn't asleep. My mind wandered. And where I wandered, I couldn't be sure. Probably because of all the curtains of night. They made it difficult to see.

Or maybe there just wasn't anything TO see.

I walked in a realm of obsidian shadow. I couldn't see a path beneath me, but my feet never once failed to meet solid ground.

"Well, well. The newborn sorceress walks in dreams, her magic lovely as pedals unfurling from a flower in the welcome moonlight," a familiar voice said.

I turned to see Phenna behind me, hovering over whatever the hell I was standing on, drifting up and down like the tide in a harbor.

She wore a yellow dress of wafting light that did little to illuminate the space around us. Phenna's long blonde hair floated as she did, swaying this way and that, not unlike the tail of a curious cat.

And suddenly, my mind splintered, like a goddamn

hammer and chisel had been set to the skull. The yolk of my Understanding spilled out across the void as both eyes rolled back into my head.

Pain raced down my neck and into my shoulders as I unleashed a stream of curses that would have put the nun who raised Jake and Elwood into a coma.

"Fuck me!" I hissed, sinking to my knees and feeling like my brain was a trampoline with 30 kids jumping on it.

Phenna laughed.

"Would that I could, but my lack of a body and your lack of being single seems to stand in the way of that. Your heart belongs to that werewolf now."

I cradled my head in my arms as white light shot through my shuttered eyelids. They were pulled tight as curtains drawn for a midday nap.

Staying like that for a while and enduring the worst migraine on Earth, I hissed. And eventually, the searing pain started to recede. But it didn't leave my imagination in its previous state.

All the walls and support beams that made up my prior mind were knocked down, expanding the corridors of my subconscious in limitless directions.

I was suddenly accompanied by that feeling of falling in a dream before I bolted up, rigid and still as a statue.

Phenna waited patiently while I took several heavy breaths, looking around in all directions.

"A Dreamscape," I mumbled. "A space for my mind to occupy while my body slumbers."

Glancing over at the floating woman, I noticed things that were invisible to me the first time we met. For starters, a massive orange flame engulfed her at all times, and it hurt my eyes to stare at it for long. Within the fire swam all the magic she'd amassed from her life residing within the Mágissa Biblia and studying for two centuries.

All that raw energy waved through the air like heat above a charcoal grill.

Curiously, I cocked my head to the right and noticed a translucent red string that hung loose between her body and mine. It pulsed with the exchange of knowledge.

"A marker to show our connection from the bargain we struck," I said. The voice was mine, but it almost felt like I was speaking in a trance. My mind was expanding from the deconstruction and rebuilding of Understanding finally coming to fruition. It was dizzying.

As my subconscious rebuilt itself to hold arcane knowledge, it felt a lot like stretching when you first get out of bed in the morning, groaning and leaning against the doorframe.

"This string allows us to find each other," I mumbled.

Phenna smiled.

"Truly. It is glorious to watch another sorceress awaken. When I awoke, I was alone in an attic with the same Mágissa Biblia you released me from. I found it to be a rather lonely experience. But somehow, seeing your eyes widen to the arcane truth hidden from mortals, I feel. . . warmed by your awakening. There is comfort here."

"Y — you were alone?" I stammered, looking up at her again and trying not to focus on the fiery magical aura.

She nodded.

"I was alone often. You see, that was preferable to being around people who refused to understand me. If you believe the minds of your time have trouble understanding that a woman may reside within the body of what they believe to be a man, imagine how much more so that was the case for me in 1816. It was a mercy that Lord Wylde allowed me to reside within his manner, away from the cruel eyes of the public. His wealth shielded his oddities from their judgment. And to hide behind that shield, I gladly became one of his oddities."

My heart sank for this woman. Any hardships I had in this century must have been multiplied by 100 for hers. Without thinking, I walked forward to hug Phenna and passed through her, the whisps of her magic trailing over me like a beaded curtain.

I turned with a gasp to find her sighing.

"No body, remember? Though, I appreciate the sentiment," she said. "Over the last two centuries, it seems that I forgot how much I missed hugs."

"Phenna. . .," I started, the edges of my eyes watering.

"Be careful with your bargains, Lilith."

I took a step toward her.

Phenna held up a hand, stopping me.

"I've brought you something," she said. "The Maiden sent me."

I raised an eyebrow. The Maiden sent her? The giant spider woman? Of course, I now knew she was far more than that. She represented a third of the Triumvirate of Understanding. A daughter, a mother, and a grandmother who sought to bring arcane knowledge to all women, and in so seeking, became beings of immense magical power, as well as the path all sorceresses walked to find Understanding.

Wow, I thought. *My brain has a goddamn wiki of magical knowledge inside it now.*

This must have been how Trinity felt, downloading the knowledge of how to pilot a B-212 helicopter. When the egg inside my mind finally shattered, all this basic lore came spilling out. I got to skip History of Witchcraft 1008 and Traditions of Witchcraft 2008 on my way to earning a sorceress degree.

Is a sorceress degree a bachelorette of science? I thought.

Unfortunately, the Understanding I gained didn't have answers for snark, which was at least 33% of what went on in my head.

"What did The Maiden send for me?" I asked.

Phenna smiled.

"Your Bouquet, of course."

Cocking my head to the side again, I stammered for a response.

"F — flowers? The Maiden sent me flowers?"

"Yes, Lilith. But these are no ordinary flowers. A Bouquet is a gift of five beginner spells that sorceresses may receive shortly after tasting the fruit of Yggdrasil."

I took a slow breath to process this. The Maiden was giving me five spells? For free? That didn't quite compute. Was this a bargain? If it was, how was I supposed to tell my mate from within my Dreamscape?

"You can rest easy, Lilith. I couldn't give you anything for free. But The Maiden, The Mother, and The Crone carry no such limitations. They are the embodiment of all Understanding. So, when they give you a gift, it is truly without strings."

With another steadying breath, I nodded.

"Do all sorceresses get a Bouquet?"

The floating woman reached behind her back, and when her hand returned, it held five passion flowers wrapped tightly in brown paper. Each flower wore a lower level of wide pedals with a second level of needle-like pedals above them. All of them were decorated in a gradient of purple and white.

"You do," she said, a coy grin poking through her words.

Phenna handed them to me, and my hands felt like pins and needles the moment they touched the paper. I nearly dropped the Bouquet.

Ravenous hunger roared into my mind once I realized there was magic stored in each flower. They all held secrets. Five different spells. And I drooled as though I was holding a slice of pizza or a carton of chicken nuggets.

"I've never been given flowers by another woman before. And for reasons I'm having a hard time quantifying, I've never looked at a set of stems and pedals like they were a bag of salty french fries before, either."

With my free hand, I reached toward the uppermost flower and then stopped.

"Do I get to pick the spells?" I asked.

Phenna shook her head.

"The Maiden chose them for you."

I raised an eyebrow.

"And how did she do that? Did I accidentally take a Fuzzfeed quiz when I was stuck in her web? Pick your favorite flowers, and we'll tell you what spells best match your magical abilities," I said, grinning.

Phenna crossed her arms and stared down at me.

"You'll see. Go on. Eat one. I know you're dying to."

My hand reached for that uppermost flower again, and at the last second, I pulled it back, my brain screaming in agony and frustration. But I tucked that frustration aside to ask one more question.

"I don't suppose one of these flowers holds the spell of flesh made clay you spoke of," I said.

Phenna shook her head again.

"That's an advanced spell, Lilith. If you desire to learn it, you had better start studying the Book of Magdylena. These spells are basic in nature. The reasons they are gifted to you now are twofold. First, a sorceress, especially one who is the fated mate of an alpha werewolf, tends to attract magical chaos and danger. These spells are meant to grant you a simple defense until you gain more arcane knowledge."

I pulled the first flower from the Bouquet. It felt like one freshly yanked from the cooler at a flower shop. Tiny drops of dew dotted the lower stem.

The magic hidden within his flower giggled like a school child carrying a pocket-sized secret that they wanted everyone to know they had.

"What's the second reason a Bouquet is gifted to sorceresses?" I asked without taking my eyes off the white and purple pedals.

"The second reason is to wet your whistle for Understanding. You will consume these and be driven by the desire to know more. A sorceress's purpose is to Understand all she can. The Maiden, The Mother, and The Crone gave their lives so that women in the future could have a measure of power for themselves."

I locked eyes with Phenna while she gave me a history lesson on sorcery.

"They watched as many men of the ancient world wielded their power foolishly and brought great strife and pain to the planet and Her people. Unable to stomach any more, the family worked tirelessly to grant women their own capacity for power. Good or evil, it mattered not. They simply wished for other girls to have the same opportunities to shape the world as kings and princes before them."

That all felt so much bigger than I believed myself to have any right to be a part of. The grand potential to inflict change upon the world had been given to me and all I wanted was to be free of my dick.

Well, there's way more to my desires than that, I thought, bringing the flower to my lips. *I also want a killer set of tits.*

"Alright, then. Here's to my first spell. Down the

hatch!" I said as though I was at brunch with a table full of other young women surrounded by waffles, mimosas, and french toast.

Gingerly placing the bulb in my mouth, I bit down on the stem, severing it and feeling an icy chill wash over my tastebuds. The taste of snow, the taste of raw cold, and the taste of cruel stalactites hanging at the mouth of a winter cave, all filled my tongue.

After I'd chewed up the stem like a piece of asparagus, words filled my mind, and I spoke them aloud, "Chilled in sight without a touch. Flesh robbed of heat, no warmth to clutch. A bite of frost and fangs of ice. Wintry flesh will suffice."

My hands grew frigid as I Understood now that with proper focus and a right nasty stare, I could render someone's flesh as cold as snow.

"My first spell. . . Frostbite," I whispered.

Leaning over, my mind freshly fed with a new spell and its required costs, I coughed, my lungs filled with frosty air. When I exhaled, I saw my breath.

"A lovely first spell. The Maiden chose well for you."

I just nodded and looked back at the flowers, already feeling hunger pangs within my mind again. It was as though I was holding a plate of cookies, steam rising from the dough, taunting me. And in a Scottish voice, my brain said, "We've had one spell, yes. But what about second spell?"

Phenna giggled.

"I think she likes it."

Grabbing another random flower, I threw it into my mouth and chewed as quickly as I could. My ears popped, and roaring laughter filled the space around me. My mouth grinned uncontrollably as more words popped into my mind.

"Words that hurt and bring the pain. Bludgeoning phrases that batter your brain. An insult so wicked it shatters the shield. Unending mockery until you yield," I said as I now Understood how to tuck daggers into my words.

It took a few seconds for the laughter in my ears to die down.

"My second spell. . . Savage Ridicule," I said, taking a breath.

Phenna put her arms behind her head as though she was lounging on a bench.

"Oh, that's a fun one. You know, I once used that spell to give Governor William King a bloody nose and a severe migraine after he referred to me as a dress-wearing vagrant," the floating sorceress said.

I snickered at that.

Grabbing the third flower, I chowed down and immediately felt like my tongue was being hit with static shocks from each tooth. My hair rose as I heard thunder booming across the sky on a hot summer day just before the storm rolled into eastern Colorado. Big old nasty clouds of lightning and hail would climb down from the Rockies and race across the plains.

"Sparks and bolts and arcs of light. Booming thunder that quakes all night. A deafening noise falls from the storm. Rattles each person, no matter their form," I said with a voice louder than any I'd heard before.

Lightning crackled in the palm of each hand, and I knew that if I slammed them together, the result would be a blast wave of epic proportions.

Willing the lightning in my hands to fade, I mumbled, "My third spell is. . . Thunderous Applause."

Phenna cleaned one of her ears with a pinky.

"Yeah, be careful not to use that one indoors. I do not know how expensive glasswork is in your time, but in mine, windows are very expensive. Lord Wylde had to replace quite a few as I studied in his manner."

Before I could say something snappy, I doubled over, sweat falling from my forehead as anxiety and fear rattled inside my chest. The right side was. . . a racehorse thundering down the track. But that wasn't where MY heart was. Why do I feel like. . .like — shit! That's where I sensed the heartbeat of my mate. She's terrified.

"I need to go. Something is wrong with Mars," I said, trying to stand up straight again but feeling winded from using so much of my arcane appetite.

Phenna's eyes flew over to the remaining two flowers. I crumbled them into a messy ball and stuffed them in my mouth like a vegetarian trying frantically to finish her salad five minutes before the restaurant closed.

My jaw exploded in pain, and a searing headache arched through my skull as I grimaced and swore.

"I'll — mother of god — figure those spells out later," I hissed with just one eye open. "Fucking hell. This must be what my poor Dragonborn felt like when I made her eat all those spell components at once."

The migraine only grew worse, and I barely heard Phenna say, "See you soon, newborn sorceress."

And then everything went dark.

BOLTING AWAKE IN A COLD SWEAT, I looked around the den for my mate, but she was nowhere to be found. It was dark. No lights trying to pierce the curtains. My phone told me it was 2:42 a.m.

I quickly threw on some clothes.

Before I could call out for Mars, a booming thud and the sound of splintering wood echoed from the porch. I could have sworn I felt the entire farmhouse shake from whatever hit the front of the building.

Stumbling toward the front door, I threw it open and spotted my mate in her bipedal werewolf form. Mars was trying to stand up from the mess of two wooden chairs she'd shattered as she hit the house.

The werewolf was covered in blood-soaked patches of fur and panting heavily.

My heart sank, but before I could run over to her, the werewolf's stare and growling voice commanded me, saying, "Get back inside! It's not safe!"

"What's not. . . safe?" I mumbled, feeling my legs turn to jelly.

A man's voice called from the driveway, his southern accent as thick as molasses. He spoke slowly with a drawl like there was not a single need to rush in all the world.

"Oh, I'm sorry to intrude, madam. But I do believe the werewolf is referrin' to me."

I turned slowly to see a wiry pale man wearing a gray button-down shirt and a black vest. His hair was brown and spiky, eyes as black as the shadows he crept from. And his stroll was as casual as a boomer dad walking through the lumber aisles of House Depot.

As he spoke, I spotted his fangs, pointed canines that were an inch longer than they should be. A bloody aura crawled all over him, from his polished shoes to his jeans to his vest.

"Vampire," I hissed, my mind Understanding the basics of a mortal body being kissed with living death, thus preserving it and caging the soul inside with an unnatural bastardization of life.

If Mars' body pulsed with the magic of wildlife and raw nature, this man walking down the driveway was the exact opposite, dry as bone dust and still as a land forgotten by time.

"A Vampire Lorde, actually, young sorceress. But an easy mistake to make for one whose mind is so. . . new to Understanding," the vampire said, putting his hands in his pockets. "Your blood smells mighty fine, all that fresh magic just a buzzin' like a fresh cup of joe in the mornin'."

I shivered as the vampire spoke. His words and gaze were beyond chilling, and I felt like I was drowning in ice water just by staring at the man.

"You may call me Beauregard. I am a simple servant of Telsyn with an even simpler message to deliver. The wraith congratulates you on findin' your mate, Mars. But as she is sworn to bring you nothing but loneliness and misery until you reveal the Wolfbone Graveyard, I'm afraid I must relieve you of this rather delicious-looking morsel."

My heart jackhammered inside my chest, but then Mars shifted into her full wolf form and stood before me, a massive beast with fur the color of mahogany. And hearing her growl lit a fire inside my guts. What was it Phenna said? The Bouquet was meant to give me some measure of defense until I could gain more arcane knowledge, right?

Well, no time like the present to test out that defense.

I Understood that all spellcraft carried a cost. And said cost could be paid one of two ways: spell components that were spent to complete an arcane purpose or a sorceress's own magic and vitality that pooled inside her. I didn't have time to gather any components, so we were about to find out just how many spells I could cast before I was drained like a tightly squeezed sponge.

"I take it this display means you don't intend to simply hand over your mate then, Mars?"

Swallowing my fear, I tried to boast as best I could with small bits of lightning illuminating my palms.

"You want my blood? Come and get it, leech," I growled.

"Well, now that is as enticin' an invitation as I've heard in weeks. Be right there, darlin'."

Gritting my teeth, I prepared myself for things to get downright ugly.

I thought, *Guess we're about to figure out what those other two spells are.*

Chapter 11

I tried to sound brave when I called the Vampire Lorde a leech. The words didn't feel brave. They felt like they dropped from my tongue as soon as I rattled them between my teeth. Now, as this Vampire Lorde slunk through the darkness toward me, icy terror gripped me.

What little fire Mars lit in my belly went out like a candle on a cold windy night.

The man advancing on us was death walking on two legs. His eyes swallowed my gaze, leaving me trembling like a wounded gazelle before a lion.

My knees buckled, and it took everything I had not to sink to the porch and start whimpering. That was the aura of fear Beauregard exuded into the night. And he'd come here to kill me specifically.

I've never had someone try to kill me before. Sure, I'd been beaten up a few times in high school. It was just part of being labeled the "campus tranny" on a rural campus. And there's a certain level of fear that comes with walking down the hallway in a skirt, feeling alone and vulnerable.

Like, at any moment, Lance Hulverick was going to pop out of a doorway and punch me square in the jaw.

But this. . . this was abject terror, staring down at the glistening fangs of a creature (because that's what he was — a creature, not a man) who was drooling over the aspect of ripping open my neck and sucking down every last drop of blood I had.

For a shocking morbid second, I briefly wondered if a vampire drinking my blood would taste the estradiol and progesterone I took each day. I suppose that was my version of gallows humor — or gallows curiosity.

People think of strange things when they believe the end is moments away. And the way my heart hammered in my chest, the way my breath came in short ragged gasps, the way my vision blurred with tears driven by madness and fear, I was certain these were my final minutes.

Beauregard was a spongey bag of bones and dead organs held together by graveyard sorcery. Every step he took, the sickening smile on his pasty face grew larger. In his eyes, I was a thick-cut steak covered in butter and salt. And the realization of being someone's dinner pushed my mind into a whole new level of outright fear.

My throat wanted to close. I desired nothing more than to run away from this nightmare that I'd found myself in. Nothing made sense. Why was something as old and cold and dead as Beauregard here to kill me tonight? What horrible sin had I committed to deserve my life being snuffed out with such violence? And it would be violent. How else would one describe the piercing of flesh and the severing of nerves to drink a person's blood while they hung limp in the Vampire Lorde's jaws? That was violence incarnate.

Another whimper from my seizing throat, and I realized my hands were shaking, fingers trying to curl inward as though they might be able to hide from the horrifying creature before my quivering eyes. The night was closing in around me, and I suddenly felt like a sheet of paper being folded and sealed in an envelope.

"Why?" I wept.

"Because Telsyn demanded it, darlin'," Beauregard answered. "And what my Lady commands, I must do. I know it doesn't help to hear this, but your death ain't personal to me. Before now, I'd never even set foot in Maine. Probably wouldn't have ever crossed paths with you otherwise. But. . . orders are orders."

When Beauregard was just five steps from the porch, my mate launched forward with bewildering speed and sank her canines into the Vampire Lorde's knee. I heard the crunch of bone and cartilage as the undead creature hissed with furious pain. He drew back a claw to strike, and just before he brought it down on Mars, she pulled her jaws up. Beauregard slammed into the ground.

After that, Mars spun, and with as much force as she could muster, flung Beauregard back down the driveway and out of sight into the trees. I heard the snapping and crashing of limbs and timber from where I stood on the porch.

A second later, a nude Mars was standing before me, having left her wolf form behind. If my legs weren't still jelly from watching the visage of death that was Beauregard strolling toward me, I might have been fascinated by how seamlessly my mate shifted skins.

My eyes traced the treeline of Mars' driveway, knowing that at any moment, the Vampire Lorde would reappear and come for me again.

Mars grabbed my face with both hands and pulled my attention to her.

"Lilith, listen, we don't have long. Go back inside. Lock

yourself in the basement. I'll buy you as much time as I can," she said.

Her breathing was ragged. She'd already been fighting Beauregard before I woke up. Something dawned on me at that moment, driving my dread to obscene levels of horror.

Mars didn't say she'd come back for me. The werewolf didn't even tell me to try and run away. My mate knew she couldn't beat Beauregard. She was just trying to coax me into a shelter that might hold up for a few minutes after he put her down.

And what would I do with those few extra minutes? Take my own life in a more peaceful manner of my choosing? Was that the only option left to me at this point? Should I be grateful for this last bit of mercy she could deliver me in the face of such overwhelming power of the night?

"Mars," I whispered, unsure of what to say.

"If he was a normal vampire, I'd have slaughtered him before you even woke up. But that beast putting himself back together as we speak is a Vampire Lorde. He's 200 years of graveyard magic condensed into a single set of thirsty fangs. I can't beat him on my own."

I shook my head, more tears drifting down my cheeks.

"Where's Buckie?" I asked.

Mars shook her head.

"I heard his truck leave an hour ago. He doesn't sleep much. Sometimes Buckie likes to go for a long evening drive if he gets restless. Beauregard must have been watching and decided to attack after he left."

When I struggled to get out any more words, Mars pleaded with me again.

"Go inside, Lilith. I love you."

But for reasons that are not all that clear to me, I took her hands in my own and pulled them down.

"I know how to use magic now. I have spells. . . ready and waiting," I whispered.

It almost felt like the magic inside of me was moving my body at that moment. But the words I spoke next were my own.

Mars raised an eyebrow.

"What are you proposing?" she asked.

"That we live to see dawn. That you will take me in your arms again and again as I pledge my adoration for you anew. . . as friends. . . as lovers. . . as mates."

The werewolf's eyes widened as she considered this, and Beauregard's voice rang out from the woods.

"Okay, now, Mars. That was awfully rude! I was quite set on letting your mate die quickly and painlessly to show this wasn't personal. But your actions and wolf-like stubbornness are encouraging me to reconsider that decision."

I closed my jaw so fast that I bit my tongue. His voice was a hand squeezing the very life and faith from my heart.

But Mars placed her forehead against mine.

"You are asking to step into a maelstrom of pain and derangement, of fang and claw. I cannot promise you that we'll survive," Mars said.

"The only promise I want from you is that you'll never stop loving me. If I know that I have your love with me until I die, be it now or in several decades, then maybe I can find the courage to fight at your side against someone so fearsome as Beau."

My mate ran her thumb over my knuckles as the Vampire Lorde unleashed another string of superlative sentences from the forest. We both heard the snapping of bushes and limbs.

"Then listen carefully, Lilith Chambers, my Little Cottontail and the fated mate born to run beside me."

Power spun from her words as we kept our foreheads

pressed together, and I felt my heart bolstering as Mars spoke.

"You are my pack. I am your alpha. Your magic is mine. My claws are yours. Your loyalty is mine. My courage is yours. Hear now the alpha's command," she growled, pulling tighter against me.

Her power flowed through my body, the raw strength of nature and wilderness shoving away the terror, the cold, and the hopelessness that had so vexed me since I locked eyes with Beauregard. Gooseflesh claimed my arms, and I gasped as Mars ran her hand down my chest.

All through my body, her courage built castles and walls. They constructed a magnificent fortress of bravery.

In response, my magic flowed through me to her, ready to be called at Mars' command. For in that moment, she was my alpha. I followed her every whim, no matter what she asked of me. Not just because I knew she loved me, but because I Understood that by her command we would live or die tonight to the best of our abilities.

Her eyes held my gaze even as Beauregard stepped back onto the property in full view.

"You are a wolf. You show no fear. You hunt the undead that trespasses in our territory. You run him down and answer every growl of his with a snarl of your own. Kill the vampire. Protect the pack. That is your oath. Swear it."

And with all of Mars' determination and firmness running through me, I put aside my prior apprehension.

"I swear it, my alpha."

Mars turned to face Beauregard with renewed drive in her eyes. And I believed at that moment, as she'd bolstered my courage, I'd given her the strength and resolve to duel this walking sack of death once more.

It's one thing to fight and defend the woman you love. There's power in that. But it's a hell of a thing to fight ALONGSIDE the woman you love. That brought even greater power.

Standing beside Mars as she again shifted into her full wolf form, I said, "I have five spells. And I can cast three with each sunset."

The last words Mars spoke before losing her human vocal cords to the throat of a howling, shaggy beast, were, "I hold him. You hit him."

We stepped off the porch and into a — actually, her description was perfect. The violence and chaos as Mars met Beauregard really was a maelstrom of pain and derangement.

But this time, I had courage and resolve. And Mars had me.

Beauregard drew first blood this round, cutting open my mate down the side. I almost flinched, but Mars' courage continued to fuel me. I hung back at a distance while the werewolf recovered and sank into a frenzy with Beauregard.

Their dance of fang and claw destroyed the farm around them. He'd grab her by a leg and drive a powerful fist into her chest. Mars would roll under Beauregard and then tear into his back.

As I watched the two struggle, instinct ran through my mind like a live wire.

"You are a wolf," Mars had said.

And I circled the two, waiting for an opening. I watched with the eyes of a huntress as Mars and Beauregard tore each other apart. I dodged, ducked, and repositioned myself again and again while they snarled.

That's when I saw what Mars was doing. She wasn't

just trying to inflict damage on Beauregard's body. She was driving him away from the farm and back toward the woods.

She was used to fighting in the forest, whipping between trees, and running through bushes. Mars was a wolf. And tonight, so was I.

Mars eventually body-slammed the vampire hard enough that he crashed into a tree, driving one of its lower branches through his chest. And the moment he was pinned, I rushed forward to strike.

Surrendering to the instinct of my spellcraft, I felt static electricity building in each palm. The flesh covering my hands glowed blue, and I surged magic into each finger. This was my raw power, spellcraft bringing the storm to a trapped Vampire Lorde.

He let out a mad hiss as I slammed my palms together in Beauregard's face. The magic I'd built in each finger exploded outward with a shockwave of lightning, followed by the deafening boom of thunder.

I blew half the skin off Beauregard's face and even an ear as the branch that pinned him snapped, and the Vampire Lorde flew off to my left. He crashed into a tree trunk before sinking to the ground with a moan of pain.

This is pack strategy, I thought. *The teamwork of wolves, of hunters driving their prey to exhaustion before killing it.*

Mars' instinct had put a point on our scoreboard for the first time tonight.

But as the Vampire Lorde rose, I knew it'd take more than what we'd just hit him with to walk away with our lives.

So, we endeavored to hit him with more.

The next round was not so different than the last with thrashing in the woods, exchanges of blood via claws and fangs. Superficial wounds that would neither immobilize nor kill a Vampire Lorde or an alpha werewolf.

Beauregard caught my mate by the throat and slammed her into a boulder. The rock shook violently under the pressure he applied, and I heard Mars whimper as her bones began to bend and groan.

"What's changed, Mars? Having your mate at your side juice you up? You still lack the power to kill me, and you still ain't strong enough to save her. An alpha derives her strength from the pack. And your pack was eradicated years ago by my Lady. All that's left for you to do now is suffer, as the newborn sorceress will when I open her from belly to chin."

Seething with rage at the sight of my alpha pinned by this trespasser, I summoned all the cold in the air around me, drawing it in with a vacuum of heat. Frost spread across the leaves and twigs on the ground under my feet.

My eyes drilled into Beauregard's wrist, the one just below his hand pinning Mars. And with the razor focus of a huntress, I willed every bit of cold I'd gathered to the joints and ligaments just beneath his hand.

Ice and chill claimed the Vampire Lord's flesh and spread across his wrist, drawing his attention and furious stare.

Cracking and splintering skin earned me a grimace of pain from Beauregard. Mars took advantage of the weakness and distraction, surging forward and sinking her fangs deep into the Vampire Lorde's wrist.

He roared in pain as the werewolf pulled with all her might and severed the very hand that held her against solid rock. Beauregard's roar of pain grew twice as loud as he held the frostbitten stump of a wrist.

While he agonized, my mate zoomed out of range. And I hit Beauregard with another clap of deafening thunder, splitting his arm to his elbow and sending him rocketing facedown across the forest floor into the side of a hollow log.

The wood of that log shattered, and Beauregard didn't move an inch.

For a split second, I dared to hope that we'd finished him. That hope built like a dim light bulb in my chest.

With the adrenaline starting to fade, my knees buckled. My vision swam as I held a hand to my head. The vitality I'd spent to cast those three spells in quick succession took its toll on me. Weakness spread through my core, like numbing waves.

Oh, I thought. *This is why spell components are so important.*

As I stood freshly drained by the arcane rituals I'd performed, I took shallow breaths, trying to focus on Beauregard.

But everything was so damn blurry and dark.

"Shit," I hissed.

I felt like my blood was low on iron, sugar, protein, and every single thing that would make a girl dizzy with a poor enough diet.

Mars was covered in matted fur, sticky with drying blood and open wounds still oozing out more of her life liquids. I was surprised to learn a werewolf's blood is just as red as mine.

But before I could say anything, a chunk of log the size of a car door flew past me. It moved like a baseball unleashed upon home plate from the MLB's greatest pitcher. I felt the wind as it missed me by inches and slammed hard into Mars.

She yelped and vanished from my sight, crashing into another tree behind me.

My eyes tore back to where Beauregard used to be, but

the one-handed vamp was suddenly standing before me, full height and menace unleashed.

"Well now, I do believe it's time to tenderize the meat before I tear you open, girl," he said, grabbing my throat.

I choked and sputtered as he slammed my head back into a tree trunk. A bolt of pain rocked my skull, and my eyes fluttered. The worst migraine imaginable flared from the back of my head.

Then, as easily as a human might toss a soda can into the recycling bin, Beauregard whipped me to the left, letting me fly forward into a thorn bush. I screamed as a hundred points of pain opened up from my cheeks to my shoulders and upper back. Ragged thorns tore into my flesh as though it were a flakey biscuit pulled fresh from the oven.

And before I could even think about crawling backward, Beauregard picked me up with his good hand again and held me upside down.

"What do you think, Lilith? You tender enough yet?" he asked. "Maybe I could break a few bones first."

The vampire dropped me face-first to the dirt, and I cried out as my neck crimped to the side, my full body's weight thrown upon it without warning. And before my entire self was upon the ground again, Beauregard drew back his leg and kicked me across the woods. I bounced and scraped over dirt with every blow bringing forth an ocean of concussions and battering pain.

The boulder where he'd pinned Mars ended up being my final resting spot, momentum carrying me and slamming my back into the rock's side.

I coughed up a spattering of blood, eyes wide open as pain rocked my body. I felt like a puppet thrown into a spin cycle at full speed. Everything hurt, and I just wanted to close my eyes forever.

Beauregard stood beside me and called down to my crumbled form.

"Are you still with me, sorceress? I can hear that heart of yours a pumpin' blood, but you're leaking like the fuckin' Titanic."

Nothing moved. And I couldn't think for more than a second at a time about which limb I wanted to budge.

I was pretty sure by the severity of pain in my left shoulder that Beau had dislocated the fucking thing.

The Vampire Lorde sat me up against the boulder and crouched.

My face was starting to swell, and I could barely open one eye.

"You see, sorceress? All that fight and pain for nothin'. Less than nothin'. I'll drain you, reattach my hand, and be well on my way out of Maine towards my next meal by the time Mars wakes up and realizes what I took from her. It wasn't gonna be personal, darlin', but then you went and made it personal. You sorceresses get a tiny taste of power, and suddenly, you think yourselves as goddesses. Then a big old monster like me has to pull you back down to Earth and remind you of just how powerless y'all are."

A rush from the trees revealed Mars pouncing on Beauregard. But he drew back his fist and smashed it into one of her lungs with far more force than he'd shown me. The Vampire Lorde had a good measure of restraint for his power.

I heard bones break inside of my mate, and it tore my heart right down the middle to hear her yelp again. Apparently, my tear ducts were still intact because my vision went blurry with waterworks.

Mars yelped as she started to fly backward from the momentum of Beauregard's hit. But he grabbed one of her hind legs and slammed her into the boulder again. She hissed in pain and coughed up a mess of blood that splattered me.

And Bouregard continued to wail on her, driving my mate deeper into the boulder, cracks in the rock crying out under the pressure of his monstrous force.

My brain sank into fear once more as I realized the difference in power between us and a Vampire Lorde. It was truly terrifying that with half a face, one hand, and one ear, the undead creature was still 10 times stronger than Mars and I put together. Every strike of his fist into her body displayed that with force. Mars wasn't whimpering now. I didn't even know if her eyes were open.

"Oh, you stubborn wolf. I am tempted to just snuff out your existence here and now. It would almost be worth it to face the wrath of my Lady if that meant I got to pay you back for how much you've irritated me tonight."

Drawing back his fist again, Beauregard spit on my mate and sighed.

Suddenly, my fear sank into the oath I'd given Mars. A fuse lit somewhere within me, and I reached for magic, a spell, anything I could use to hurt this fucker.

My mind swam back to the memory of that Bouquet that Phenna passed on to me. And I realized when I grasped for those last two unknown spells that I'd been wrong in my initial Understanding.

Those final two flowers I ate didn't represent basic spells like the others I'd been gifted. They were two halves of a much more powerful spell, entirely separate from the arcane rituals I'd named with Phenna.

When I reached for that spell inside me, only darkness answered. Hunger. The urge to devour. A gnashing of teeth, magically speaking.

I shuddered and pulled back. This didn't feel like the other spells I'd cast tonight. I couldn't comprehend what was stirring inside me, writhing like worms in my intestines. But two things happened that pushed me straight into the black of that unknown spell.

Beauregard struck Mars across the jaw, and I heard someone whisper in my ear, "Ravage him."

The fuse inside me met a powder keg, and I gave myself over to the spell. Darkness swam across my vision, and I saw the massive ball of graveyard magic that was Beauregard's power, his core.

Where everything else around me dimmed, that tightly wound ball of gray light at this core that gave him his strength, his endurance, and his ability to whip an alpha werewolf like a ragdoll was the most delicious-looking morsel I'd ever laid eyes on.

I was alarmingly aware of the lack of magic within me, having spent my three spells for the night. But what I was about to do to Beauregard required no magic on my part. This spellcraft was vicious and took everything it needed from whatever I attached it to. The ultimate magical siphon.

Beauregard was a shiny car, and I was about to drain the fuel from his tank. Obsidian veins of hunger crawled down my right arm and turned the flesh on my hand solid black. My open palm became a magical black hole, eager to tear into a magical source and bleed it dry.

The ground under me cracked open, and nearby trees and bushes cried out, life attempting to flee the ravenous open wound I'd become.

"Ravage him!" the voice hissed in my ear once more.

I rose just as he slunk over Mars' body, fangs fully extended and ready to drink of my mate. Dead leaves and dry twigs flew into a cyclone around us as I snarled, and thrust my blackened hand toward his throat.

His eyes widened as I grabbed the Vampire Lorde and

pulled him away from Mars with surprising strength and an unspeakable need for his magic. With a mad cackle, I drew his energy into my body.

I tasted death and the graveyard magic that'd created him two centuries ago. It took everything I had not to gag on the taste of sludge and tainted soil. Beauregard hissed and snarled as I drained him. He tried to tear free of my grip, but his power fled, and the Vampire Lorde knew it.

The air around me grew acrid, and trees and bushes withered to dust the more magic I siphoned from Beauregard.

Power like I'd never felt before bolstered my previously empty reserves. But I quickly realized that I could not entirely contain such a vast amount of magic. My body, as a vessel, was too young and new.

But at the same time, I didn't know how to stop the siphoning spell. Nausea roiled my stomach, and fever quickly took me as I cried out. The chilled pain brought about by swallowing so much graveyard magic raced to the core of each bone in my body, and I laughed all the louder driven by the madness of so much energy swirling in and around me.

Inky tears raced down my face, but the spell's hunger did not cease.

"Please," I whispered to the spell, but nothing responded.

Fear filled Beauregard's now-milky eyes as his skin pulled back, and he started to desiccate. He opened his mouth to. . . what? Plead for mercy? Give me his final words? I never found out because after an agonizing few minutes of siphoning, his magic was finally gone, corpse of a body devoid of energy, core dimmed after exactly 207 years of "life."

With nothing left to eat, the spell ceased, and I could

do nothing but fall back as the chill of death finished spreading through every inch of my body. I was never meant to use that spell. And if I was ever stupid enough to cast it, I wasn't meant to survive.

"Mars. . .," I whimpered before my head slumped left, and I went limp, buried by the very death that gave Beauregard so much strength.

Chapter 12

The air was warm, not quite sticky. Sunlight beckoned me to open my eyes but punished me when I did.

"Ow. Shit. Who turned the sun up on the thermostat?" I asked, taking 30 seconds to realize that didn't make any sense.

I was. . . swinging? Was I in the air?

My vision was filled with two large trees, one behind me, and one in front of me. And as the wind blew, I started to sway back and forth.

Looking down, I finally realized I was in a hammock. And this thing was old. It creaked in the wind, and I didn't exactly trust it to hold my weight. Climbing out was an ordeal, but I finally managed to do it without falling on my ass.

"Where. . . am I?" I asked no one in particular, looking around with wide eyes at a very different farm than the one I'd passed out on. "This isn't Mars' farm."

A familiar man's voice sent chills down my spine.

"No, darlin'. That's because it is mine."

Spinning, I found Beauregard standing behind me and

looking. . . alive? He was clothed in overalls and a brown shirt with muddy boots. His once-spiky hair was greasy. And the man's skin was positively tan, soaking up every bit of sunlight it could.

I flinched as terror seized my heart, and I reached for magic to blast this man away from me.

"Hold up! Easy now," he yelled, throwing up his palms. "I ain't here to hurt ya. I'm not even sure I could."

I didn't retreat, and his words took several seconds to process. It helped that he wasn't moving, just standing there with his hands up.

"What do you mean? How did I get to your farm? Did you drag me here after I passed out? Where is my mate?!"

My questions only grew more frantic as I asked them. And Beauregard just stood there scratching the back of his head.

"Well, shoot. Um, guess I'll just take those in order as best I can. I can't hurt you here. We appeared on my farm after you swallowed all the magic in my body and left me a desiccated husk. And I reckon your mate is back with your body. I know I didn't kill her."

His calmness was so eerie, as were his soft brown eyes. Wait. Why could I see his eyes? When he attacked us on the farm, they were solid black.

"Beau, are you. . . still a vampire?" I asked.

He just snickered and shook his head.

"Naw, Lilith. In this place, I appear to be human again. And I forgot what it felt like. . . standing in the sunlight's warmth, being near living creatures that didn't fear me, and feeling a beating heart with warm, living blood in my veins."

The ex-vampire's eyes showed nothing but relief as he inhaled deeply and stretched.

Looking around, I found we were standing in a pasture

with a large herd of black and white cattle gathered across the way, grazing and lazing in the afternoon sun. The air smelled of livestock and manure.

My eyes found their way to an old white barn in the distance with a couple of horses waiting to be let out of their stalls. Opposite the barn across the farm was an old shack of a farmhouse. It looked nothing like Mars'. The roof was slanted, some of the windows were broken, and the chimney was half-collapsed.

When I looked back at Beauregard, I found the man with his hands in his pockets, just staring at me. And there wasn't an ounce of hunger in his eyes. Just. . . calm.

"Okay, maybe you can explain what's going on in more detail? I don't have a clue how I went from siphoning your magic to waking up on your farm."

Beauregard stepped over to one of the oak trees I awoke under. He pulled out a crumpled home-rolled cigarette from his pockets and lit it with a match.

Leaning against the tree, the ex-vampire inhaled, then sighed and let the smoke out of his lungs.

"Mother Mary does that feel good. . . to just. . . feel warmth in me again. Warm air, warm tobacco, warm sunlight, warm blood. A man can forget what all that feels like after a century or two of being dead."

He spoke slowly. I'd forgotten how much of a drawl some Southerners carried with them. Beau's accent was always thick and his words plentiful. But here, he seemed to be savoring every minute he could get in this field of cows.

Over by the barn, a small boy with similar hair to Beauregard's ran into the building with a bucket. He was jumping and giggling.

"That'd be my little sister, Adelaide," Beauregard said, turning his head to look at her. He chuckled and shook his head. "My word, I forgot how excited she'd get to feed the horses in the mornin'. You could hardly keep her out of the barn."

I scratched my head while Beauregard talked. And then something dawned on me. Beauregard must have sensed my realization because he turned back to me and nodded.

"Yup. She's like you. And I was the only one she ever told. Mom and Dad call her Atticus, and she says nothing. They tell me to look out for my little brother when they take the wagon into town, and I say nothing. What can we say? What words could we use to tell the world who she is and what she feels that wouldn't get her whipped and beaten? Nothing."

Sighing and feeling the weight of Adelaide's world, one that refused to give her a place to exist as herself, one where no Lord Wylde was coming to save her, one where she lived and died with just one man knowing who she truly was, I nearly wept.

"So, Lilith, when I told you that my attack wasn't personal, I meant it. I would never drink the blood of someone my little sister would have been friends with."

I turned to face him.

"Then why?" I asked, barely managing to choke out the words.

"Because Telsyn ordered me to. And I was powerless to disobey her."

Confusion spread across my face as Beauregard talked. I needed more answers. Fortunately, he seemed prepared to offer them to me.

"Telsyn is a wraith, Lilith. She's a powerhouse of magic and a higher class of undead than I ever was. Vampires typically do their best to avoid wraiths. And it's usually pretty easy because there aren't many of them in this world to begin with. But if you have the misfortune of stumbling across one, they enslave your will and drag you into their schemes without a hint of struggle."

I took a deep breath and tried to process this new information. Beauregard looked at the ground, a pained grimace on his face as he remembered Telsyn.

His voice lowered to a damn near whisper. And tremors rattled his throat as Beauregard spoke to me. His eyes went somewhere neither of us wanted to be.

"Wraiths. . . they. . . dissect your soul. They're both undead flesh and spirit simultaneously, an unstable union of abominable abilities. It makes them remarkable tormenters. When a wraith enslaves a vampire, they reach into their very soul with spectral talons. And they just start scraping tiny pieces off."

I gasped.

"It's pain, but more. Because you don't bleed, you don't scream, and you don't have any way to make it stop. Except to capitulate. When Telsyn had her nails running down my soul, I wanted to claw my own eyes out. I wanted to tear out my tongue. I wanted to run my fingers through a paper shredder. And none of that would have compared to the agony she inflicted on me. Wraiths don't get tired, Lilith. So this just keeps going until you submit. All that power you've been building through the years. . . it becomes theirs to wield as you're chained to their dominion."

Beau took in a sharp breath with a hiss and shuddered. I watched the man's flesh quiver as he relived the godawful things Telsyn did to shatter his will and take control.

For the first time since I'd met Beauregard, I was tempted to walk over and pat him on the shoulder. But something kept me anchored to the ground I stood on.

"In truth, I'm glad you killed me, darlin'. I'd been that

miserable bitch's puppet for the better part of two decades. And now I'm free, for the little bit of time I have left."

Raising an eyebrow, I asked, "What do you mean 'little bit of time you have left'?"

Beauregard pointed with his chin over toward the barn, and I turned to see what he was looking at. But the barn was gone, swallowed by an encroaching fog.

"What's happening?" I asked, dread filling my guts like a mud puddle during a downpour.

"To you? Nothin'. You'll wake up here in a little bit, and I'll be long gone. Off to wherever a murderous Vampire Lorde goes when they finally kick the bucket."

I ran my fingers through my hair and tried to make sense of everything. But my mind was spinning with everything Beau had told me. It wasn't simple to sort through.

"You still have questions, and I don't have much time left. So I'd suggest you make it quick, newborn sorceress."

Shaking my head, I closed my eyes tight and tried to think. How fast was the fog moving? What would happen when it hit me? Would I vanish? No! No. I needed to calm down. He said I'd be fine. And for some reason. . . I kind of trusted him. The ex-vampire was different here.

It was whiplash to pass the fuck out fighting Beauregard for my life and wake up on a farm where we were apparently swapping life stories. Er — well, maybe not swapping. I hadn't told him anything about me yet. Did I even have time to?

"I feel like I've asked this question three times now. Can you please walk me through exactly what happened to me?"

Beauregard finished his cigarette and put it out, crushing it under his boot. Then, to my surprise, he pulled out a second and lit it with another match from his pockets.

Were his pockets just full of matches and cigarettes? No. Focus.

Taking a deep drag, Beau closed his eyes.

"Your spell, which was quite a whammy, by the way, ripped every bit of magic from my body, leaving it a centuries-old corpse. No graveyard magic? No vampire. But a Vampire Lorde carries within them an entire lake of magic. And in terms of containers, your body is akin to a soda can. Understand?"

I cocked my head to the side and tried to visualize all that.

"The graveyard magic you swallowed from me overwhelmed you. Hell, it should have killed you. But the fact that you're still here, in my memory, shows that you must still be breathing somewhere out in the world. Your mate is probably doing everything she can to keep you that way."

"Okay, so I killed you by draining all the magic in your body. It overwhelmed me. I passed the fuck out. And now I'm standing here in one of your memories? How does that work?" I asked.

Beauregard looked over at where the shack was, and when I spun to follow his gaze, we were both greeted with fog. My heart rate picked up a bit more at that.

"Well, I'm no expert on siphoning spells. I can only assume you pulled a piece of my consciousness into your body along with all that magic you downed like a pitcher of beer at the possum supper."

Note to self, I thought. *Never EVER attend whatever the hell a possum supper is. It sounds disgusting.*

"So. . . what? I swallowed your soul?"

Beauregard laughed, which I thought would be an unnerving sight. But he just looked and sounded like a man enjoying life, one of those people you see at the park feeding ducks bread. They're not in a rush or upset about anything. They're just enjoying life in that moment. That's what his laughter reminded me of.

"No, darlin'. You just got a piece of my thoughts is all. And a sentimental piece at that. And while we've been standing here chattin' like a couple of church ladies after the service, your body has been digesting me."

Looking up, I noticed the fence was gone now, and the herd of cattle had moved closer to us, almost as if they could sense what was closing in. Beauregard put out his second cigarette and stepped closer to me. I didn't move away.

"Before I go, I'm going to tell you how to beat Telsyn."

"W — why?" I stammered.

"Because she made the last two decades of my life hell. You and that werewolf are going to make her pay. I know what she took from your mate, and I know what she almost took from you. So listen up."

I did just that.

"A wraith isn't from our world. Of the Five Realms, theirs is the worst. Dryer than any bone or desert you've ever seen. It's a miserable, decaying, stagnant home. And Telsyn will do anything to keep from being sent back there. But you can kick her ass out and lock the door. You just need to find the object she's bonded to and destroy it. It's the one thing that anchors Telsyn to this world and the only way you'll ever be rid of her."

That just raised more questions.

"What is it? WHERE is it?" I gasped as the fog swallowed all the cattle and moved in closer. I started to panic, even if nothing bad would happen to me. Vanishing backgrounds aren't a great indicator of situations you should remain calm in.

Beauregard smiled as his sister ran out of the fog like it wasn't even there. She appeared to be around nine years old. Her eyes were blue like the sky, and Adelaide's smile gave the sun a good run for its money. She was just so excited to see her brother, clinging to his leg like a tree in a flood.

"Beau! I found you!" she giggled.

Beau picked up his sister, spun her around a few times while laughing, and then sat her on his shoulders, which only seemed to have grown while we talked.

There wasn't much pasture around us now.

"Yeah, hon. You found me. Good job. You feed the horses?" he asked.

She beamed.

"Yup! I even got Grumpy to eat this morning."

"Well, now, doesn't that just speak to your talent? You're a regular horse whisperer."

Adelaide just smiled all the wider, and it was infectious because I did as well.

"Who is this?" Adelaide asked.

Beauregard pointed at me with his chin.

"Well, this here is Lilith. She's got some work to do, and I just wanted to help her a little bit after our fight."

Adelaide's smile disappeared like the sun behind rain clouds, and she whispered something close to Beau's ear.

"Why were you two fighting?" she asked.

I cleared my throat.

"A mean old monster told us lies, and made us angry at each other. But we talked it out, and we're friends now," I said in the most reassuring voice I could.

Adelaide nodded real slow.

"And now I'm gonna go find that monster and kick her ass," I said, punching the air.

Beau's little sister giggled and then stopped before looking horrified.

"Momma says we're not allowed to say that word. We have to say 'behind' instead."

I grinned.

"Well, then, I'm gonna go find that monster and kick her behind."

That earned me another beaming smile from Adelaide. She laughed and then turned to look at Beauregard, who appeared as happy as the day his sister came into the world. It took everything I had to keep from tearing up at what she said next.

"Is it time to go?" she asked.

Beau nodded without dropping his grin.

"You bet, darlin'. Oh, Lilith. One more thing. I know asking you a favor after our fight is a bit of a faux pas. But you're the only person who can do anything about it now."

"Name it," I said.

The ex-vampire took a deep breath before answering. The fog was inches away from us now, and I felt clammy air moving up my skin, inch by inch.

"My sister's buried in Kansas City, a little graveyard called Green Valley Cemetery. Her surname after getting married was Thimbleton. If you're ever down that way. . . would you mind getting her a new tombstone with the right name? I always wanted to do it, but I was too ashamed to approach her grave as a. . . well, the thing I became. I didn't want our reunion to happen like that."

I couldn't stop the solitary tear leaking down my face as Adelaide turned to wave at me.

"Bye now!" she said, still sitting on Beau's shoulder.

I waved back as the fog finished its job.

"Kansas City will be my first stop after Telsyn is gone, Beau. I promise."

And then everything was gone. Myself included.

UNLIKE THE LAST place I awoke in, here I felt cold. And it was dark. A hefty weight lay upon my chest, and warm breath spilled over my face.

When I opened my eyes, I was staring at a large snout with a black rubbery nose on the end. It twitched as my breathing slowed. Only then did I realize the weight on my body was a massive wolf.

Gods, she was heavy. But she was warm. And I . . . couldn't seem to stop shivering.

A mess of blankets and pillows curled around us.

I'm in the den, I thought, looking up at the couch walls surrounding us.

My teeth chattered, and fuck me did every bone inside my body ache. One of my shoulders was bandaged.

Right about the time I started to realize my bladder was going to explode, I saw my mate's eyes snap open, golden irises locked with mine.

The thump of a wagging tail soon sounded through the den.

"Hey, Mars," I croaked. My voice sounded like sandpaper. I was simultaneously thirsty as fuck and needed to piss an entire lake out of my bladder. "Look, not that I'm not happy to see you first thing in the. . . whatever time it is. But can you let me up? I'm busting."

When the wolf growled and narrowed her eyes at me, I snapped.

"Yes, bed rest. I get it. But unless you've got a piss jar tucked away in these blankets and a French man to throw it at afterward, I think you need to let me up."

Mars didn't immediately move, and I was about to shatter like the Hoover Dam in an action movie.

Desperately looking at the bathroom door, about 15

feet to my left, I began to struggle beneath the wolf's weight, feeling more aches spread through my body. And then, before I knew it, I vanished from under Mars and reappeared just outside the bathroom door where a large shadow spread across the floor.

I heard Mars hiss in surprise and rise to her feet as I turned around to face her.

"What the fuck?!"

My mate looked over at me and then back down to the bed I'd been lying in, burying her nose in the sheets and pillows and sniffing loudly.

The entire vanishing and reappearing took a split second, and it felt like being in one of those dreams where you're falling just before you wake up.

One moment, I was on solid ground. Then, I was a weightless mass flowing from one shadow to another before feeling the floor beneath me again. In the blink of an eye, I'd gone from flat on my back to across the room and standing on my feet.

Before I could further contemplate what I'd done, my bladder knocked on the door and said, "Hey! Remember me?"

I exchanged glances with Mars as a new chill washed over me, my teeth chattering again.

"Just. . . we'll figure this out in a minute. Be right back!"

And then I did to that toilet bowl what God did to the Earth just after Noah built his boat.

A few minutes later, I was washing my hands. Casually glancing up at myself in the mirror, I screamed at the girl staring back at me.

"Oh, what the FUCK?!" I yelled.

The Lilith staring back at me was not the same woman

I'd been before draining a Vampire Lorde of magic and passing out.

"Why the hell do I look like I want to skin a bunch of puppies for a fur coat?"

The woman staring back at me had her usual black hair to the right. But the entire left side of her hair was now a ghostly white. And if that wasn't enough, my eyes didn't match. My right eye was its typical brown, but my left eye was the palest shade of blue imaginable. Like — it was almost white and could barely be labeled a blue of any kind.

I had new age lines under my eyes that I didn't recognize, and my skin was covered in bruises. Okay, that last part checked out. I'd been kicked through the forest like a soccer ball by Beauregard.

Either way, my reflection looked like I'd aged about a decade or two in the span of one fight. I know it was stressful, but geez! This couldn't have been normal.

Stepping out of the bathroom, I started to say, "Hey, Mars. We need to talk ab—"

But I was cut off by a pair of grizzly arms being thrown around me. Then, I was squeezed to the point of near death by my mate who'd resumed her human form.

Here I was torn between smarting off about the tight hug and folding into my mate's body heat. Because dammit, why couldn't I get warm?

Mars buried her nose in the crook of my neck and then spent the next few seconds smelling me from head to — well, head.

"I missed you," she said in a husky breath. And before I could respond, Mars was licking the bite marks she'd marked me with on our first night. My legs started to buckle for multiple reasons.

"I missed you, too. But now I miss my shiny black hair

and my previously youthful complexion. What happened to me?" I asked. "My body feels like it got run over by a bus during a blizzard. My brain feels like an old sponge. And my core just refuses to get warm. How long was I out?"

Sighing and placing gentle hands on my shoulders, Mars said, "You should sit down. Things have been screwy since you died."

My eyes widened.

"Since I what?!"

Chapter 13

"You died, Lilith," my mate said, her eyes tearing up. I couldn't bear to watch her cry, not the woman my soul had learned to pine for in a matter of days. Not the woman who made me feel wanted for the first time in my life. Not the woman who loved me so deeply that I couldn't stop questioning what I'd done to deserve her.

So, I buried my face in her neck and threw my arms around the werewolf. My shoulder still felt a bit stiff.

"That's twice now that I've felt your heart stop beating in my chest. Most mates only feel that once. . . at the very end."

Mars trembled. All that strength she wielded with the raw power of nature dropped to the floor like shattered glass.

I held her tighter as the werewolf started to sob louder and come undone.

"I finally found you. Years of searching for my fated mate, and you popped up at a festival, right under my nose. I've been so happy, Lilith. Holy shit, I haven't told you how happy I've been since you danced into my life.

And that just made it hurt all the more when your heart-beat went silent . . . again."

My eyes watered, and I felt the telltale sign of tears racing across my cheeks and over to the edge of my nose, the same route they always took.

"The thing all those musicians sing about. Madonna. Cher. Whitney Houston. The love their notes echoed on and on about. I finally understand, how another individual can make you feel so complete, so whole. I've been missing a piece for 30 years, and here you are. I feel. . . full. And I just want more of you. More and more and more, Lilith. But I'm so fucking terrified that you won't be here to give me more, that I'll lose you like I lost. . . like I lost. . . everyone."

That last thing Mars said was more of a quiet hiss than an actual word.

"I'm sorry, Mars. I'm so sorry. I don't mean for these things to keep happening," I cried as the two of us sank to the floor, still clinging to each other like one of us might fade away if released.

For a minute, the only sound in the room was our combined breathing. The shared vulnerability between two souls made to exist together before they were born apart.

And even this felt good. It felt right to be scared together, to cry over a near-death experience that almost cost us the very thing we'd been searching for our entire lives.

My heart thumped harder as Mars and I held one another. I almost willed it to beat all the louder so Mars would feel it with such confidence as to know I wasn't going anywhere. I closed my eyes tight and swore on all that I was, all that I'd gained, all I'd learned, that she wouldn't lose me completely. Not for a very long time.

We settled down, still holding each other. Silence kept

us company as the shadows around the den stretched and moved with the sunrise outside.

Grief born from terror eventually gave way to joy over mutual survival. And when my arms could no longer stay up, I sighed and wiped my last tears away.

"Let's get some breakfast and talk," Mars said. "I need coffee before I say more feeling words."

I smirked as Mars helped me stand. My foot let me know it'd fallen asleep with pins and needles poking everything from my toes to my ankles.

Fuck me, I thought, trying to straighten it out and almost willing the blood to go back where it needed to be. That's how it worked, right?

"Don't tell me you're one of those cliche people who are addicted to coffee," I said, lightly tapping my foot on the floor and wincing as it tingled all the more.

Mars raised an eyebrow.

"How is being addicted to coffee a cliche?" she asked.

I shrugged.

"Well, lots of people are. They make it part of their personality. It becomes a cliche," I said.

"So, because lots of people enjoy something, it's automatically a cliche?" Mars asked, leading me toward the kitchen.

"I mean — no, it's not the enjoyment or popularity that makes it a cliche," I said, scratching my head. "It's more that so many people make their coffee addiction part of them. They buy mugs that say things like, 'But first. . . coffee.'"

Mars turned back to face me in the hallway.

"But you drink coffee," she said. "So doesn't that also make you cliche?"

I scoffed.

"No — because I don't make it part of. . . like," I

sighed. Being dead had apparently robbed me of my words and logic.

Mars just grinned at me and waited while I sputtered.

"Shut up," I mumbled, bumping her shoulder as I walked by.

Like the merciful mate she was, Mars let it go, knowing she'd won the — well, I wouldn't call it an argument or a debate. She won the moment. And thankfully, she was a gracious winner.

The werewolf walked into her kitchen while I stood off to the side, unsure of what to do. Heavy wooden cabinets hung bathed in morning sunlight from a huge window over the sink. A white dish drainer sat to one side, the rubber mat underneath angled for any remaining water to drip back into the sink.

Mars poured water into her coffeemaker, and we stood quietly waiting for it to leak out enough bean juice for the two of us.

When the coffee was ready, my mate went to the cabinet farthest from me and pulled down two mugs. She filled both.

"Cream or sugar?" she asked.

"Naw. I'm good with black coffee," I said.

Setting my mug on the counter next to me, I caught Mars smirking again. I scrunched my face in confusion, trying to figure out what had her in such a snickering mood.

Finally, I gave up and grabbed my coffee. The white mug had simple black lettering on the side that said, "But first. . . coffee."

I nearly dropped the damn thing as Mars burst out laughing. Rolling my eyes, I sighed.

"Yes, yes. Haha. You got me good, Mars."

My fingers wrapped around the steaming mug, and I closed my eyes, trying to absorb all the warmth from the drink. Gooseflesh erupted on my arms, and for a moment, I felt like I'd gotten a fraction of a hot shower, just holding my coffee.

I took a deep breath of Rich Roast Vanilla Blend and held it in my lungs, hoping I could steal heat from even the air I inhaled. My core still refused to warm up. And I wasn't awake enough for my Understanding to explain what happened to me.

Mars scooted closer when I set the mug down after a tiny sip. She gently grabbed my chin and ran a thumb over my lips. It sent shivers from my spine to my toes. Guess I wasn't going to get rid of the pins and needles feeling this morning.

"I missed you," she said, with such tenderness that I almost choked up again.

I was wanted. Even though I was physically present in her home, Mars still missed me. I hoped she missed how I looked at her like a goddess posed on an altar. I hoped she missed how I giggled at the awful jokes my brain released into the world like a kid gently placing a toy boat into a pond. And I really hoped she missed fucking me within an inch of my life. Although, maybe now that I'd died, she would restrict herself to fucking me within a meter of my life.

"Your body. . . just refused to stay warm. And I was terrified. So Chocolate, Chip, and I all took turns laying with you to share our heat. Seems like it helped."

"I will never complain about you laying on top of me," I said. "And thank you for bringing me back. Whatever you did after I died seemed to work."

Mars raised her eyes to my hair, now half black and half white.

"I can only imagine what happened to give you hair like Death the Kid."

"I'm not sure. I just feel so cold and tired. My core can't seem to warm up. I'm left craving warmth like some kind of extra hunger. And where my Understanding should have kicked in by now to tell me what the fuck happened, nothing is clicking upstairs."

My mate pulled my face closer and licked the side of my cheek. Then she kissed me lightly on the lips.

"You've basically been unconscious for two days. I think your body is still recovering. It'll kick things on one piece at a time. Sort of like the different switches being flipped as the power came back on in 'Jurassic Park.'"

Pausing, I frowned.

"Just out of curiosity, have you read *Jurassic Park*?"

Mars cocked her head to the side and answered without thinking for even a split second.

"Why would I? There's a perfectly good movie I can watch anytime I want."

My eyes widened.

"Please tell me my mate isn't someone who refuses to read," I said.

Mars raised an eyebrow.

"If I tell you that I don't read all that much, what will you do?"

"Judge you for falling in love with a librarian," I blurted.

The werewolf pulled away from me and raised her hands into the air. Then, with as dramatic a voice as she could muster, the newly-born soap opera star said, "Judge me if you must, Lilith. But I'll remember that next time you want me to assfuck you over the side of my bed."

And before I could retort, I heard a man cough just as a heavy boot hit a squeaky patch of kitchen floor.

My neck slowly turned in horror to spot Buckie standing in the kitchen doorway with a large box of Sunken Donuts. His expression could best be described as, "What a terrible day to have ears."

Mars walked over to grab the donuts like nothing had happened. And inside, I felt my brain sinking to my stomach in hopes that I could somehow cease to be if I just willed it hard enough.

Unfortunately, I continued to exist. And Buckie continued to stand there like a statue, arms still raised as if he was holding the box of donuts long after Mars took them to the counter.

How much trouble would I be in with Mars if I died a third time? Because it was starting to look like the best solution to my encroaching embarric attack. That's what I called a panic attack resulting from such strong embarrassment that I wanted to erase my memory by several minutes.

Buckie refused to make eye contact with me as he said, "Glad to see you're up and about, Lilith."

Then, he turned and walked away as I heard barking outside. When Buckie opened the door, presumably to walk back to his cabin and rinse his ears out with bleach, two pounding sets of paws thundered in the kitchen.

Chocolate and Chip ran around me, sniffing and jumping. They bounced and barked as if to celebrate my return to the living. I kneeled to greet them, which was a big mistake because Chip simply body-slammed me to the floor.

And as I lay flat on my back, I was sniffed and licked by competing wolves, each eager to prove to me that they rarely left my side while I was unconscious and my body was trying to hypothermia itself.

"Where were you two brave beasts when I was being

attacked by a vampire, hmmm? I specifically remember being told you two would protect me on the farm," I said as Mars lightly barked at the wolves to let me up.

Mars took a sip of her coffee and said, "They were with Buckie. He apparently had the worst timing ever for his late-night drive, and they climbed into his vehicle the moment he opened the door. So, he took them out toward Katahdkin for a run."

Part of me was frustrated we didn't have the werestag and two wolves to join the fight. But the other part of me, the colder half that struggled to maintain more than two consecutive seconds of warmth, realized they'd have ended up as cannon fodder.

Mars survived the fight because I unleashed a powerful new spell that took Beauregard by surprise. And I survived the fight because. . . because. . . well, I still wasn't sure.

Maybe adding a half-dozen rings of pure sugar to my belly will help kickstart my Understanding, I thought, taking another drink of my coffee.

I made short work of three chocolate-frosted glazed donuts before downing half my mug of coffee. Was it supposed to be scalding going down my throat? Yes. Did I flinch even a little? No. That should be a little alarming, right?

As I eyed an éclair, which we called Long Johns back in Colorado, I paused long enough to ask Mars, "Will you tell me what happened? After I went down for the count?"

Mars was on her second donut. But when I asked my question, she froze and looked at the floor, anguish spreading across her face. She placed the donut on a napkin, seemingly losing her appetite for a moment.

With a long sigh, she ran her fingers under the sink to rinse them free of sugar and icing.

"I should be able to tell you pretty easily, Lilith. After

all, I've only replayed the scene in my head a thousand times while you were unconscious."

Crossing the kitchen, I took Mars' hands in my own.

"Please. I need to know. It might be the only way I'll find out what happened to me. . . what's still happening to me. I know you're scared of revisiting memories of my death. But, babe, look into my eyes. Feel my fingers on yours. Smell my scent. I made it back. I'm here with you at this moment. You know how the story ends. I just need to know what middle chapters I'm missing."

Mars pulled a hand free and ran her fingers through the white side of my hair. She hadn't commented on whether I smelled different after dying. And, honestly, I was too scared to ask.

I gave my mate all the time in the world to think before answering.

At last, she spoke, eyes still on my hair.

"After whatever you did to Beauregard, the air around you grew thick with some kind of smog. It smelled like rust and decay. Your hair started to twitch. And then your whole body spasmed. It was struggling with the magic you used. I watched as you fell backward. I listened as you belted out an ear-piercing scream. And then. . . your body jolted upward and expelled a huge wave of magic, bigger than anything I'd ever witnessed. The trees and bushes around you withered in seconds. The soil turned a sickening and spongey brown. And then. . . just as your body came to rest, your heart stopped."

I could only stare at my mate while she talked. And as her words sank into my ears, somewhere deep inside the recesses of my mind, I felt my Understanding whir to life.

"Show me," I whispered.

Mars took my hand and led me out to the patch of forest where we'd fought Beauregard. I. . . couldn't believe my eyes. Dead leaves and dried bark covered the ground. Everything smelled horrid. A skunk on its worst day couldn't match the odor.

Covering my nose, I looked around for any signs of life. But an entire patch of the forest was dead, as far as I could see.

Standing in the woods, I closed my eyes and felt. . . nothing. There was nothing living in this patch of the forest anymore. No magic. No plants. No animals. Walking further into the trees, I ignored Mars calling my name.

My breath was all I could hear now. My heart ached. I was on the verge of sobbing. Around me, the skeletal remains of squirrels, rabbits, and birds dotted the tree floor.

Every step I took felt like wading into sewage, even though I knew it was just soil beneath me. All of a sudden, I leaned over and puked, coughing up at least half my breakfast and coffee. Nausea and twitching wrecked my body as Mars started to run toward me.

I held up a hand to stop her.

"Fine — I'm fine. Just. . . stay over," I said, trying to get enough air in my lungs to finish that sentence.

To her credit, Mars waited patiently, though I felt her heart racing in my chest. Seeing me retch in the place where I died couldn't have been fun.

Standing up and taking a few breaths to steady myself, I looked around at the poisoned land. My Understanding told me what happened. It wasn't all that complicated. Hell, Beauregard had explained it pretty succinctly at his farm.

"I siphoned Bearegard's graveyard magic. . . all of it. But there was too much for my body to handle. It over-whelmed me. When you saw me convulsing, that was my body trying to expel what I'd ripped from the Vampire

Lorde. And when I pushed it out. . . the forest paid the price."

Mars came over and lightly patted me on the back while my brain worked out the rest.

"The white hair, aged skin, the changed eye colors. . . they're all symptoms of my body going into magical shock. After my heart stopped, what happened?"

My mate started to pull me out of the forest, and when we got back to the front of the farm, my gaze traced the porch. I guess while I was out, Mars and Buckie had fixed the windows and door. Though the porch still bore signs of our fight. Scratch marks, warped boards, and pieces of debris from the shattered porch chairs.

"Well, Buckie came back around sunrise. And neither of us could get close to your body for at least an hour after that. The magic you expelled was too thick in the air. It rotted our flesh when we got within 10 feet of you. We had to back off and wait for our bodies to mend. I was losing my shit because your heart wasn't beating for several hours.

"And then. . . out of nowhere, I felt it again. Quiet at first, like a baby bird gradually hatching from an egg. I wasn't even sure it was a heartbeat. But then I heard you breathing. By noon, we had you moved into the den. You were breathing but still cold to the touch. That's when Chocolate, Chip, and I took turns sharing body heat with you."

I nodded, putting the pieces together.

My brain continued to whir as Understanding dawned on me like a real-time epiphany. Puzzle pieces fell into place, and I could only blink in astonishment as facts built themselves like a staircase in my mind's eye.

"I think I get it now," I said, as Mars brought me back into the kitchen and chopped me up an apple.

Taking small bites while my nausea subsided, I cleared my throat.

"My body healed itself."

"How?" Mars asked. "Can all sorceresses do that?"

I shook my head.

"No. I mean — yes, some spells can repair the physical body. But I don't know any of them. Instead, I seemed to have stolen a few abilities from Beauregard, keeping them for myself, even as my body vomited out the vast majority of his graveyard magic."

Mars finished the donut she'd put down earlier and grabbed another.

"So. . . that shadow thing you did in the den? And the healing? Those came from Beauregard?"

I nodded.

"As best I can tell, yeah. He dislocated my shoulder, and it hurt like a bitch. But it feels mostly normal now. Just a bit stiff. I guess while I was talking to Beau on his farm, my body was slowly mending itself with the power it ripped from him."

Mars stopped mid-chew.

"I'm sorry. Did you say. . . talking to Beau on his farm?" Mars asked, mouth full of cake donut.

Finishing my apple and downing the rest of the cold coffee remaining in my mug, I nodded.

"While you were keeping my body warm, my mind was trapped in a memory with Beauregard on his farm. I guess I'd siphoned it away with his magic. He was human again."

Mars shook her head, swallowing the donut.

"How the fuck is that even possible?"

Outside, a murder of crows cawed as they flew over the patch of forest I killed. Briefly, I wondered if any of them had nested there. I wondered if I'd ruined the trees they called home.

Washing my hands, I started talking without facing Mars. I told her everything Beau said to me, from his sister's life to his enslavement and his final request to me.

By the time I finished, Mars was seated in a chair with her face in her hands.

"Holy shit," she whispered. "That's a lot to process."

I pulled up a chair next to her after pouring myself another mug of coffee. Mercifully, the pot had still been warm, so I'd held the glass in my fingers for a few minutes, stealing what heat I could.

Snuggling close to my mate, I rested my head on her shoulder and just stared at a half-eaten loaf of wheat Mars had in her breadbox.

From across the house, I heard a loud buzzer sound from the laundry room. I guess the dryer was finished running.

Outside, I listened to the dogs running around and barking as they played with each other. They didn't go near the driveway. I didn't blame them.

"I'm sorry I destroyed part of your forest, Mars," I whispered.

That seemed to snap her out of her trance because Mars straightened up and kissed my forehead.

"Don't even. That was a fucked up night we were both extremely fortunate to walk away from. Some land is a wicked small price to pay. Listen to me, Little Cottontail."

So, I did. She held my full attention. I parked my gaze in her honeyed eyes and waited while Mars gathered her strength to speak again.

"I've lost you twice now. And I've regained you twice now. Each loss taught me just how important you are to me and how utterly desperate I am to cling to you and keep you in my life."

I was shaking from the cold, but Mars was quivering from the memory of my death. Neither was what we wanted to feel, so we moved even closer.

We needed to share more than just a moment or heat or touch. Mars and I had to share life because that was the gift we'd both been given after an attack that should have ended us permanently.

"You heard her name. Telsyn. She's a godforsaken horror that shouldn't exist in this world. But she does. And because she does, Telsyn was able to rip my entire pack from me when I was a whopping 12 years old. They're frozen in time on an island off the coast of Lubec, and I've spent every moment of my life since trying to find a way to free them. My parents, my friends, my pack, they were all taken from me. And honestly, Lilith, some days, I just didn't want to keep going. Once or twice, I wanted to drink a vial of liquid silver, just to make the loneliness and hurt stop."

I grabbed Mars' hand and squeezed as tightly as I could.

"But you didn't," I whispered, hoping to god that she felt me as much as I wanted her to. The thought of knowing my mate carried such crushing loneliness left me wanting to fight the entire world. And I would fight the whole world for her, from a planet all the way down to a single vampire. She was worth it because Mars had deemed me worth loving first.

"But I didn't," she said. "And I found you. For the first time in my life, you chased those feelings away, Lilith. You made me want to keep fighting, not just to free my pack from their curse, but to protect you as well. I treasure you, Little Cottontail. You send me over the moon. And I cannot bear the thought of losing you to the storm of madness we find ourselves in."

Pulling Mars down into a slow kiss, I stroked her hair and moved to her lap. We'd set our coffees aside, content to steal warmth and spit from each other.

"You need to stop thinking about how you lost me and start thinking about how I found my way back to you. Because I'll always come back to you, Mars Dubois. No magic, no monster, no force in the 'verse can keep me away from you indefinitely. So, if you ever lose me again in the future, take a breath, and know it's only temporary. You're worth fighting my way back to every time, my ferocious protector, my howling moon and stars. I'll love you and return to you always."

Mars pressed her lips against mine again, running her thumbs over my cheeks. We paused to remember the promise we'd made to one another, one no vampire or wraith would ever break.

When we finally pulled away to breathe, I asked Mars, "Has anyone called my phone about the library being closed for two days?"

She shook her head.

"No, I put a sign on the door that said it was closed because you had pneumonia."

I cocked my head to the left.

"Quick thinking."

Mars shrugged.

"Eh, you learn how to make fast excuses when you're a werewolf. You'd be surprised how many full moons take you away from planned events."

I smiled and then thought for a moment.

"Well. . . pneumonia is a hell of a thing. That can keep some folks out for an entire week," I said."

My mate looked confused.

"What do you mean?"

"I mean. . . I could conceivably be away for an entire week with your cover story."

"So?"

Pressing my forehead against Mars', I gently kissed her nose.

"So you can use that time. Take me to Lubec, and I can break this fucking curse on your pack once and for all."

Chapter 14

After waking up from death, I spent the rest of the afternoon doing refreshingly little. My body was still healing courtesy of a Vampire Lorde's powers, and apparently, those abilities were a little slower in a mortal body. But they were chugging along like a freight train.

So, I took it easy. I walked a little bit between the deer pens while Mars checked the fences and fed them. She gave me a bucket of corn and let me feed some of the does, which was a giggly experience.

I call it that because I couldn't stop giggling. Their pink tongues just kept scooping up more kernels as six or seven does crowded around my bucket. A few even started sniffing my pockets, hoping I had a secret stash of corn (I did not).

After I fed the doe, Chocolate and Chip stayed glued to my hips as if they felt guilty for being away when I died. And I spent a good portion of the afternoon playing games with them and petting the wolves. They absorbed every drop of attention I was willing to give and kept begging for more.

Finally, after Mars fixed a venison stew that helped warm my core a bit, we retired to the den, and I was buried in fluff from three wolves.

Staying warm through the night was not an issue. But remaining alone in my thoughts proved to be a challenge.

SOMETIME AFTER CLOSING MY EYES, I found myself in a different den entirely. This den was deep underground, and the last time I visited, I'd arrived in the jaws of a massive wolf, the same wolf who towered over me now.

The smell of old bones and mostly-eaten carcasses greeted me like an old woman angry to find you on her doorstep. And I responded in kind, fighting the urge to cover my nose with my sleeve. I didn't want to insult my surprise hostess by telling her this den smelled like skunk anus.

Darkness covered most of the cavern, but pale blue lights filtered down from some stones above, giving me enough leeway to make out shapes and shadows, especially when said shapes were big enough to swallow me in one gulp.

Off to the right, I spotted two wolf pups curled together in a bed of pine needles, leaves, and tree bark. They were each about my size, which only added to the unnerving feeling of being here.

The massive wolf above me angled her snout downward, glowing amber eyes locking with mine.

"H — hello," I stammered.

The last time I met The Mother, I didn't Understand. I had yet to eat of the Yggdrasil Tree. But now. . . I could feel the beast, magic radiating from her like heat from an open stove. It was overwhelming in a grand sense, my mind realizing just how big of a difference there was between her abilities and mine.

A massive beast of steel-colored fur with the odd white patch here and there, The Mother did not seem all too impressed with me. So. . . not much had changed since the last time I'd seen her.

"Once more you find yourself in my den. Let us hope you carry a tad more wisdom than when last we spoke," she said.

I bowed my head because I didn't want to be eaten.

After a beat, The Mother snapped, "Wisdom and silence are not the same thing."

Feeling my chest, and my throat seize up, I tried taking several breaths to calm down. But it's hard when you're facing something so big. I was speaking to a carnivore the size of a blimp, and beyond that, she carried the magical density of a neutron star.

"May I ask why you summoned me here?"

The Mother cocked her head to the side.

"How do you know that I did?"

Willing my hands to stop shaking, I looked up at the giant, shaggy wolf standing before me, eyes piercing and hungry. Not hungry for flesh. . . but something else. So, I cleared my throat, paused to get my thoughts in order, and started to untangle the mess of my Bouquet from The Maiden, the spells I'd been gifted.

Sitting around and resting for most of yesterday left me with time to think. And the great thing about Understanding is that I had the power to reason through most magic and logic. The privilege of surviving a battle was the ability to analyze and learn from it. And that's what I did in between play sessions with Chocolate and Chip.

"The Maiden sent a Bouquet to me with three spells of her choosing, delivered by a sorceress named Phenna."

"And what does that have to do with me?" The Mother asked.

Blinking, I moved on to the next part of the story, trying not to be rattled. But the warmth I'd gained from Mars' stew and sleeping with a werewolf and two fuzzy companions was slipping away in my fear. I didn't want to be here, knowing what The Mother was and represented.

Tightening my knees so they didn't buckle, I sighed.

"Sometime before Phenna received the Bouquet, you added a spell but broke it into two pieces so I wouldn't be suspicious about how different your gift was from The Maiden's. The spells she selected for me were relatively simple. Yours. . . I wasn't ready for."

The Mother shook her body, hairs longer than me falling from her coat. Under my feet, the ground rattled a bit from her movement.

I felt like I was watching a horror movie, just waiting for the jump scare. The stringed instruments played hauntingly in the background while my adrenaline kept me wired and ready to jump at a moment's notice.

"Are you accusing me of something, young sorceress?" The Mother asked. And if a wolf could raise its eyebrow, she would have. There was an implication in the tone of her question. Tread carefully now. Accusations against powerful people often lead to the accusers shuffling off their mortal coil. If they were lucky, it would be a quick shuffle.

So, my voice dropped to damn near a whisper when I next answered.

"Oh, no. I would never be so foolish as to accuse you of anything. You're so wise and powerful. Accusing you would be tantamount to suicide."

That earned me a slight chuckle. And I do mean slight.

"Flattery and wisdom are also not the same thing," The Mother said. But she didn't tell me to fuck off.

So, I continued, steeling myself under her withering and impatient gaze.

"Right, where was I? Ah yes, the siphoning spell you gave me. It was in a much different class of power and complexity than those spells from The Maiden's Bouquet. Using it killed me."

"You certainly seem alive enough to be chittering at me like a drunk squirrel," The Mother said, slowly blinking.

This was the wolf telling me. . . get to the point.

Taking a small step to the left and hearing the joints in my feet pop (how tightly were they pulled?), I clasped my hands together in a new effort to keep them from shaking.

"My being alive is a fluke I remain grateful for. So, I guess my question is really. . . why did you give me that spell?"

The Mother yawned, and I got to see all 84 of her teeth in two separate rows. I swallowed nervously.

"So. . . the only real proof you have that I gave you this spell is it was more powerful than the other spells in The Maiden's Bouquet? Why are you convinced the spell came from me instead of The Crone?"

I scratched my head.

"Because using that spell didn't feel like I was draining a bug caught in a web or squeezing the life from a rodent and swallowing it whole. Casting the siphoning spell felt like I tore into the Vampire Lorde I was fighting and ripped his magic away. It was wolf-like in nature."

The Mother remained silent for a minute.

I spoke up once more.

"The last time we spoke, you were ready to kill me because my answer to your question showed a lack of wisdom. I disrespected your magic with a flippant answer and was only spared because I'm a werewolf's mate. I can only hope that by solving this much of your arcane puzzle, I've displayed enough wisdom to gain some measure of respect from you during this visit."

The Mother shocked me by laughing, and seeing a wolf open its jaw to chortle was as unnerving as anything else a massive beast could do. Her belly rumbled with laughter, and I took a measured step back.

"Respect? No, you do not gain my respect by solving half of a mystery. Imagine how ridiculous it would be for you to watch an ant carry a gain of sand halfway back to its nest and then turn to you for applause."

I swallowed nervously again.

Then The Mother surprised me by slowly lowering herself to the cavern floor and crossing her front two paws after a long yawn.

I squinted and noted that The Mother looked tired. And it wasn't that she'd expended some great measure of magic to be so exhausted. It looked more like the conversation she was preparing to have drained her.

When her amber eyes found mine again, they were a touch less fierce than when I first appeared in the den.

After a lull, The Mother said, "Tell me what you did to him."

I didn't need to who she was talking about, even though every fiber of my being wanted to Understand her connection to Beauregard and why she cared so much to summon me here in the middle of the night.

"He was going to kill me. Beauregard beat the everloving shit out of me, made me feel like I was being ground into the forest floor. Nothing Mars and I threw at him put the vampire down for long. But we lasted long enough in the fight to burn away his patience. That was when he decided to kill Mars. Emptied of my own magic, I threw open the gates, and cast your spell."

"And?" The Mother pressed me, more drawn into my story than I could have ever imagined possible.

Why did she care? Here she was, one-third of the living embodiment of all the magic sorceresses have ever used, are currently using, and will ever use. And The Mother almost seemed desperate to know what I, a lowly newborn caster, had done to this vampire.

I assumed she would reveal their connection when I finished answering her questions. So, I stuffed my burning curiosity aside and continued the story.

"The spell necrotized my entire hand. And I was suddenly ravenous for the massive body of graveyard magic that gave Beauregard the power to easily put down a werewolf and a sorceress. I latched on to that man and took everything he had. He was a fucking husk when I finished. But my body couldn't handle swallowing all that graveyard magic. I'm told it killed me and a large piece of the surrounding forest when my body rejected the lion's share of Beauregard's power."

The Mother scoffed.

"Did he scream? Sound like he was in pain when you drained him?" she asked, quietly.

I could only nod.

"Good. That's less than an abysmal creature like he deserved but more than I ever expected him to get."

My stomach twisted at her tone. For all the magnificent power The Mother carried and shared with lowly mortals like me, here, at this moment, she sounded like any other mom in agony.

My story finished, all that I was going to tell of it, anyway. I didn't dare give The Mother some sob story about Telsyn torturing Beau or how he had to watch his little sister live a lie her entire life. Those were so far removed that they couldn't even be called extenuating circumstances. Not to the anguished mom before me.

"January 9, 1912, in a city your kind calls Dallas, my son was growing his family. His name was Aidan, and he repaired boots for a living. Not the boots of cowboys, but of bankers and architects, the shoes wealthy men wore through the streets, where the biggest obstacle was an over-sized puddle or a slick of mud," The Mother said, staring off into space like she was telling this story to the walls of her den instead of me.

I glanced over at her pups, both still asleep despite their mother's laughing seconds ago. How did The Mother have a human son? Did her wolf pups grow up to become humans? Or did she become human and give birth like any other person in my world? My brain was hungry for answers, curiosity cooking my brain like crumbled beef in a cast iron skillet.

"Aidan was a good kid, worked hard, never took a shred of magic. He was determined to live his life in the way of mortals, to build something with his own two hands, his own strength and cunning. He begged me, pleaded to leave the Yggdrasil Forest. No matter how many times I told him about the pains of mortality, the toll that world exacts from a soul, he remained bright-eyed as ever, determined to make something of himself in a world that believed less in magic with each year gone by."

My knees ached, a dull pain, but at least they weren't shaking anymore. I wasn't vibrating in terror like I had been. All the fear had drained out of me, and I was only left with expectant melancholy as The Mother's tale continued. We both sensed where this story ended, but only the massive wolf before me could get us there.

The Mother took in a deep breath before she continued.

"Finally, I decided to let Aidan go. Because a mother only ever wants for her children to be happy. That's all we desire. We can be sad. We can be furious. We can be mournful. But as long as our kids are happy, everything else in the world eventually falls into place. So, I let him go. He left and worked hard, day in, day out. Somewhere along the way, he met Kayla. Oh, you should have seen how big she made him smile! All the teeth. You could count each one when he grinned at her side.

"He came to me one day, saying, 'Mother, I've met the most joyful soul. And I want to be with her. I want to be part of the reason she's so happy.' So, I said, 'Go, my son. Be with her. Be her joy.' And he did. Oh, he did. My boy gave Kayla everything she wanted, including a beautiful baby boy they named Dylan, after her grandfather."

I covered my mouth and drew short breaths to keep from crying. Because, again, we both knew how this story ended. And try as I might to imagine any other conclusion to Aidan's tale, a persistent shadow over his fate would not be chased away. Not with all my power. Not with all The Mother's power.

She continued, "Dylan was born on January 9 at 5:13 p.m. I couldn't wait to meet him. My heart swelled with cheer picturing Aidan bringing his baby to the Yggdrasil Forest. That baby boy came into the world as loud as thunder, but Kayla and Aidan were beside themselves with glee. After the birth, her sweet tooth struck, and Kayla asked her husband to run out and grab her a few baked apples."

My hand was pressed so tight to my mouth that I almost forgot to breathe. The Mother's voice was all I could hear in that den. Not even the snoring pups were loud enough to register in my attention right now. She held it all. And I suddenly knew how she felt, urging me to continue my story about killing Beauregard.

"You remember me saying my boy wanted to be the reason Kayla was happy?"

I slowly nodded.

"Well, to that end, he left the hospital and visited three different markets before finding a single baked apple for sale. Tired as sin, my son held that apple tightly as he raced back to the hospital to give it to his exhausted wife."

And that's when the story hit me with heartbreak. I could sense it coming from a mile away. I wanted to look at the cave floor but forced myself to lock eyes with The Mother. Her eyes were glossy, and then water made its way to my vision as well.

"A foul creature found my son a few blocks from the hospital. I don't believe many words were exchanged between them. But that horrible, bloodsucking fiend dragged my boy into an alley and ripped his throat wide open. Before Aidan's body hit the ground, I felt his heart stop. Ask me what a mother does when her child's life slips away, like blood dripping down into a sewer grate."

I didn't want to ask her.

"Ask. Me," she growled.

Prying my fingers from my mouth, I managed to choke out, "What does a mother do when —"

The Mother interrupted me, rising with a wicked roar.

"She howls, Lilith Chambers. She gnashes her teeth. She crashes into trees. A mother does everything and anything she can while writhing with grief."

Then, softly, the massive wolf before me whimpered, "He took my boy, my sweet boy, who hadn't done an ounce of harm to the world. Aidan was gentle. He was thoughtful. And above all else, my son was happy. He should have lived to see young Dylan grow up and have his own kids.

He should have died an old man, giggling and holding Kayla's hand as he exited the mortal world with her tender kiss on his cheek. Instead, he left your world screaming and choking on a vampire's mandibles."

Whatever I thought of Beauregard at that moment, my heart quivered in a puddle of its own tears.

This happened in 1912? I thought. *That was long before Telsyn got her claws into him. He chose to kill Aidan on his own.*

Except. . . did he? Does a lion choose which gazelle to kill? Or do they simply get hungry and hunt according to instinct? It's not like the lion pauses to decide, morally, which prey deserves to live and which deserves to die.

But that didn't satisfy The Mother. Nothing would. . . until I ripped Beau's life from him as he had done to Aidan.

"The only thing I've wanted, truly wanted, for the last century, was that animal's untimely demise. But I had to wait. That's the thing about agelessness, you see, you do a lot of waiting. People always fantasize about what they'll do with forever, this, that, and the other stuff. But it's mostly waiting. And at last my waiting. . . came to an end. The Crone told me your string was destined to intersect with the man who killed my son."

My string? So, The Crone was the one out of these three with some gift for prophecy. How vast or limited it was, I'd probably never know.

Cautiously, with the timidity of a field mouse, I asked, "Why couldn't you go and kill Beauregard?"

The Mother sighed and lowered her head to her paws, lying down again.

"When my daughter, my mother, and I performed our ritual and became The Maiden, The Mother, and The Crone, we amassed a truly dizzying amount of magic. What we would later learn is there are. . . let's call them cosmic rules to godhood. If any of us ever wanted to return to your world, we'd have to surrender almost all our power. There's a ceiling to how mighty one can become in the world of mortals before they're forced to depart from it."

I nodded, trying and failing to imagine what such a power scale looked like or how it worked in practicality. Telsyn was powerful enough to curse an entire werewolf pack. But apparently not so powerful that she met this proverbial ceiling The Mother described.

"So. . . I did the only thing I could. I armed you with an arcane tool that would either kill you or kill my son's murderer. So, imagine my surprise when I summon you, and you stand before me. A 'fluke' you called it? Perhaps. In the end, my only concern was the slaying of that cretin. And now, you tell me he's well and truly gone. My waiting is, at last, finished."

In a few seconds, my sadness turned to anger, and I clenched my fists. Heat returned to my body as I stifled a growl.

Mars was nearly killed. I fucking was killed. And this bitch strapped a grenade to my back and hurtled me at Beauregard without a second thought? She didn't even have the courtesy to look relieved that I survived!

My blood boiled, but I recalled how The Mother's teeth felt against my flesh when I first landed in her open mouth. I decided then and there it would be best if I didn't give The Mother a reason to return me to her jaws.

Still, a nagging sense of injustice pecked at my brain. I died in that fight, and Mars suffered for it. At the very least, I deserved something for our shared pains and troubles. I'd just have to be extremely careful getting it.

Choosing to push my luck, I inhaled deeply, and said, "I killed Aidan's murderer."

The Mother's gaze intensified, and I felt the fire in my chest withering under it. Still, I pushed forward.

"What of it?" she hissed.

My fists clenched all the tighter, fingernails digging little crescent moons into my skin.

Still, I held onto my calm. I pulled from the memory of a chilled core, one that struggled to keep warm even after returning from death.

And, I said, "I would call killing Aidan's murderer a service."

The Mother's gaze hardened further, and I felt her hackles rising.

"Is that so?" The Mother asked, each word as crisp as a frosty autumn morning.

I nodded.

"And since you spoke of grand cosmic rules for people who obtain godhood, I believe there's one about returning the favor to anyone who performs a service for you."

Quiet fell through the den again.

All I could hear was the sound of my own beating heart. It grew louder and louder while The Mother thought about my words.

"Bold move, Lilith Chambers, she named for the First Wife. So what would you ask of The Mother?"

I felt my breath catch in my throat. Holy shit. Was this going to work?

"Let's just say my mate has her own Beauregard we'll soon have to deal with. As I slayed your son's killer, I want you to annihilate the wraith who took my mate's pack away. And I mean, rain down fire, nuke from orbit just to be sure."

The Mother rose to her feet upon hearing my request, and my heart plunged into my guts. Did I ask for the wrong thing? Was she going to come over here and tear me to pieces?

My fear ended up being unfounded, though, as the giant wolf slowly walked to a watering hole across the den. She lowered her head into the underground lake, dug around for something, and then padded over to me, giant drops of water dripping down on the cave floor.

The Mother lowered her jaws to me, and I saw a long silver spear gripped in the edge of her teeth. Well — it looked long to me. To her, it appeared she was holding a toy weapon from an action figure.

Gingerly, I took the weapon, and as its full weight fell into my grasp, my arms buckled. The damn thing was weighed down with more than just physical material. The very magic of this spear added to the weight.

I felt like I was holding the bar of a bench press. And I didn't work out much.

The spear's sleek silver pole ended in a fierce point. From bottom to top, the spear must have been seven feet long. It was awkward to hold.

"If you want to call forth that much of my power to slaughter your mate's enemy, you'll have to guide it from my world to yours. Whatever you stab with this spear will call my magic down like a bolt of lightning, obliterating your target and reducing it to cinders. You can only do this once, so do yourself a favor, and be accurate. Make your shot count, Lilith Chambers, she named for the First Wife."

I nodded.

"Thank you," I said.

"Don't thank me, sorceress. I'm not doing you a favor. I'm merely repaying a debt as the cosmic rules state I must. Now go. I've given you all I'm going to."

THE NEXT MORNING, Mars was mystified to find a spear in the den with us. But I explained everything as best I could, and she took me at my word. Mate privileges.

We wrapped the spear in thick paper, tied it with string, and loaded it into the truck bed. Then, we piled into the old farm vehicle.

As the engine growled to life, Mars turned to me and said, "Are you ready to see my pack?"

"Gotta meet my future in-laws someday. Might as well be now," I said.

Are they still in-laws in the case of fated mates?

Mars ruffled my hair and started down the driveway. Before long, we were on the road to Lubec. I had a curse to lift, and a wraith to exterminate if she showed her face.

Watching the evergreens roll by outside my window, I leaned my elbow against the passenger door and thought, *All things considered, I think I'd rather have pneumonia.*

Chapter 15

Brego charged toward Lubec like a loyal farm truck on a mission. And dammit, we WERE on a mission, the most important I'd ever set out on in my life. By tonight, I hoped to have my pack again.

And if I rubbed noses with even one of them, it'd be because of the amazing mate I met just days earlier. Looking over at the sorceress, I couldn't help but smile. Her long black hair was pulled back into a ponytail, and the green wool jacket she wore fit her form snugly. My gaze lingered on her breasts for maybe a few seconds longer than was safe given that I was driving.

"W — what?" Lilith giggled nervously, heat rushing to her cheeks. My god, she was adorable. She'd been through so much shit in the last week, things that would have driven any normal person full-speed into lunacy.

And yet, she'd somehow come out. . . mostly intact. On top of bargaining memories to a book-bound sorceress, gaining access to magic, and being killed by a Vampire Lorde, she still managed to look innocent and flustered as my hungry eyes lingered on her.

That look came despite the times I'd ravished her. Not that I could help it. Little thing was in the waning days of heat for me, and I wanted every drop of her I could get.

I grinned.

"Just thinking that coat makes your tits look great," I said.

She scoffed.

"Mars Dubois, how dare you say such inappropriate things to me! I am merely an innocent passenger in your vehicle," my mate said in exaggerated tones of piety.

Shaking my head, I chuckled and watched as we passed a car with Massachusettes plates.

Summer's over, Massholes, I thought. *Go back to Boston and let Mainers enjoy our state until the next tourism season, will ya?*

Lilith took my hand, which chased all manner of foul tourist thoughts away, and brought my attention back to her. And not just her, but all the pheromones her body had filled my truck's cab with.

The sweet little thing had already been bred this morning before we left, and I was chomping at the bit to have another taste of Lilith. Her scent had more than imprinted on my memory over the short time we'd spent together. And it kept changing in subtle ways, when we danced, when she became a sorceress, when she devoured a vampire's magic, each drastic moment altered her flavor.

Without looking over at my mate, I said, "The strap I rode you with this morning would seem to prove a surprising lack of innocence on your part, Lilith Chambers."

The sorceress dropped my hand and placed her palm over her heart. Her outrageous tone grew louder.

"Saying such slanderous things! My goodness, your words are filthy enough to almost make a lady faint. And if using foul words wasn't enough, you also hit me with my full name."

That's when I turned to my mate with a raised eyebrow and said, "Hey, you full-named me first. And while you are every bit the woman I am, the things you've begged me to do to your naked body have shown me you ain't no fair lady, bub."

Lilith struggled to stifle her snicker, but she managed to keep her nun routine together.

"Pray tell, if I am not a fair lady, then what am I?"

I didn't even hesitate to answer that one.

"You're my bitch, Lilith. A werewolf's bitch who yearns to be mounted and spent in the throes of carnal passion."

Pausing to hear the hitch in her breath as I spoke, I found myself all the more amused by her arousal. And the great thing about being a werewolf was that your mate couldn't hide shit from your heightened senses.

I heard the wrinkling fabric from her pants as Lilith tightened her legs. I smelled the moisture of increased saliva on her tongue. And I felt her body temperature rising ever so slightly when I pried that pious hand from over her heart, kissing it gently. Actually — given her new core temperature, rises in body heat had become even more obvious to me.

Lilith's cheeks were flushed, and she stared deeply into my eyes, all the while squirming from my words. Her own eyes had changed so much since I first carried the Little Cottontail back to my truck on Wylde Night. My mate's brown eyes both used to be so dark, the same color as antlers I'd harvest on my farm. Now? Only one remained that color. The other was a blue so pale it could have come from a husky's skull.

She'd told me her body looked different from the shock of overwhelming graveyard magic. Anyone who might have thought there was a small age gap between us, a 30-year-old werewolf dating a 25-year-old librarian, would no longer have any complaints based on our appearances. With the shock her body went through dying, Lilith now looked a few years older than me.

I didn't know if her body aged a decade while magic pieced it back together, but my love for Lilith had only grown since that fight.

"Oh, I'm your bitch, am I?" Lilith said, bringing my attention back to the present.

"You heard me," I said, squeezing her fingers tight.

Her grin turned downright devious, and she unbuckled her seatbelt as I shifted into fourth gear to pass a logging truck.

"You trying to test your vampiric healing against being thrown through the windshield? Or are you just that eager to stress test my heart by dying again?" I asked, raising my eyebrow even higher.

But my mate didn't put her seatbelt back on. She did something even more dangerous and moved her hands over to the button and zipper of my jeans.

"Whoa! Hey now. What are you —" I stammered, struggling to keep my eyes on the road.

"Being your bitch," Lilith interrupted.

Scooting into the middle seat and burying her nose in my hair, Lilith licked the side of my neck and whispered, "Mars, I have a confession to make."

My mouth suddenly felt dry, and I struggled to respond in a timely fashion.

"W — what's that?" I finally asked.

Another whisper.

"I intend to stress test your heart. But probably not in the way you're thinking."

Lilith's fingers unfastened my button, lowered the

zipper, and slid into my pants. Gooseflesh crept across my arms.

I spun to see Lilith and prepared to ask my mate once again what the fuck she was doing, but the sorceress caught my cheek with her free hand. She gently pushed it back until my eyes were on the road again.

"No, no, Mars. Your mission, should you consent, is to keep the truck from crashing. The rules are simple. You can make all the noise you want while you're fucked. You can feel free to writhe in pleasure. But you cannot stop the truck prior to orgasm."

She kissed my cheek and inched her fingers deeper into my jeans until they found the bottom of my panties. I gasped.

"Do you consent, baby? Nod once for yes. Shake your head for no."

There's no way she's going to do it, I thought.

"You're willing to risk our safety like this?" I asked. But my tone betrayed any illusion I'd projected over safety worries. I wanted her to do this. It was one of the hottest things I could think of, and Lilith absolutely saw through my bullshit.

"You told me you bounced back a few hours after the fight with Beau, so unless Maine has a silver processing plant alongside this particular highway, I'm not too worried. Between your werewolf healing and the vampiric regeneration I stole, I'm willing to bet we'd survive any sex-related crashes."

The final shred of my feigned worry mounted a pathetic last defense as my hands gestured to the truck around us.

"And what about Brego? I don't think my truck has healing magic to save it if we total the poor thing."

Lilith gave my chin a long, slow lick before answering,

and I wanted so badly to turn and bite her lower lip. I gritted my teeth as a shiver of pleasure ran down the back of my neck.

"If Sam and Dean can rebuild Baby several times throughout 15 seasons, I think your truck is capable of at least one glorious resurrection. Stop stalling. Am I doing this or not?"

We passed a Maine State Police vehicle, and I nervously waited for the officer to do a U-turn in the rearview mirror. Thankfully, the trooper kept driving out of sight.

I've never been so happy to see my tax dollars at work, I thought before finally answering my mate.

Doing some mental math, I figured we were about an hour outside of Lubec. Perfect.

"It's 106 miles to Lubec. We got a full tank of gas, half a pack of cigarettes, it's misty out, and we're wearing sunglasses," I said.

"Guess I'll hit it," Lilith chuckled.

Fuck, was there any more beautiful sound than the laugh of your mate? Dad used to say that all the time. The only reason he did anything in life was to make Mom laugh. He used to say there was no better sound to him in the whole world. I always gagged at the time, but as Lilith giggled in between each soft kiss upon my cheek, I think I finally understood what my father meant.

"What are you giggling about?" I asked, catching some of Lilith's infectious laughter.

"I just can't believe I'm about to do this," Lilith said. "I've always wanted to, but I've never felt brave enough."

I downshifted, and after a few more kisses, I asked, "I make you feel brave?"

"So fucking brave," Lilith said, taking off her coat.

That did something special to my heart, and if I didn't

know Lilith was about to fuck me as I drove, I might have started tearing up.

Werewolves mostly found their fated mates in other wolves. It was just statistics. But once in a while, a werewolf found their mate in a regular vanilla human. And there would always exist a worry in those werewolves that their mate would grow to fear the power imbalance. In those moments of doubt and worry, the most soothing balm in existence was hearing a mate say their wolf made them feel safe. . . even brave.

My heart throbbed in renewed love and passion for the Little Cottontail who'd stolen my affections.

Any other person who went through just one of the things Lilith had faced this week would have run away screaming. But not my mate. No. She felt brave, in part, because of me. And that left me feeling like a million bucks.

Of course, when Lilith started to tease me through my panties, I quickly felt like two million bucks.

I pulled my foot off the accelerator briefly.

"No, no, Ms. Big Bad Wolf. If that needle falls below 50 miles per hour, I'll stop playing with you until you speed up again," Lilith said with a teasing tone.

Marshaling the willpower of a goddess, I forced my foot back onto the gas pedal and reworked the clutch. As the truck went faster, so did Lilith. Her fingers continued to tease me until I was good and wet. Then, my mate moved her lips to my neck where her kisses elicited a soft moan from me.

We took a curve in the road a little fast, and Lilith had to readjust her fingers. It took a few seconds to get them back where we wanted them.

When I'd soaked through my panties, Lilith flattened

her palm against me and slid her fingers under the band of my undergarment.

She wasted no time parting my lower lips and sliding a finger inside me. This caused my left arm to crank the wheel enough that we briefly crossed into the other lane. Thankfully, no cars were around to meet us. I fought Brego back into our lane and stifled a louder moan.

This was becoming dangerous. . . and I was getting more turned on by the second. I took shallow breaths as Lilith adjusted her wrist and slid a second finger inside me.

I briefly lowered my head in a sweet hiss and fought to put my eyes back on the road.

"Fuck. I love the sensation of pushing inside you and feeling you squeeze around my fingers," Lilith said, her voice full of heat. "There's no place my fingers would rather be than in your tight. hot. wet. cunt." She put a fine point on each of those last four words.

My foot slid off the gas pedal again involuntarily, and Lilith's fingers stopped moving.

"Come on, Mars. You know the rules," she said.

Getting my leg to cooperate took twice as much work. My core tightened, and I wanted nothing more than to ride my mate's fingers.

But I couldn't do that and keep Brego driving. So, I had to wait for Lilith to move her fingers again.

As the needle passed 50 MPH once more, she picked up the pace.

"Holy shit, Little Cottontail. Oh my god," I mumbled, feeling waves of pleasure wash over me from, not just Lilith's fingers scissoring inside of me, but the thrill of knowing we were racing down the road.

Being in motion was partially frustrating because I wasn't in control. I couldn't press myself against Lilith's fingers. But there was also a new excitement I'd never felt before. The raw danger of trying to keep control of a pickup truck while my mate fingered me. It was. . . exceptional. I tightened my legs as my mind sank into a sea of oxytocin.

"Focus on the road now," Lilith said as the truck's wheels briefly danced with the white line at the edge of the highway.

I fought to center the vehicle.

My mate took my hand off the gear shift and slid it under her shirt. It took a little finagling, but road sex was an imprecise science. Lilith and I knew to be extra patient with each other while we explored this fun and potentially deadly new activity.

Lilith pressed my fingers against the bite where I'd marked her. And we both felt an extrasensory wave of pleasure wash between us. The kind of powerful link between a werewolf and her mate. One might even call it a kink link. You know, if sex scientists ever discovered lycanthropes and decided to study their intimate activities with human partners.

I bit down on nothing while another moan built in my throat.

"Fuck! Lilith, I'm getting close," I warned.

"Close to Lubec or close to coming?" she asked.

I shot her a fierce glare and realized my mate could have taken that line of questioning even further. Thankfully, Lilith wasn't bratty enough to try.

Because fuck that. I didn't have the patience to deal with that level of sass in a partner. God knows I tried. I dated this one girl from Vermont for a week, but after the second or third "make me," I just rolled my eyes and left.

Make yourself, I remembered thinking that night as I drove back to Pine Springs and silenced my phone.

When I was on the cusp of losing myself, Lilith pulled her fingers out.

"Excuse me. Your alpha commands you to put those back right the fuck now!" I growled in agitation and impatience.

"Patience," Lilith said, slapping my thigh. "Now lift your ass."

"For what?" I asked, voice nearly cracking.

Lilith cocked her head to the left and gave me a blank stare.

"Every second you waste asking silly questions is another second you're not getting road head," she said.

My eyes widened.

"You're not serious."

"If you don't want an orgasm while driving 60 miles an hour, keep saying things like that," Lilith said, crossing her arms.

What else could a girl do? I complied.

Pulling my feet off the clutch and gas pedals, I stabilized my legs and gingerly lifted my ass. As Brego coasted down a hill, we didn't lose much speed.

"This is nuts," I hissed as Lilith carefully worked my jeans and underwear down.

"You wanna get nuts?" she said. "Let's get nuts."

I rolled my eyes.

"Are you going to eat me, or . . .?" I asked, which just brought a whole new wicked smile to Lilith's face.

It took her a bit to find the right angle. I heard my mate's neck pop as she tilted her head, but she didn't groan or grimace in pain. Lilith held my thigh with both hands and moved her face closer to my cunt.

I could smell Lilith's precum, its light salty odor mixing with the deep, musky scent of my own juices. She'd dampened her gaff.

We hit a small bump in the road, and before I knew it, Lilith's face met my pussy.

Effective enough, I thought moments before her first lick up the center of my cunt.

I shivered as she pulled back just far enough to speak a few muffled words. I think they were, "Fuck. You taste good."

Then, Lilith squeezed my thigh even tighter and showed me just how excited she was to bring me to orgasm on the open road.

My mate lapped at me, doing her best to work with the angle she'd been given. And, sure, it wasn't as steady or optimum as it would have been in my bed or against the barn door, but Lilith made it work. Or maybe it would be more accurate to say she worked it. She worked it really fucking well, lapping at me, paying close attention to my gasps and the clenching of my legs.

It didn't take long before I was back at the precipice again, moaning over the growl of the engine.

"Ohhhhh, yeah. Right there, Lilith. Right there!" I keened.

Moving my right hand from the gear shift to the steering wheel, I took my left hand and pressed it against the back of Lilith's head. Then, I gently pushed her face further into my pussy, burying her in my juices.

If I expected this to slow her down at all, Lilith surprised me and paid special attention to my clit.

That sent a shockwave through my core, and I could barely keep my eyes open and on the road. I wanted nothing more than to look down at the beautiful dyke licking and sucking me to queendom come.

Instead, I revved the engine and moaned loud enough that it reverberated off the entire cab of my truck.

"Lilith, I'm about to —"

She cut me off and quickly said, "You better fucking howl, Mars."

The sorceress pulled one hand off my thigh and inched it downward while she continued to dip in and out.

Meanwhile, my dam was breaking, and a raging river was gushing around inside me, my entire body quivering in bliss.

Sliding a finger inside of me, Lilith curled her digit while writing cursive over my clit with her tongue. The effect was an earth-shattering orgasm that pulled tight every muscle and ligament in my body.

"Lilith. Sweet mother of god. Yes!" I howled.

My legs curled against the seat, leaving the truck to coast for a while. As I huffed and tried to catch my breath, Brego finally came to a rest, and I maneuvered the pickup truck across the white line so we could stop on the highway shoulder.

"How fast were we going at the point of orgasm?" Lilith asked while my brain swam in the afterglow. It took me a few seconds to stop seeing stars and remember words exist.

"Um. . . I dunno. I think we were past 70."

My mate smiled and rested her head on my shoulder.

"Hot damn," Lilith said. "That must be what that one song is about."

I peeled open an eye and looked down at my mate.

"What song?"

"Radar Love," Lilith said.

Cackling, I pulled out my phone.

"I haven't heard that one in ages. Let's see if it lines up with our recent sexperience," I said. "Hey, Ciri, play 'Radar Love' on Spotifee."

We sat and listened to the entire song, nodding along with the beat and enjoying each other's warmth while more fog rolled over the highway. That logging truck from earlier passed us, and I smiled. We'd catch up later.

As the song ended, I shrugged.

"Maybe that IS what they were singing about," I said.

Lilith opened her eyes and leaned back over in her seat. The sorceress popped her neck.

"Oi. Hopefully, vamp healing takes care of cricks in the neck," she said.

I just laughed and looked at the highway. We weren't far from my pack now. Just another few miles up the road, a boat ride across the bay, and we'd be there.

"Hey, Mars?" Lilith asked.

"Yes, Little Cottontail?"

"If we do manage to free your pack today, will they be able to, um, smell. . . recent activities?" I asked.

My eyes shot wide open as I considered the first thing my parents might notice about my mate would be how she'd given me road head. What a fantastic thing to smell first thing out of the ice.

"Well, shit," I groaned.

That realization is what motivated us to detour and find a truck stop with a shower.

We got back on the road afterward, and I shuffled around in my seat, trying to make my new stiff pants more comfortable.

"These fucking things are awful. I can't believe I dropped $80 on truck stop jeans," I moaned.

Lilith just giggled and ignored her new jeans. She was still riding a wave of euphoria over being told where the women's showers were by the cashier.

As Lubec came into view, my mate took my hand.

I glanced over at her.

"So what made you wanna try that?" I asked.

"Well, I figured we were both kind of tense over the

pressure of trying to break a curse. Thought that might take our minds off it and help us relax."

Pulling Lilith's hand over, I kissed the back of her fingers.

"Damn fine job," I mumbled.

Lilith basked in the praise of her cunnilingus skills until a new thought entered her head. She turned back to me as I parked the truck.

"If your parents ride in Brego, won't they also smell —" she started before I interrupted her.

"The pack will ride back to Pine Springs with Uncle Pierre," I snapped, trying very hard not to imagine an uncomfortable and awkward ride back to the farm with them smelling what we did in here.

My mate scratched her head as I looked out over the docks and into the sea.

"Who's Uncle Pierre?"

Getting out of the truck, I handed Lilith her wrapped spear and said, "The saltiest man on this side of the Canadian border. C'mon, he's going to love you."

Chapter 16

"So, the young pup finally brings her mate to meet Uncle Pierre! I cannot believe it took this long," a fisherman said, taking me in a bone-crushing hug. He spoke with a thick Québécois accent and smelled like low tide.

I wiggled helplessly in his embrace.

"Yes, sir. That's me. Mars' mate. It's nice to, ugh, meet you, Mr. Pierre."

He let me down and waved a hand dramatically in the air.

"Bah! None of this 'mister' stuff. You're my niece's mate. Just call me Pierre. Uncle Pierre if you need to cling to some title or formality. And look at you! A real beauty. The magic of a sorceress. What a charming present the universe gave my silly niece."

Mars crossed the pier and snatched me back just as Pierre was kissing the back of my hand. I blushed because no one had ever talked to me like this before. A light giggle escaped my throat. It was all too much, the fisherman's outfit, the breeze around the dock, his thick accent, and the energetic mannerisms of an eccentric man. . . I was tickled by the meeting.

And yet, I also Understood getting a better look at Pierre that he wasn't human. His movements were good mimicry, but his walks, swoops, and gestures were too fluid. His eyes were a little too pale. And his breathing seemed a tad strained as if the air I needed wasn't something he thrived on. It was simply something he could make do with until he slid beneath the waves again.

"You're merfolk," I said, eyes widening as Mars pulled me into her arms.

Pierre made an exaggerated gesture of shock and looked around the dock as if I wasn't talking about him.

"Merfolk?! Where?!" he gasped, his head swiveling around from left to right. "I've always wanted to meet one. They say merfolk bring good luck to those who cross paths with them."

Mars rolled her eyes.

I looked over Pierre again. He was rail-thin and wore a ballcap covering neatly trimmed hair. He could have been in his late 50s or early 60s, but I suspected age wrapped around him a bit deeper than that. The magical wiki in my brain kicked into gear, and I suddenly knew that merfolk could easily live to be 300.

"Trying to find my gills?" Pierre said, laughing as he caught me staring.

I blushed all the harder and coughed out a, "No!"

He grinned, revealing teeth that were angled backward, more toward his throat than a human's would be.

"You won't find any, young sorceress. We breathe through our skin underwater. Flesh equals lungs beneath the waves," he said. "And now that I've answered your unspoken question, perhaps you'll satisfy my curiosity."

I froze, expecting some super invasive question about my body, more out of habit and experience than suspicion about Pierre's character. Some folks believed learning someone was trans entitled them to all kinds of secrets about our bodies, medications, surgeries, and more. And those people can go fuck themselves. You wouldn't ask a cishet man about his dick while riding the bus. Don't ask about mine.

Then, to my surprise, Pierre narrowed his eyes.

"Why is your blood so cold? I can feel the water inside you and Mars. Yours is. . . a bit frosty, no?"

Sighing in relief that this was his question, I waved my hand.

"Long story short? I ripped all the magic out of a Vampire Lorde trying to kill me and Mars. Some of that power stuck around and seems to have changed me."

Pierre nodded.

"And I'm guessing that magic also explains why your hair is like Rogue's. Kind of funny, isn't it? You took someone's power, and now you've got black and white hair like hers?" Pierre said.

I just blinked at the fisherman.

"I'm not sure what it says about me that upon seeing my changed hair, my first thought was Cruella. And yours was one of the X-Men."

Mars laughed and ruffled my hair, which sent shivers of pleasure down through my shoulders. Goddamn, I swooned under her touch. Leaning into Mars and closing my eyes, I heard her say, "Don't mind Pierre. He's been reading X-Men comics since they were introduced in the '60s."

When I opened my eyes again, I sassed the merfolk and said, "Figured you'd be more into Aquaman comics."

Pierre's face went grim, and my heart nearly stopped.

"Wow," he said. "You didn't tell me your mate was

such a bigot, young pup. I'm kind of disappointed. That's a bit insensitive to say to someone like me, don't you think?"

My heart sank into my guts, and I stammered, "Wait. No. I didn't mean it like — "

But Mars interrupted me.

"Don't be mean to my mate, Uncle Pierre. You've known her for 10 minutes, and you're already harassing her? Fuck off."

The grizzled seadog burst into laughter, his boisterous chortle filling the entire pier and echoing out over the waves.

"Oh, I'm sorry, Lilith. I'm sorry. I couldn't help myself. We merfolk love to joke, yes? Very much with the jokes."

My throat loosened a bit as I started to breathe again. Then I walked over and slugged him in the arm.

"Don't do that! I was fucking mortified that I'd insulted my mate's uncle."

Pierre held his hands in mock surrender.

"Sorry. So sorry. I had to. I hit Mars with the very same joke when she first came to live with me. I had to see if her mate would react the same way."

I slugged his arm again.

"Meanie!" I lobbed the insult at him like a curse. "C'mon, Mars. We'll find a different boatman to take us to the island."

The fisherman blinked and then crossed his heart with his hands in another dramatic gesture.

"Oh, of course. It is not me you have come to introduce your mate to, but my boat! How silly of me to assume you'd drive to Lubec for any other reason than to commandeer my vessel," Pierre sobbed while looking at Mars.

To her credit, my mate's eyes were a little downcast

upon hearing that. So, I slugged Pierre a third time for good measure.

"Stop it! You're being mean again," I huffed. "Uncles are supposed to be nice to their nieces. And if you don't start being nice to my mate, I'll hex you so bad that your skin becomes allergic to saltwater."

Pierre rubbed his arm, pretending as though I'd severely wounded him.

"You drove four hours to beat up an old man and steal his boat. What a crime. WHAT A CRIME!" he sobbed.

Then, he started laughing again. And as grumpy as he'd made me with his ridiculousness, I broke down and laughed alongside him. Mars joined us in chortling as well, and before long, we were three cackling clams yucking it up on the little pier.

Seagulls flew above us and called out obscenities while I wiped tears from my eyes. I hadn't laughed this hard in a while.

"Okay, Sea Hawk. Show us your boat. We're ready for adventure," I said, wrapping my elbow in Pierre's.

He bowed his head and gestured toward the end of the boardwalk.

"But of course, mademoiselle. Right this way," he said.

And suddenly, I was right back to heated cheeks. Maybe hearing French did something to me. I'd have to ask Mars to try speaking it to me when we got back to the farm.

Ten minutes later, we were on our way to the island where Mars' pack had been cursed. I had the spear tucked under my chair. The island before us was the single greatest sight of tragedy for my mate, and I'd asked her to bring me there. She faced her darkest moment at my request and all in the hopes that I could break Telsyn's curse.

The waters were calm as Pierre's boat powered through a mild current to Treat Island. In the distance, I watched the small landmass grow closer to us, a spec of green and brown among the grayish bay.

Nobody spoke until I turned to Mars and finally asked, "Honey, will you tell me why Telsyn cursed your pack? Maybe hearing the story will give me some clue about how to break it."

My mate leaned back in her seat and sighed, keeping her eyes on the island. I took her hand, and still, she did not look at me.

Mars' gaze remained forward, on the place where her past and future would meet.

Pierre kept his eyes on the water, not daring to speak a word. He was a character in Mars' story, but he was not the storyteller. That role was reserved for the alpha of the Dubois Pack.

"Telsyn appeared before my pack on two occasions. On her first visit, she called us witless dogs and demanded that we show her the Wolfbone Graveyard."

I was suddenly filled with so many questions but kept them in check, waiting patiently for Mars to continue her story. She coughed and cleared her throat.

"The Wolfbone Graveyard is an ancient cemetery my pack has guarded for centuries. The first werewolf who journeyed to Vinland with Leif Erikson a thousand years ago is buried there, along with hundreds of my ancestors. It is a sacred space for members of my pack, overflowing with magic. Telsyn, of course, wanted to devour it all like the wraith she is."

Suddenly, the number of questions rumbling around inside my skull exploded. The first werewolves to reach North America came from Nordic peoples? Was the Wolfbone Graveyard the same cemetery Lord Wylde went searching for in the woods before disappearing for good? Did Mars expect me and her to be buried in the Wolfbone Graveyard when we died (hopefully far from now)?

Still, I bit down on my tongue and listened to the rest of the story.

"When Telsyn visited my pack a second time, we knew she'd come for blood. My father, Randy Lee Dubois, gathered the whole pack on Treat Island, wanting to make sure no innocents were involved in the bloodshed to come. And when Telsyn appeared amid the quiet dark to demand our ancestral graveyard, our alpha, with all of us at his side, looked her dead in the eye and said, 'No.'"

A strange pride built in Mars' voice as she told this part of the story. Her chest puffed out. It almost looked like my mate was getting ready to stand and howl.

Even though she knew how the story ended, this moment was powerful. It blazed in her memory as she recited it to me.

"His exact words to Telsyn were, 'I deny you the sacred gravesoil of our people. Your teeth of shadows will find no wolf bones to gnaw on this night. Not while we stand united against you.' Enraged, Telsyn called forth a powerful curse. I watched as every wolf on the island stood defiant as spectral ice encased their flesh. My mother, just before the curse took her, let forth a fierce, guttural snarl. The snarl was a promise, Lilith, that one day the Dubois Pack would be free, and we would bring ruin on that wraith. I am that promise."

Taking both of Mars' twitching hands into mine, I folded our fingers tightly into my lap. And those fierce amber eyes turned to me.

"WE are that promise, Mars. You're not alone anymore. I am your mate. I am your pack. And today, we're going to free the rest of them."

It took a few seconds, but Mars grinned.

"Damn right."

The dock at Treat Island came into view, a tiny, weathered structure that appeared ancient. It looked like something built as a hobby by someone who had a pond in their backyard. A dad who wanted his kids to have something they could dive off into the water.

Tearing my eyes away from the island, I kissed Mars on the cheek and asked, "Am I allowed to know why Telsyn's curse didn't freeze you? Was there some limit to her magic? Or were you protected somehow?"

The grin on Mars' face faded. I watched her eyes sink back into the sensations from that horrible day. My mate looked like the echoes of werewolf screams and sounds of freezing flesh were swimming around her ears.

"I wasn't protected, Little Cottontail. Nor was I spared. My curse was just different. I, a 12-year-old pup, was forced to watch everyone I knew and loved endure the agony of being frozen alive. Telsyn knew I'd spend my entire life trying and failing to break the curse, tormented simultaneously by the hope I'd see my family freed and the continued denial of that miracle. Eventually, I think she expected me to break and offer her the graveyard's location in exchange for lifting the curse."

Folding myself against Mars and shivering from the sea breeze, I whispered, "But you wouldn't do that."

"But I wouldn't do that," she agreed.

Pierre cut the boat's engine as we drifted closer to the dock. I watched the shallow water washing up against the island's edge as if the ocean was constantly reminding the little island, "I could swallow you at any time. You remain because I allow it."

Above us, gray clouds filtered in, occasionally blocking the sun before letting its rays return. Shadows ran over the dock as Pierre tied the boat off on an old post. A "No Trespassing" sign stood at the edge of the dock.

"The usual, Mars? Wait here until you return?" the fisherman asked, stretching.

"Keep the meter running," Mars said softly, kissing Pierre on the cheek and hugging him tight. "With any luck, you'll be returning to Lubec with more people than you brought here."

Kissing my mate on top of her head, Pierre whispered, "Best of luck, ma fille."

Mars stepped past me up onto the dock as I watched Pierre pull out a paperback. He licked a thumb and opened to the middle of the book. The book's spine revealed its title: *A Hunt of Her Own* by someone named Elena Abbott. I made a mental note to Foogle that author later.

I slowly stood and slung the spear over my shoulder via a tiny strap we'd fashioned with its wrappings.

Offering her hand, my mate waited to pull me from the boat, and even this left me feeling flushed. A dyke chivalry I'd waited for my entire life. Mars smiled seeing the effect being treated like some kind of dainty, fragile thing had on me. And I'd have wagered actual money she made her own mental note to do that more in the future.

But that was the future. We were in the now. And now, I had a wraith's curse to lift.

Feeling Mars' strength gently, but firmly pull me up onto the warped boards of the small dock, I noticed my breath hitch in my throat. To add to the effect, Mars pressed me against her chest until I slowly looked up into her carnivorous gaze.

"Not one moment have I regretted snatching you away from that sad little man in the art gallery," she said against my ear.

"And not one moment have I regretted being dragged away to the home of a mighty werewolf," I whispered back, lightly licking my mate's cheek.

"Come along, Little Cottontail. I have some very important people to introduce you to."

I allowed myself to be led up the dock and onto an island where more wolf tears had fallen than raindrops from the sky.

We entered and walked through a forest of evergreens that seemed to stretch north to south for most of the island. I stepped over a crumpled beer can and a fallen bird's nest from a season or two ago.

The air grew colder the further we got into the island, and I could feel Mars' footsteps slowing and growing heavier. She trudged forward holding my hand. In my chest, alongside my heartbeat, I could feel hers. It beat like the engine of a race car zooming around the track. And I wondered then if her mind was doing the same thing, replaying every scene of her pack frozen in the eyes of a little girl.

A 12-year-old watched her beastly parents, who, until that moment, had been untouchable. A mighty alpha and his mate who led a pack of creatures that, united, could take on any foe.

But the foe they stood against wasn't something of this world. It was a creature from a horrific place of stagnancy and decay. Somehow, it'd crept into our world, our good and magical world of living souls and innocent people who thought monsters were just the stuff of bedtime stories.

That abomination stared down a pack of fierce predators and petrified them one by one. Mars stood by powerless to stop it.

And in one moment, I knew her intense hatred of Telsyn. Because if a werewolf was a makebelieve monster to humans. Then a wraith was a makebelieve monster to werewolves, something so twisted and depraved that it could only exist in the imaginations of scared storytellers.

These were the scariest monsters one could think of, unless, of course, we were talking about Republicans, in which case, wraiths and werewolves were only the second scariest monsters they could imagine, behind trans folks.

Tall grass tickled my knuckles as we left the forest behind and came to a clearing where the pack came into view. From a distance, they looked like large ice sculptures. Up close, they looked like shivering and pained human beings, most of them frozen in a moment of rage and agony.

Mars' hand tightened around mine as she led me into a circle of petrified werewolves. They didn't even have time to shift before the curse washed over them.

My mate led me to a man who stood baring fangs and ready to attack. The man bore a striking resemblance to Mars, and I figured this must be her father. The alpha was frozen in a tank top and stained jeans, amber eyes pointed skyward to his then-attacker.

Roger Lee's shaggy brown hair was caught in a wave around him as he prepared to rush into battle. He'd pushed Mars' mother a few inches behind him. Perhaps he'd felt the curse building.

Adeline Dubois stood staring into the sky, trapped in a perpetual snarl as Mars had told me in the boat ride here. Her sandy blonde hair was pulled back into a long braid with a silver ring embedded in the bottom.

I'd heard Mars describe her mother as a bit of a hippy once, and aside from the snarling pose, she looked it with her sundress and black tights.

"Hey, Mom. Hey, Dad. I'm back," Mars started as I

kept staring at her parents. It sounded like she was trying to keep from crying.

I stood close and waited while Mars took a deep breath and prepared to say what she needed to.

"I just wanted to stop by and introduce my mate. This. . . is Lilith Chambers, the woman who holds my heart, the girl I was made to love before I took my first breath."

Stepping up next to Mars, I looked at Roger Lee and Adeline. And where I expected to feel awkward or embarrassed to be talking to people who couldn't hear me, I instead felt a natural relaxation sinking into my muscles.

The most macabre, maudlin part of my brain expected this to feel like talking to statues. Instead, an instinctual part of me recognized these two as. . . something akin to family. They were pack.

Mars' bite marks on my body pulsed in their presence.

My mind told me I was standing in view of my mother and father. And I guess when Mars and I got married someday (Gods, that was a strange phrase to think about), they would be my parents. Er — my werewolf in-laws.

Bowing my head, I said, "Hi, Mr. and Mrs. Dubois. My name is Lilith. I — I'm in love with your daughter and pleased to meet you both."

Mars snickered, catching me by surprise.

"If you call them that when the curse breaks, I guarantee Mom and Dad will give you shit for it. Just be ready," she said.

That seemed to break the tension in the air, and Mars looked back at her parents.

"Lilith is a sorceress. She's going to try and break your curse. Then you can come home with me, and see the farm I've built. I have so much to show you, show the rest of the pack. So please. . . just hang in there a little bit longer."

My eyes swept over the six frozen werewolves, and although I recognized a powerful magic at work . . . something wasn't quite right.

The effects of the curse were here, of course. And that was supposed to draw the attention and eye. The people affected by the curse were the focal point.

Telsyn's spell wanted all of Mars' attention to be focused on her pack, I thought, my Understanding firing into high gear.

As long as she thought the entire spell was built around this core group of six frozen werewolves, Mars would never find out how to break the curse.

"What do you think?" Mars asked.

I rubbed my chin.

"I think. . . we're only seeing the effects of the curse, not the actual curse itself."

Mars raised an eyebrow.

"What does that mean?"

I took a deep breath.

"It means, I need a better look at the magic around me. I need you to step back while I cast my siphon spell and trace the origins of this curse."

Mars did as I asked, stepping out of the werewolf ring.

Taking a deep breath, I reached inside me for the spell that ripped every scrap of magic out of Beau and killed me in the process. Its eyes opened somewhere deep within, curious as to what I'd be feeding it with now.

This arcane craft wasn't like the other spells I wielded. It almost had a life of its own. I shuddered remembering the hunger that came from seeing Beauregard's magic and the intense need to devour it all.

I attempted some manner of control, and it felt like trying to leash a polar bear.

"Easy now. Calm the fuck down," I grimaced while Mars looked on, concern filling her eyes.

"I'm okay," I said, noticing her anxiety building in the other side of my chest, where I felt her heart beating. "Just taking it slow."

Grabbing my right arm, I tried to control my breathing and unleash the spell in minor increments. I didn't need to siphon anything. What I sought were the eyes that allowed me to see raw magic so I could know where to aim the siphon.

Under my clothes, I felt my tattoos crawling across my body. Letting the spell flow down my arm, I watched obsidian veins creep toward my hand. With a squelching noise, the flesh of my hand rapidly decayed, its skin turning from a creamy white to a jet black. A magical black hole opened in the palm of my hand, eager to devour magic. Lots of magic. Any magic. It wasn't picky.

Holding it back, I tried to focus on the ocular portion of the spell. I didn't need to swallow magic. I just needed to see it.

"Is your hand. . . supposed to look like that?" Mars asked from somewhere to my left.

"That's the siphon spell. It's fine. My hand doesn't look like this when I finger you," I said through gritted teeth, using humor to try and keep my attention in the present. I didn't want my focus to be swallowed by the bottomless void inside of me eager to devour nearby energy.

Mars scoffed in disbelief.

"My parents are RIGHT THERE," she hissed.

"Relax. They won't be the next time we fuck," I said.

At last, I seemed to get some control over the spell — or at least its effects on my body. My vision swam and then seemed to narrow as a sea of gray washed over everything. Hues and finer details drained from my field of sight, leaving the wolves, the trees, and the ice colored by varying shades that ranged from ash to slate.

Taking a steadying breath, I lowered my hand and looked around.

Mars' core burned bright orange with the living magic of nature, an energy that made her every bit a human and a wolf. It was wild and feral, playful and fierce, leaping and hunting. If I expected my siphon to start reaching for her magic, I was shocked to find no such urge to drain her.

Why? I thought. *I was so quick to latch onto Beauregard.*

And through Understanding, the answer dawned on me. This spell is of The Mother. It's powerful, but it can't override my loyalty to my mate. That connection is too primal and deep within me for sorcery to touch.

On top of that, The Mother being a giant wolf understands and values the importance of mates, I thought. *Even if I annoy her, she won't move to harm me or Mars because she knows we're fated to be with one another.*

Looking over the frozen werewolves, I spotted a sickly vein of pale blue magic buried at the bottom of each ice chunk. The werewolves themselves all possessed a slumbering orange magical core similar to Mars, but it was diminutive from years of dormancy within the curse.

It's like their magic is in stasis, I thought.

The werewolves weren't breathing. They were. . . trapped in a stage of deep sleep. The curse was designed to keep them encased.

"I don't mean to sound like a broken record, babe, but are your eyes supposed to be all ashy-looking and gray? You look like a follower of Kaecilius," Mars said with a bit more concern in her voice than before.

It took a minute for me to respond as I was busy examining her frozen pack.

"I'm fine," I said. "Looking at. . . the curse. Tracing it."

Words were hard to form when I concentrated on maintaining a single aspect of the siphon spell. It felt like trying to carry on a conversation while staring at a bacteria sample under a microscope. My eyes were focused on tardigrades, and my ears were trying to listen to someone behind me talk about how much better *Ready Player One* was as a movie than a book.

Mars didn't say anything else after that, so I went back to looking at the wolves. The ice encasing all six of them was unnatural. The substance formed quickly and carried the consistency of steel. It wouldn't melt on the hottest day nor chip if struck by the sharpest ice pick.

But as I suspected, this was merely the effect of the curse, rather than the base of the spell itself.

The curse's anemic icy roots flowed from the base of each chunk of ice and twisted together into a sickly blue rope a few inches under the soil.

Keeping my eyes on the buried roots of the curse, I started walking out of the clearing.

"Where are you going? Lilith?" Mars asked behind me.

I ignored her, not willingly but unconsciously as I put every ounce of myself into maintaining the siphon spell. It kept wanting to power off since I wasn't actively feeding it with magic to devour.

The spell inside me growled in annoyance.

I ignored it and continued walking south back into the evergreen forest. The curse's roots ran under logs, between shrubs, and over creekbeds.

Mars eventually gave up trying to ask questions and followed along quietly behind me, doubtless curious about where I was walking.

It was slow going, and I lost the trail once or twice. Following a buried cable was difficult work when you had to maintain a spell just to see it. Sweat beaded on my forehead despite the chilly sea breeze that raced through the forest around us.

My legs started to buckle when I finally arrived at the hornet's nest of magic that was the curse's source of power. It was a sickening silver that pulsed outward from a large rock the size of a car door.

Pointing at the rock half-buried in soil, I said, "Mars, can you please flip that rock over?"

She didn't question me, puzzling how best to get a grip on the rectangular chunk of granite. When she figured it out, I watched my mate flex her strength and grunt. The rock didn't want to budge at first, but she didn't give it much of a choice.

Rending it from the earth and sending dirt and previously buried insects flying in every direction, Mars roared as it came loose.

Flipping the rock over, she tossed it back down to the ground. The immediate area shook with a resounding THUD as the rock crashed back down into the soil.

She gasped as I finally powered down the siphon spell. We didn't need magical vision to see the curse's source.

Glowing silver markings covered the now-visible rock surface. Wraith-like aura washed over us, a nauseating power far greater than standing in the presence of Beauregard. It penetrated us to our very core.

I fell to my knees while Mars leaned over and grabbed a tree trunk to steady herself.

"W — what is that?" Mars asked. "And why the fuck didn't I notice it before?"

Trying not to hurl, I glanced over a silver sigil that took the form of an ouroboros with a glowing open eye in the middle of the circle.

The eye had a single tear and the buried root I followed here attached to that solitary tear via a few thin, yet powerful strands of magic.

"That nasty piece of spellcraft is the source of Telsyn's

curse. It's what keeps your pack encased in otherworldly ice. The curse is designed to remain hidden nearby so all of your attention remains on the frozen werewolves and ignores it," I explained.

My head felt like it was filling with quick-drying concrete. The curse was fucking toxic and roiling my arcane senses.

Mars took a few steps back and pulled me with her.

"Okay. Can you disable it?" my mate asked.

And I sighed, looking over the cursed rock again.

Shaking my head, I covered my eyes with my hand that since returned to its normal color.

"That thing is ridiculously powerful, hon. I thought maybe I could siphon the magic's energy and lift the curse, but it's so much stronger than anything I've felt aside from The Maiden, The Mother, and The Crone."

"Is that why my nose is bleeding just standing this close?" Mars asked.

I nodded.

"If siphoning Beauregard was like swallowing a firecracker, siphoning this spell would be like swallowing a grenade. There's no way I'd survive, even with stolen vampiric healing. My whole body would explode outward in a mess of spilled lasagna," I said.

Mars pulled me a few more feet away. The longer that curse stayed exposed, the worse its effects upon us grew.

"What do we do now?" Mars asked, stifling a retch.

I scratched my head, my Understanding doing the depressing math.

"You have a difficult choice to make. I don't have the power or capacity to stop this curse."

Mars raised an eyebrow and looked down at me with suspicion.

"What's the difficult choice? Because if you think I'm

going to let you bargain with Phenna or someone else to lift the curse, you can forget it. Some werewolves may stupidly stumble into bargains with greater powers, but I ain't one of them, bub."

I closed my eyes and pulled the spear off my shoulder, unwrapping it slowly.

My mate stood there with her arms crossed.

"I can't stop the curse, but The Mother can. Her power can blunt force that curse from existence. It'd be like dropping a nuke on a cobra, but it'll break it all the same. If I pierce the ouroboros with this, it'll free your pack. But you'll lose the one weapon we have that can kill Telsyn. So, my love, you have to choose. Do you want your parents back today or Telsyn's guaranteed death at some unforeseen point in the future when our paths cross?"

A flash of anger rushed across Mars' face as she considered the possibility that the gun she was prepared to fire at her mortal enemy could lose its bullets.

Her body shuddered with several stages of grief before me all at once. She drudged her boots into the earth at the same time she ground her teeth.

Every part of me wanted to comfort my mate. I desired nothing more than to step forward and throw my arms around her.

She ran her fingers through her hair and gritted her teeth while two ideas warred inside her. Revenge or reunification.

We might find Telsyn tomorrow. We might find her 10 years from now. There was no way to know for sure. Mars and I had no guarantees.

The werewolf clutched her fists and let out a roar that rattled the trees around us. I was sure Pierre heard her back at the boat.

Mars fell to her knees and sank her fist into the ground, striking it repeatedly.

I stayed where I was. This was an internal battle that I couldn't interfere with. Mars couldn't think I was trying to sway her to one choice or the other. When she was finished I could comfort her, but not before.

At last, my mate reached a conclusion. "Set them free," she whispered. "I want my pack. Please, Lili. I just want my family back."

Gripping the spear, I steeled my resolve.

"I will do everything I can to grant your wish," I said. "Because you're my mate and I love you."

Turning toward the stone, I walked over and raised the pointed end of the spear above the rock. Then, I drove the spear down toward the Ouroboros sigil, determined to end this curse once and for all.

To my surprise, the spear tip stopped inches short of the rock, an invisible force catching the weapon's point and freezing all motion. Then, an equal force to the one I attempted to unleash threw me backward.

I wasn't prepared for the possibility the curse would protect itself, and I paid for it, falling ass over face and coming to rest several feet from the stone, my world spinning in a haze of dizziness.

"Son of a bitch," I hissed.

"Lilith!" Mars shouted, rushing over.

I held up a hand which stopped her.

"I'm fine. This is just going to require a bit more force," I said, getting up and taking a deep breath. My ribs were throbbing from where I'd struck the ground.

"Are you sure?" Mars asked.

Ignoring her, I rushed forth, determined to keep the promise I just made. I got a good running start and drove the spear down with all my momentum. Like before, some invisible force stopped the spear tip just before it struck the sigil. And that force was turned back upon me, flinging me backward.

"Hrrnnnggg!" I grunted, flying back into an evergreen tree and slamming into its trunk, pine needles washing over me and clawing my skin.

It took me a little longer to recover this time, and Mars helped me up.

"Maybe we should reconsider. . .," she started, but I cut her off.

"More force," I hissed. "Go stand over by the rock and be prepared to toss me."

"Excuse me?" Mars gasped.

I stared at her, fury building inside me.

"I'm not going to lose to this curse, Mars. Now, please, go stand over by the rock. I'm going to run at you, and I want you to toss me as high as you can. Then I'll let gravity end this."

She looked from the rock back to me.

With a frustrated sigh, my mate reluctantly did as I asked. I gripped the spear with both hands and backed up about 15 feet. Running through the trees as fast as I could, I watched as Mars cupped her hands near the ground. Throwing my left foot into her grip, I felt her werewolf strength work and hurl me up into the air until I was above the evergreens.

Gripping the spear tight, I pointed it downward and rode the gravity straight down into the rock.

Predictably, I was stopped. It felt like my entire body struck an airbag in a car crash. Then, before I could react, the curse hurled me back up into the air, right back where I came from.

"Motherfuckerrrrr," I screamed, eyes closed as I shot

over the trees and came rocketing down into the sea several feet off the island's shore.

The frigid water soaked me to the bone, and I nearly lost the spear. But my rage only grew.

"Lilith! Enough. We need to rethink this," Mars shouted, running out of the treeline and stopping on the shore as I inched back to dry ground grinding my teeth. "Seriously, you're covered in scrapes and bruises. Please stop. This isn't working."

"It. Will. Work." I said, stressing each syllable.

In my mind, I just kept picturing Mars crying in front of her frozen parents, gripped by the loneliness of survivor's guilt. Inside that muscled goddess who loved me for reasons I couldn't begin to explain, there was a scared 12-year-old girl worried she'd never see her pack again.

I'd given Mars a glimmer of hope on this trip, and I'd be damned if this curse would strip even that from my mate.

"I just need more speed," I hissed, stepping into the shadow of the nearest tree and folding myself into the darkness with a vampiric ability that was suddenly more instinct than technical understanding.

Feeling myself meld into the shadow in an instant, I raced down the line of trees at a breakneck speed I'd seen Beau use on the farm.

Gripping the spear tight, I carried all the vampiric shadow momentum with me, preparing for a clash that would be nothing short of epic.

"I'll break this fucking curse or my neck trying," I yelled, driving that spear downward with more power than I'd used thus far.

This time, the air shimmered as the curse struggled to match my output. And I hoped for a divine moment that this would be the breaking point. But to my crushing dismay, I was driven backward again, with equal force to what I'd used.

"No!" I yelled, again flying backward. "Not this time."

Using the curse's momentum, I dove into the nearest shadow, spun around an evergreen, and slingshotted myself back at the rock with even greater speed.

It seemed like a foolproof idea until the curse blocked me again, and I felt the back of my skull crashing into tree bark.

If I'd upped my game on approach, how much more so did the curse? It was like no matter what I tried, it held the upper hand.

Never before had I moved as quickly as I had during that last approach. And even that was rebuffed.

I felt blood dripping down the back of my neck as Mars rushed over and snatched the spear from my hands.

"Okay! That's enough," she said with a choked voice.

But I wasn't done. Not by a long shot.

I felt vampiric healing piecing together the back of my skull, at least enough to keep me conscious. The sickening sound of an eggshell being put together filled my ears.

Beau, you ridiculously Southern son of a bitch, your powers only get more useful to me, I thought, once I had coherent brain patterns again.

Snatching the spear back from Mars, I turned to look at her and winked.

"Have faith in your mate. This is what I came here to do. I just need to push a little harder. I felt the curse give way with that last drive. It's not all-powerful. I can do this," I swore anew.

Mars took my face in her hands.

"I don't want you to splatter yourself to bring my family back."

"No splatter. I promise," I said.

Facing down the rock again, I called to my magic, and it answered, responding to my need. It wasn't a spell, per se. But I could use my magic to push my physical limits a little further if I blanketed myself with raw energy.

No idea how long I can keep it up, I thought. *But I felt the curse bend. It has limits. I just have to shatter my own to breach it.*

Picturing my magic wrapping around me like a suit of armor, I felt the energy stretch and crawl over every inch of me, spreading gooseflesh wherever it reached. When, at last, my magic smothered me with a sheen of violet light, I gripped the spear tight and walked back to the shadows of the treeline near the water. I gave myself as much of a runway as I could.

In my head, I told myself the shadows leading up to the cursed rock were the tarmac of an airport, and I was a jet about to launch myself forward at full speed.

Folding into shadow once more, I kept my magic burning as much as I could. I threw myself at the stone with reckless abandon. No speedometer could track me. I was raw velocity, and the spear was my sharpest point.

I met the curse head-on as the ground around me rumbled with power. My spear tip came within centimeters of that rock's surface before the spell mustered enough power to drive me back.

This played out over and over again, me burning my candle as bright as I could at both ends. I attacked the stone from every conceivable angle, direction, and speed. Each time, I was thrust backward into trees, into the sky, and into the ocean. I skipped across the ground like a stone over pond water. I bashed my limbs into tree trunks.

My body became a human punching bag of raw force. Still, I waved off Mars' growing concerns and rose each time.

Time went by, and I felt myself slowing, my magic depleting.

That fucking curse just wouldn't break, no matter how hard I charged ahead.

Eventually, night fell, and I was healing from a shattered knee, breathing like an asthmatic in a paper towel manufacturing plant, when Mars barked, "For god's sake. ENOUGH. Your alpha orders you to fucking stop."

My knee slowly pieced itself back together, and I thanked the gods for adrenaline, which I was apparently on my last few milliliters of.

"I can. . . do this. I swear. Just one more run," I huffed, one eye closed. Scratch that. One eye swollen shut.

"You can barely stand! No, you can't do this. You've tried. I've watched all day, growing increasingly worried. Well, no more."

With spite, I grimaced, feeling aches and pains running down my legs as my knee finished healing, and stood.

"See? I can stand. No 'barely' about it."

Mars rolled her eyes and grabbed my shoulders.

"Stop. Please. For me."

My heart quivered as those same imagined scenes of a young Mars crying before her frozen pack replayed in my exhausted brain again.

"Please, Mars. I promised. I can do this," I said, reaching for the spear that she'd taken from me again.

She shook her head.

"No, Little Cottontail. You can't."

My face sank, but when I tried to lower my gaze to the ground, my mate grabbed my chin and pushed my attention back up until our eyes met.

"You can't do this," she said, again. "But we can."

The werewolf pointed to the sky just as the clouds parted, and silver rays from a full moon washed over us. I just stared at it until my brain clicked with Understanding.

"You can change anytime you want," I whispered.

"But I'm strongest on nights when Silver Eye is wide open above me."

With those words, the werewolf stood tall over me. She kicked off her boots and threw her shirt to the side. I watched ripples of fur sprout from beneath her flesh, splitting the skin open as my mate gave way to the bipedal beast within.

Her fangs extended, her spine elongated as a bushy tail formed, and razor claws claimed the edge of each finger.

And where my mate usually wore a thick coat of mahogany-colored fur, her fur was now tinged in an effervescent gold, the same shade as her eyes. Mars' muscles expanded, and she stood at least nine feet tall now.

"Holy shit," I whispered, feeling her raw magic running and spreading through the trees around me. It ran and leaped in every direction like a pack of wolves chasing down a herd of caribou.

"Blood of Fenrir. . . rise," my mate growled so deep the sand around me rippled.

Holding out the spear, I understood that Mars meant for us to throw all we had into one final thrust. What I had left. . . was fumes. And yet, my faith in us didn't waver for a moment.

"I love you," I said, meaning it with every fiber of my being.

Mars leaned down and ran her tongue up the whole side of my face, and fuck if that didn't do things to me.

"We can do this," I said, placing a hand on the ground. "Sorry, island. I need to borrow some of your energy."

Siphoning the very life from the forest we stood in, I felt the trees and bushes wither around me.

"Cursed be the land a wraith sets foot on," I hissed, my magic slowly rebuilding itself.

Mars and I approached the cursed stone with the surety of our purpose. And with every ounce of combined power we had, we thrust our spear downward toward the stone.

The curse, bless its heart, rose to meet us again, ready to drive me back. But this time, I had the backing of my mate, the unleashed Blood of Fenrir coursing through her veins hungry for victory over a dread that'd held her pack prisoner for far too long.

That fucking curse pushed back with all the power Telsyn had granted it. But when that force reversed to meet us, Mars and I refused to budge. So, the curse thrust upward all the harder.

We stayed anchored, driven by our twinned desire for unyielding victory. No compromise. No defeat. No survival for this curse.

As we let loose a unified scream of frustration, the ground around us began to quake and splinter, dead trees falling to the ground, and birds all around the island scattering, fleeing our wrath.

"Come on, you fucker!" I yelled all the louder, unleashing every single drop of magic I'd siphoned.

Waves around the island stirred as the curse started to hit its upper limit, unraveling at a furious pace. But even that wasn't enough to satisfy our growing arcane bloodlust.

Mars and I pushed harder still, the spear tip inching ever closer to that stone.

At last, with a massive shattering of cursed energy, the magical field around the stone that'd fought me off all day gave way. Our combined stubbornness and endurance claimed victory, thrusting the spear down into the rock and splitting it right down the middle.

With little fanfare, the spear superheated to the point that we couldn't hold on. Above us, the night sky ripped open, and a massive hole of unbound space became the tunnel, through which, The Mother's magic flowed. It raced down toward us in an arc of brilliant magenta light.

The combination of approaching magic beyond my comprehension, the shattering of the curse, and the tight grip of exhaustion resulted in a smearing of consciousness that didn't quite capture every moment that followed.

But I'm pretty sure three things happened next:

1. I grabbed Mars with the last bit of my strength and folded us back into shadow to get the hell away from the cursed stone.
2. Some minutes later, amid all the smoke and rubble, Mars said something about hearing the ice cracking.
3. Before Mars could carry me to her newly freed parents, an inexplicable chasm opened beneath us.

And that fucking void consumed us both, body and soul.

Epilogue

I don't know how long I was out. But I do know that I stirred first. Maybe it was another win for the vampiric healing that just couldn't seem to quit on me. Either way, I remember looking up into a night sky full of doors where the stars should have been.

Mars and I appeared to be lying on a hardwood floor of some kind. I was vaguely aware of walls or the shape of something similar around us.

Some part of me was bleeding, but I wasn't sure what.

And then came her voice, creeping into my ears like a stream of ants. I twitched and groaned with every sentence she spoke.

"Oh, you foolish little creatures. You went and did something to anger me, didn't you?"

"Hello?" I choked out, my voice like sandpaper.

"Yes, yes. I am here, your unexpected hostess. I'm sure I don't need to introduce myself. Surely you know my name, yes?"

I racked my brain for Understanding and found little available, so I took a wild guess.

"Telsyn?" I hissed.

"Wow. You are an intelligent sorceress. No wonder you found and broke my curse," the voice sassed me.

"What do you want?" I asked, feeling my annoyance starting to stir.

The voice from. . . somewhere sighed.

"I want the Wolfbone Graveyard, sorceress. And I'm prepared to keep you both here until you're driven mad and surrender it to me in a desperate plea for death."

The doors above us were spinning and swirling across the night sky now. Where the fuck were we?

"I bid you welcome to the Evermanor, Lilith Chambers. You and Mars Dubois are my first guests. Be honored."

And for the life of me, I just didn't feel all that honored.

Afterword

Alright, that's a wrap on my first monsterfucker book. I never thought that'd be a sentence I'd type, but let's be honest, we all saw the path leading here eventually. Now, please don't be too mad. I know this is a cliffhanger, probably my biggest one to date (if you don't count Sierra's ending in *A Bargain for Wings*). But I promise, y'all will get endings to both of those cliffhangers in 2025.

And my goodness! 2025 is so close as I write this final letter to you, my beautiful readers. This time last year, I was publishing *My Aunt, The Vampire*.

So, what's next? Well, if you join my Discord, you'll know my next book is a project called *Dragonturned*. It'll be a dark dragon romance about a disgraced knight falling in love with a flame sorceress as they both try to protect their princess from assassins.

I'll have regular chapter updates posted on my Kofi starting in January with the full book probably being published in March or April.

After that? Who knows. Fuck, I'm tired. All this month, I've been working two jobs and trying to finish this book.

Maybe I should finally rest like Soph and Arra keep trying to convince me to do. (HA, GOOD ONE!)

For those worried about my health (and bless your hearts for caring), I'll only be working one job in January. So, *Dragonturned* shouldn't have any interference. In my spare time, I'll have an apocalypse DnD campaign to run and a new season of *Beastars* to finish. So, I'll be staying plenty busy.

Thanks for being patient with my wild writing pace and reading my books!

In the meantime, tell your friends you love them, play in the snow, and buy that pretty new tarot deck.

Later, bub

- Autumn

About Autumn

Autumn Wolff is a very gay lady. And she's a woman of few simple interests. When she's not writing stories about girls kissing each other, Autumn is likely reading stories about girls kissing each other, playing Dungeons and Dragons, riding her bike, or watching a movie. She and her wife live near the ocean and consume more pizza than four turtles mutated by ooze. Autumn may not have the biggest living space, and it may never have enough bookshelves, but it's home.

Other Autumn Wolff Books

A Bargain for Sanctuary

Bride of the Elven Innkeeper

My Aunt, The Vampire